DRY ROT

DRY ROT

A Sage Adair Historical Mystery
of the Pacific Northwest

S. L. Stoner

Yamhill Press
P.O. Box 42348
Portland, OR 97242

Dry Rot

A Yamhill Press Book

Copyright 2013 by S. L. Stoner

Cover Design by Alec Icky Dunn/Blackoutprint.com
Interior Design by Josh MacPhee/Justseeds.org

Publisher's Cataloging-in-Publication

    Stoner, S. L.
    John Sagacity Adair : dry rot / by S.L. Stoner. —p. cm. —
    (A Sage Adair historical mystery of the Pacific Nortwest)

    ISBN 978-0-9823184-6-1
    ISBN 0-9823184-6-4
    ISBN 978-0-9823184-7-8
    ISBN 0-9823184-7-2

    1. Northwest, Pacific—History—20th century—Fiction.
    2. Labor unions—Fiction. 3. Detective and mystery stories. 4. Martial arts-Fiction. 5. Historical fiction.
    6. Adventure stories. I. Title. II. Series: Sage Adair
    historical mystery.

    12 11 10 09 08 07 06 05 04 03 02 01

    PS3619.T6857J64 2012   813'.   QBI11-600235

This Book is Dedicated to
The Women and Men of Yesteryear Who Walked Out On
Strike,
Risking Everything To Win A Better Future for All of Us.
And, to Those Who Will Strike In The Future

Their Hearts Full of the Same Fears And the Same Hopes.

These Are the Heroes

ONE

October 1902, Portland, Oregon

A FAT RAINDROP SMACKED THE BACK of his neck and slid down his spine like a cold knife edge. "Damn," Sage grumbled, twisting his collar tight for about the tenth time in the same number of minutes. He hated the rain. Snow was better any day. It might cake a man's trousers but at least it didn't seep through every seam. He stared east, into the sullen gray wall of cloud obscuring the Cascades. For weeks now, the Pacific Northwest sky had drizzled endlessly, turning the ground into a slurry of mud and moldering leaves.

The sneering voice inside his head said, "Well, fella, it's not like you're forced to be here." True. Back at his restaurant, the pipes carrying city-supplied steam heat would be radiating warmth, driving the damp against the window panes where it belonged. He was here by his own choice. When asked by Vincent St. Alban to help the striking construction workers, Sage immediately agreed. He'd known when he signed on as a labor movement operative that physical discomfort was part of the package. While restauranteur John S. Adair could retreat to the dry warmth of his exclusive eating establishment, Sage Adair, the labor union spy, had to stick it out right beside the men he hoped to help. Two weeks of unremitting rain, however, was starting to douse his enthusiasm for the job.

He studied the dozen or so men shuffling back and forth before the construction office, their steps stiff with cold, their shoulders bowed low under sodden coats. Each miserable day was exacting a toll. One man losing heart and walking away. Another finding work elsewhere, his apology trailing behind him as he trudged up the road and out of sight. No table bumping spiritualist was needed to predict the outcome of their efforts The labor strike was nearly lost.

Sage stood a bit apart from the strikers, alongside the nearly impassable mud road. For the most part, the friendly strikers paid him no mind. They knew him as the dark-haired, droopy mustached kin of their union president. "Nice enough guy, steady but kinda quiet," Leo told him that was the group's overall opinion of Leo's "nephew."

Lockwood, himself, had readily accepted St. Alban's offer of Sage's assistance. The three of them had settled on Sage playing the role of "Sam Graham," Lockwood's just-passing-through nephew. Sage's only tangible "assistance," thus far, had been food boxes anonymously delivered to strikers' front doors. He wanted to do more for the men yet no real opportunity had presented itself.

The men, making their stand at the road's end, were protesting long work hours and starvation wages. The hardheaded construction contractor Abner Mackey and Earl, his even more hardheaded son, worked the men seven days a week for as long as there was light. Mackey Construction and Lumber Company was the largest, most powerful construction contractor in the city. The thinking was that this was a do-or-die chance for all of the city's construction workers who also needed better hours and pay. If the Mackey strikers won, other construction companies would also adopt an eight-hour day, six-day work week rather than risk a similar strike—especially since the Mackeys couldn't undercut them on labor costs. If the strikers lost, it was just as certain that those same construction companies would fire every pro-union worker, keep wages low and continue to load the hours on without mercy.

So far, none of their tactics had tipped the balance in favor of the striking men. Instead, Sage watched from the sidelines as that balance kept tilting relentlessly in the bosses' favor.

His back stiff from standing in one place, Sage ambled a few paces toward the gully where a stream was raging. Leaning against a pile of waste lumber, he closed his eyes, allowing the surrounding sounds to send him somewhere else—an early spring day, a scented forest, the fir canopy overhead sighing in a steady breeze.

Another freezing, wet drop slithered past his collar, snapping his thoughts into the present. The rushing sound in his ears was not the breeze slipping through tree branches. It was the sound of muddy water shooting down the nearby gully. All across the city, similar streams scoured debris from banks, attacked tree roots and surged against trestle timbers until they thrummed.

Sage sighed and opened his eyes to study the Mackey lumber mill's office at the road's end. It was a one-story, rectangular, unpainted wooden building fronted by a covered porch. Out of that building they operated the mill, tallied profits and dispatched men to construction jobs. Beyond the office building lay the sheet-metal-clad mill and lumber-filled yard. That complex extended north and south along the Willamette riverbank, covering a plot of land over 300 feet wide and 600 feet long. A high barbed-wire fence blocked the far end, a gate in its middle giving wagons access to the yard. The same fencing ran along the north side of the dirt road all the way up to a warehouse building at the top of the muddy lane. On the mill's east side, the river's flood made docking perilous. To the south, the mill's bulwark against trespassers was more barbed wire—this time stretching to the edge of the gully's swift flowing stream. The river, mill, unruly stream and barbed wire fences all combined to prevent trespassing onto the mill property and created the cul de sac where the protestors circled. Not a safe location for the strikers if the Mackeys resorted to violence. Nonetheless, this was their workplace so the workers needed to make their stand here. Still, it was worrisome. This location was a trap if the standoff between boss and worker turned bad.

The hinges on the office door creaked open, causing the men to turn hopefully toward the sound. Sage straightened. He too searched for some positive sign in the faces of the union's bargaining team. Leo didn't prolong the suspense. He gave his head a doleful shake. No compromise, then.

"Son-of-a-bitch," a nearby man said under his breath. Most of the other men said nothing, just squished through the mud toward Leo. In days past, after talking with management, it was Leo's practice to mount the wooden soapbox he carried to the picket line each day and report on the negotiations. This bleak morning, Leo didn't raise himself above his men. Instead, he rested a scuffed boot on the soapbox and spoke softly. Sage stepped forward. Leo caught the movement because he gestured for Sage to move closer.

"It's like this, men. Mackey and his son think they're sitting pretty right now. What with the rain, there's little construction underway. You all know that, because of this year's gol'darn heavy rains, we'd have been sitting home a good bit even if we weren't on strike." A few nods among the men acknowledged the truth of Leo's observation. Late fall and winter always made for lean times in the construction trades.

"So, the Mackeys don't feel that they need to negotiate with us about working a six-day week or an eight-hour day. They intend to wait us out. Come spring, if we last that long, we'll be in a better position. Again, some of the men nodded.

Leo paused to search the pinched faces of the handful of men who stood looking up at him, their lips faintly blue with the cold. "Autumn isn't an ideal time to go on strike. I guess we all realize that now," he said. Again, a few nods.

"I say we burn the rascals out. The idea of a little heat right about now suits me just fine," shouted one of the younger men. He was someone Sage had previously marked as a hothead.

Leo raised a gloved hand to silence him. "I know how you feel. Think, men, if we engage in violence, you know we'd be playing into the Mackey's hands. As long as we remain law-abiding, public sympathy will keep with us. We don't want to lose that."

The men began to grumble. "My kids can't eat sympathy. I'm tired of nothing happening," said one.

"I might as well go home and start breaking up the furniture for stove wood," grumbled another.

The rumble of the mill's huge steel door sliding open snapped everyone's attention in that direction. Men on horseback poured out of the black maw as two men charged out of the office to drag the fence gate wide open. Fear rippled though the strikers at this unexpected sight. One of them, spying the wooden staves gripped by the horsemen, caught on. "We're done for, men! Run for it!" he shouted just as the horses leapt forward, their riders' heels slamming into their sides.

Sage bolted for a big leaf maple that canted out over the nearby gully. With a leap, he reached its nearly horizontal trunk and began shinnying out along its length, praying that his added weight wouldn't bear it down into the hurtling water. Other men tried sprinting up the middle of the road, only to have the mud grab their boots and slow them down. As the horses overtook them, the riders' staves swung downward to hit the men's heads, shoulders and backs. Screams, shouts and whinnies mixed with the sounds of roaring stream and drumming rain. Sage looked for one of the policemen who'd been standing sentinel these past few weeks. For the first time, every one of the helmeted officers was absent. "No damn surprise there!" Sage muttered.

From where he lay clinging to the tree trunk, Sage watched a man lose his footing and sprawl face down into the mud. Seconds later a horse's plunging hooves slammed down onto the man's back. The downed man screamed and the horse reared in surprise, its rider fighting for control.

Farther up the road, the man Sage had labeled a hothead halted his dash toward safety and looked back. After flicking a glance forward, the hothead wheeled and reversed direction, snatching up a length of board. He charged at the horse, using the swinging board to force the horse into shying away from the downed man. The rider jerked the reins, using his boot heels to spur the horse up the road and out of sight. The rescuer flung his board aside and began pulling the fallen man from the mud.

Another drama grabbed Sage's attention. About a hundred yards from his tree trunk, a striker was running, knees pumping high, through the brown weeds that covered the narrow space between the mud road and sloping gully bank. On his heels trotted a black horse, its rider swinging a long stave. The fleeing man was struck so hard he stumbled, lost his balance and tumbled end over end down the bank until he splashed into the raging creek fifteen feet below. Even before the man's terrified shriek reached his ears, Sage was slithering backward down the tree trunk. He raced along the top of the bank, his eyes combing the ground for a sturdy board or stick. At last he spotted a large tree limb and snatched it up, gauging its strength and length even as he tugged it toward the turbulent water. The limb should do. It had to.

Upstream, the man thrashed about, at least five feet from the bank, a pocket of trapped air ballooning his coat, keeping his head above the roiling brown water. His arms flailed, slapping the surface as he fought to keep his face clear even as the torrent bore him swiftly and irrevocably toward the swollen Willamette and certain death.

Slick mud underfoot prevented Sage from finding the stable footing needed to pull the heavy limb along with him. He gasped in desperation. Finally, with an "oh hell" oath he jumped over the edge of the bank, landing on his butt, the limb's big end clutched to his chest. Limb and man swiftly slid down the bank and into the water. Luckily, his boot heels hit firm gravel instead of plunging into a hole. Sage struggled to his feet, looking upstream to see the man careening toward him—now less than four yards away. Grunting, Sage struggled to lever the limb onto its butt end. Once there, he swiveled and dropped it into the water so that it pointed upstream toward the man. Flinging himself atop the limb's butt, Sage fought to hold it parallel to the stream's edge and to keep its tip pointing into the current that was trying to rip it from his grasp. With a jerk that nearly tore it from Sage's hands, the man first hit and then clutched at the limb.

Sage struggled to maintain his hold, gasping as water pelted his face with such ferocity it was impossible to tell whether it came from sky or stream. Still he held on, digging his heels in and leaning back so that the limb twisted downstream as if connected to a wheel hub. Arms quivering, Sage wrested the limb so that the current began pushing it parallel to the downstream bank. The man clutching its slick surface floated behind. At last the man's feet seemed to find purchase on the bottom, because he began pulling himself up the limb against the current toward Sage. His weight was exerting less of a drag except when he briefly lost footing and floated. By this time, Sage lay on his back against the mud bank, panting, his knuckles dead white and cramping as he fought to hold the limb, his eyes riveted on the man struggling toward him, willing him to make it. And he did. He was there, within reach. Sage grabbed him and pulled him onto the muddy slope of the bank. Gratefully, Sage released his hold on the limb. It shot away fast as a loosed arrow.

"Hoo whee," the man gasped, as he lay on his back, his chest heaving. "I thought for certain sure I was a goner. Thank you, Sam. I owe you a beer. Heck, I owe you a whole barrel, I surely do."

"Don't be thanking me just yet," Sage gasped, as he tried to stand upright on the slippery slope. "There's still those goons on horses to evade and being's as we're so damn soggy, we'll move like two old buffalo. Not much chance we'll outrun horses."

Both men looked toward the safe haven that lay less than thirty feet across the stream. No. Neither one wanted to chance that escape route. As one, they swivelled to look upstream where a thicket of bramble canes snarled the hillside, running from the top all the way down into the water, completely blocking escape in that direction. Escape downstream was also hopeless because that route took them deeper into the mill yard where, as trespassers, they'd be fair game for Mackey's goons. As if yoked together, both men faced the hill and began climbing, clutching at bushes to pull themselves up. At the bank's top edge, they lay on their bellies and slowly lifted their heads, to peer up and down the road. What they saw nearly startled them both into sliding backward.

"It's the police," Sage said, dread in his voice. The police, after all, had been suspiciously absent when the thugs attacked the strikers. The police presence now likely meant they intended to finish the thugs' job. He'd seen police turn on striking workers before. Given the policemen's low wages, bribes proved quite effective in getting the police to act on the boss's behalf. Sage climbed to his feet but stayed close to the gully's edge until he recognized the big man leading the small phalanx of helmeted policemen down the cul de sac.

TWO

Sergeant Hanke, a friend and sometimes collaborator in Sage's various escapades, was striding toward them, the churned mud sucking at his boots, a fierce scowl on his face.

The big sergeant's blue eyes widened momentarily when he recognized Sage. He knew John Sagacity Adair didn't belong in this part of town, wearing muddy workingman's clothes. Adair was, after all, the proprietor of one of Portland's most elegant eateries, Mozart's Table. The surprise vanished immediately from the policeman's features. It wasn't the first time he'd found the restaurateur in strange garb and circumstances.

Hanke addressed Sage's companion. "What's happened here?" he asked. "Why are you both soaked to the bone? Tain't raining all that hard for a change."

The other man struggled to push words out between chattering teeth and stiff lips. "One of Mackey's goons riding a damn big horse knocked me into that hellish stream down there. Sam here saved my life. Otherwise, I'd be halfway to the ocean by now. Where in hell's acres were you coppers when they rode down on us?"

Hanke's face reddened as he struggled for a response. Finally, he said, "Matter of fact, mister, we're the new shift. Probably the other shift misunderstood the time we planned to report and they quit early by mistake." The glance he sent toward Sage suggested, once they were alone, he'd voice another explanation.

"Ha!" the wet man snorted, "You coppers are in league with the Mackeys. You cleared out deliberate. Don't try to tell me different."

Good thing my friend here is mouthing off to Hanke and not to some other copper, Sage thought. Lip like that usually brought a club smack against the ear.

A commotion at the top of the cul de sac saved Hanke from formulating a response. A band of shabbily dressed men rounded the corner at a shuffling run, most clutching two-by-four boards with six-inch spikes driven through one end—serious threats to any horse and rider.

Hanke and his men spun to face them, their billy clubs rising up in two-handed readiness. Hanke quickly stepped to the forefront, raising his hand to halt the approaching group. "Whoa, men. Nothing is happening here. Lay down those boards. Everything's all over."

The group was mostly strikers, with a few regular customers from the nearby saloon mixed in. Its apparent leader, a striker named Chester Garrett, halted the group when he saw Sage. He lowered his augmented two-by-four, saying, "It's all right, men. That there is Leo's nephew, Sam. He's the one we came for—him and Jimmy there."

"It's a rescue party you've mounted then?" Hanke asked. When Garrett nodded, Hanke relaxed, lowering his billy club and motioning for the men behind him to do the same. "You acted right and proper, men. Now that you've found them, you need to take them someplace warm. They ended up in the creek and both are soaked through. Pneumonia's a danger unless they dry out fast." He gestured around at the empty *cul de sac.* "No point in hanging around here now, everything's over. The riders are gone."

Minutes later, the entire strike line was in the saloon, glasses of belly-warming whiskey in the shaking hands of the two creek battlers. Sage swallowed one shot before borrowing a dry coat from the bartender. He set out for the hospital, leaving Jimmy behind to regale the others with a blow-by-blow story of his rescue from the creek. Sage needed to talk to Leo. The union president was at the hospital, they told him, standing vigil for Rufus, the man trampled by the horse.

Sage saw immediately that the news wasn't good. Anguish etched deep lines in Leo's face. He said, "Rufus doesn't feel anything in his legs and he's busted up inside. The doctor thinks that the horse broke Rufus's spine. They don't think he'll live through the night."

Leo sat on a wooden bench, his back against an outside wall. High in that wall, small-paned windows provided a faint light that only emphasized the gray pallor of Leo's face. Still, fiery anger smoldered inside the strike leader because Leo's next words rang throughout the room. "Those sons-of-bitches meant this to happen all along. They didn't want any settlement today. Mackey just played with me, taking his time, gabbing, keeping me distracted, until his worthless son maneuvered his murderers into position. I'll see that old man in hell, see if I don't!"

Leo's threat grabbed the attention of the black-garbed nun who was working at a desk situated near the entrance of the waiting room. The nun bustled over. Alarm creased her forehead below the white band of her wimple though she kept her voice gentle, "Now, sir, I know you are upset about your friend, but we do not allow such talk here. St. Vincent's is a Christian hospital."

Leo looked down at his clenched hands and nodded meekly. "Sorry, ma'am," he said. Her eyes gleamed sympathetically and she patted his shoulder before gliding back to her desk. He leaned toward Sage, "All my men want is an eight-hour day, a six-day workweek and enough wages to feed, clothe and house their wives and kids. Why must they suffer and die for such a righteous cause? What kind of God allows this? Christian or otherwise?" Leo's questions hissed with anger.

Sage said nothing. It was one thing to come up with theological answers after leisure contemplation. Another thing altogether when a good man lay dying for no moral reason. He wasn't the first to die either. Legions had already died for shorter work hours and better wages. He knew that, before they won the battle, many more would die. Why indeed? Thinking too deeply about the heartless, senseless greed behind those deaths felt like a descent into hell's inner workings. Sage stepped back from that abyss. He'd made promises to people, to St. Alban and, more immediately, to his mother and Fong. Promises that relied on an enduring belief in greed's eventual defeat at the hands of justice. Now, more than ever, he clung to that belief because if he let it go, Rufus's suffering would become meaningless.

Sage laid a hand on Leo's shoulder, "I don't know, Leo. It seems that's the way of life. We make the choice—we either permit wrong to continue or we make an effort to stop it—two diverging trails. No one forced Rufus to make the choice he did. It was always up to him whether he stayed or abandoned the fight. He chose to stay. And, Leo, I believe that some day the humanity of brave men like Rufus will prevail."

"You tell that to him, lying in that hospital bed with his back broke. You tell it to his children, to his wife who is going to lose her husband and be left to raise their little kids all on her own. I'd like to see you try," Leo said bitterly. "I can't. I'd choke on those castles-in-the-air words right now."

Later that day, Sage sat at the small table near the kitchen door, fingering the waxed ends of his carefully groomed mustache. Sam Graham no longer existed. Two stories overhead, the rough clothes worn by Leo's "nephew" lay discarded on the floor. He looked down at the spotless white shirt and fine broadcloth suit. His clean fingers touched the white blaze above his right temple, the concealing lamp black once again scrubbed out.

He stared into the middle distance, thinking that transforming his looks did nothing to stop Leo's bitter words from repeating inside his head, again and again. Sage wondered, exactly what do you tell a woman whose husband is dead and whose children now face a life of poverty? How could he— sitting in his fully-stocked kitchen, in his expensive restaurant, in his wholly-owned building, really know what she was facing or how she felt? He was in a position to make the choice between a comfortable life and one of struggle. Most working folk never had that choice. As if on cue, Fong's voice sounded in his head, "Choice always good, especially if you make right choice."

So, he, Mae and Fong made the choice to follow St. Alban, who was a hero to many. Originally in the mine workers union, St. Alban had seared his lungs in a Colorado mine fire he'd entered to save trapped miners. For that, miners and others in the labor movement fondly called him "the Saint." In the years since his heroic deed, the raspy-voiced St. Alban continued to earn workers' respect, making them willing to follow him wherever he believed the labor movement needed to go. His goals were simple: Decent lives for working people, job security and an end to rampant greed.

When Sage felt optimistic, he saw the gains, the small steps toward simple things like more healthy working conditions and wages high enough to keep food on the table. The advance was slow, carried on the shoulders of people like Rufus who risked everything—families, homes and their lives. When their efforts paid off, their families, coworkers, neighbors and the entire city, benefitted. Healthy workplaces, decent livelihoods and the time to enjoy being part of a family and community "raised everybody's boat," as his mother would say.

Gradually the kitchen din increased as Mozart's cook, Ida, and her helpers, efficiently prepared the evening supper. At the other end of the room, a linoleum counter containing a big enamel sink stretched the length of the wall. A new girl, apron cinched around her waist, was vigorously scrubbing bowls and utensils, her cheeks rosy from the effort and the heat of the kitchen. Nearer to hand, a coal-fired cookstove sat in the middle of the room next to an equally large linoleum-covered preparation table. Ida herself stood at the stove, stirring pots and issuing instructions over her shoulder to the two waiters as they grabbed full plates from the warming oven and bustled out the swinging door into the dining room. A single electric light shone on the scene, its dim glow wavering whenever a draft touched its hanging wire. This dim globe was the only electricity in the building.

Though if Mae Clemens got her way and, eventually she would, the ugly dangling wires would festoon the kitchen's ceiling.

Sage filled his coffee cup, sat again and returned to brooding, waiting for his mother to return to the kitchen. Leo was right, he concluded. Sometimes, words gave no comfort. Sometimes comforting platitudes choked like dust in the throat.

Sage looked toward his mother, Mae Clemens. She stood in the alley just outside the kitchen door. The lack of curtains on the back door and adjacent glass side panels allowed him to see her clearly. The sight could still make his heart twinge because of all the years he hadn't seen her. Ramrod straight, her head erect beneath a twisted crown of slightly silvered raven hair, she was conversing with a ragpicker. The stranger wore a heavy, serviceable brown overcoat. He'd stuffed his baggy canvas pants into scuffed boots that laced up nearly to his knees. Layered flannel plaid shirts flashed color from beneath his drab, unbuttoned coat. Nearby, his two-wheeled handcart waited, bulky burlap bags filling its bed, parallel wooden shafts resting on the ground.

Taking advantage of a rain break, the man pushed his tattered black hat back, exposing a broad, lined forehead. The weak sunlight traced the arching ridge of his long nose. With his untrimmed beard and deep-set brown eyes, the man resembled those East European Jews who intently conducted business on New York City's crowded streets. The ragpicker's age was hard to figure. Outdoor living aged a face well before its time. He looked maybe about ten years older than Mae Clemens. Around sixty-five. Too old for street living in this dismal weather. Sage hoped the ragpicker had a warm place to sleep.

The man spoke and Mae Clemens nodded emphatically and stood listening as he talked on at length. When the ragpicker finished speaking, she clapped softly, spoke a few words and patted the man's sleeve. Glancing toward the kitchen, she caught Sage's gaze upon her and smiled. Turning back to the man, she again touched his forearm and said something that made the ragpicker shake his head. She whirled and hurried up the stairs to enter the kitchen.

Sage started speaking only to stop when she raised a hand, saying "Just a moment, Mr. Adair, I need to collect food for

Mr. Eich. He's likely to roll off before I get back out there." Sure enough, the man outside was pulling on knitted gloves that covered all except the tips of his long boney fingers. He bent down, hefted the shafts and the cart began to roll.

Meanwhile, Sage's mother swiftly sliced and wrapped slabs of roast beef and bread in waxed paper and headed out the open door. By that time, the ragpicker's cart was already out of Sage's sight, its departure marked by the sound of its iron-clad wheels rattling over the alley's potholes. The cart sounds paused, only to begin again before disappearing beneath the distant rattle of trolley and dray.

Sage's mother appeared and mounted the steps at a slower pace, the food parcel gone. "Coffee, Mr. Adair?" she asked on her way to the large pot keeping warm in the back corner of the stove.

"Yes, Mrs. Clemens," Sage responded using her maiden name. They'd promised Vincent St. Alban to keep their relationship secret while working for him. Initially, that precaution felt unnecessarily theatrical. After all, their previous work for St. Alban had taken place in the mountain hollows of Appalachia where people knew them. Here in Oregon, though, they knew no one. An incident the previous June, however, forced them to acknowledge the wisdom of St. Alban's insistence on secrecy. An adversary, desperate to forestall exposure of a land fraud, had set alarm bells clanging when he pressured Sage for details about Mae Clemens. That unsuccessful attempt to warn Sage off reinforced the idea that their relationship made them vulnerable.

She slid into the chair opposite him and leaned forward across the table. "That was Mr. Eich I was talking to," she explained in a low voice.

"Mr. Eich, huh?" Sage repeated in an equally low voice. "What did Mr. Eich, the ragpicker, say to turn you all agog?"

She tightened her lips and lifted her chin. "I am never agog. If you must know, not that it is any of your business, he recited a poem and I listened. That's all."

"A ragpicker poet, that's a new one on me. Where does his inspiration come from? The bottom of the dustbins, the holes in his shoes?"

Her shoulders twitched in irritation and her tone was snappish as she said, "Neither one, Sage. I am sure that his ideas come from his own experience just like yours do. And, he cares about justice, right and wrong just as much as we do."

"Sounds lofty. Is he any good as a poet?"

"Sometimes. Today, though, he recited a poem by a woman named 'Sarah' somebody. About children watching from their factory window as the rich men golfed." She flapped her hand dismissively. "Enough of Mr. Eich. What happened today at the strike?"

He told her, downplaying the danger to himself as he related Jimmy's near drowning. He also described the deadly assault on Rufus and the man's poor prognosis.

"Humph. Just plain lucky they didn't knock you into the crick too. As I recall, your swimming ain't worth a darn." She stared into her mug of coffee. "Riding unarmed men down doesn't exactly fit the character of the Abner Mackey that *The Gazette* praises in its society pages," she mused. "From what they print, you'd think him a kindly, benevolent old coot."

He said nothing and they sat in silent, gloomy contemplation until she shook it off. "Sitting here wallowing in bad happenings won't change a one of them. Best we both keep moving forward," she said and stood, radiating vigor as she snugged tight her apron strings and waded into the kitchen bustle. Her departure left Sage with the task of figuring out how to move the strike effort "forward" after such a serious setback. No question—he held the dirty end of the stick when it came to assigned tasks. Still, her words suggested an idea.

An hour later, Sage was mounting the steps into the *Daily Journal* newspaper offices. Once inside, he navigated between tightly packed desks where reporters clacked away on their typing machines. When Sage finally reached the relative peace of the publisher's office, he found Ben Johnston bent over his desk, fountain pen feverishly scratching corrections across typed copy.

Johnston gave an irritated growl when the door opened only to grin when he saw Sage. "Sorry, to sound so unfriendly, Adair. Those yahoos in the other room stick their head in here every couple minutes to interrupt me with one question or another. I am trying to work this article into shape before it has to hit the presses. Seems like there's been an interruption in the middle of every sentence." Johnston gestured to the empty chair before the desk. "John, mighty good to see you! Sit, sit. What brings you out?"

Johnston's warm welcome was typical. First and foremost, Sage was a big investor in Johnston's feisty newcomer of a newspaper, *The Daily Journal.* They planned to break the fifty-year monopoly of the establishment newspaper, *The Portland Gazette.* Secondly, more than once, Sage had demonstrated an uncanny knack for churning up stories that increased *The Journal's* circulation. So, there was good reason for Johnston's pleasure at seeing Sage.

An anticipatory glint brightened Johnston's eyes when Sage pulled a sheet of paper from inside his coat. Sage handed it to Johnston who pushed his glasses up on his nose and began to read, concentration wrinkling his forehead.

Johnston laid the paper aside. "Not bad writing for an amateur reporter. Is it true?" he asked.

"Absolutely, every word. I was there. Will you print it, Ben?"

"I've no problem doing that, as long as you vouch for it. I'm sorry that the poor young man is in the hospital, though. Doesn't sound like there's much hope for him. Too damn bad. Anyway, Adair, I'll print this story. *The Gazette* certainly won't touch it. Those Gazetters hate unions and they're too caught up in being la-di-da to care whether working people get hurt. Fact is, more than likely we'll see their article blaming Rufus for what happened to him."

Johnston leaned back in his chair, interlacing his ink-stained fingers over his lean stomach. "The Mackeys know *The Gazette* is behind them whatever shenanigans they pull. I'd take bets that *The Gazette* will never publish one word of criticism against either the Mackeys or their thugs. That class of people guards each other's secrets like a prairie killdeer warming her eggs."

Johnston snapped erect in his chair as if coming to a sudden decision. His pen tapped Sage's article. "I'll print it all right. I hope some good comes of publishing it."

Sergeant Hanke sat in Mozart's kitchen, waiting for Sage's return. Usually, Hanke took some time rolling his words out. Not this time. "Your nearly-drowned friend back there at the mill made the right call," he said, his wide face glum. "I just happened to stumble across the policemen assigned duty at the strike. Found them hiding out in the back of Roxy's Saloon. From the looks of things, somebody bought them beers so they'd stay there. It made me think something might be about to happen. So, I grabbed a few men and headed on down to the strike line at a fast trot. Just sorry we didn't show up before the horse stomped that one striker."

Hanke was a dedicated police officer who took it hard whenever his fellow officers failed to display a similar dedication. He still wanted to believe that his fellow officers were as honest as he was. The downcast German soon took his leave after surprisingly declining a piece of Ida's dried-apple pie. The big policeman had never refused that offer before.

Late in the night, sleep eluded Sage, driven away by worrisome questions tumbling one after the other through his mind. How long until the strikers and their families gave up? How long before they abandoned the strike for other jobs, or even worse, crossed the picket line, hat in hand, to beg the Mackeys for a second chance? If something good didn't happen soon, he would not blame the striking men for giving up the fight, walking away—leaving it for replacements to fill their jobs, working endless hours for a pittance.

When worry stopped bedeviling Sage's thoughts, he relived the horror of that huge beast rearing above Rufus's unprotected back. More than once, that vision snapped him alert when he began to drift off. So, Sage lay there, staring at the ceiling until finally fixating on a single question: What was the meaning of his own work if, in the end, it meant that Rufus sacrificed his life for a failed strike?" Sage tossed, turned, and punched his pillow repeatedly to no avail. Sleep stayed elusive until after midnight.

THREE

SHEET RAIN SLAMMING INTO THE WINDOWS woke Sage. His pocket watch, lying open on the bedside table, indicated he'd slept for less than an hour. He listened as the rain, driven by a fitful wind, pelted soft, loud, then soft again. His work as a timber beast in the Pacific Northwest woods gave Sage the opportunity to experience rain's every manifestation—fat globs, fine droplets, sleet, snow, even feather light mist. Whatever shape it took, every wet molecule proved pernicious in its ability to penetrate layered woolens down to warm skin. For endless days, he'd watched as the rain relentlessly pelted leaves, trickled down limbs and trunks—seeping into the earth—making the ground soggy, sodden, and finally muck. He'd sheltered with other loggers beneath dense fir boughs during the worst of it, as they spit tobacco and told each other bear, cougar and Sasquatch stories. The stinking dank of crowded lumber camp bunkhouses was worse. There, his joints soon ached from the dampness permeating the walls and he felt helpless, then angry, when a winter contagion swept through, leaving loggers lying dead atop their hard plank bunks.

He shut off those grim memory pictures. Tonight, he was warm and dry although the watery drum of raindrops, dripping gutters and the squish of wheels in the street below filled the night beyond his windows. It was turning out to be an incredibly wet fall and, even though winter hadn't yet hit, many lowland stretches lay beneath roiling water. The vibrant red and intense yellow of maple leaves had quickly given way to the duller red-brown leaves of the oak. Now, even those were falling beneath the onslaught of constant rain. Sage burrowed deeper under his quilt, retreating from the fierce sounds assaulting the window glass and fixing his thoughts on spring sunshine and the scent of roses .

Half a mile south, Herman Eich, the ragpicker, lay in his narrow iron cot, his back propped up by pillows. Woolen gloves, finger tips removed, kept the damp away from his arthritic fingers as he held a small book tilted so as to best capture the oil lamp's spluttering light. Tattered blankets, rescued from dust bins, snugged tight across his body up to his breastbone. Two flannel shirts and a woman's discarded shawl kept his shoulders warm while a faded night cap covered his ears. In the corner, dying embers sparked within a small potbellied stove as salvaged wood collapsed onto itself. Soon, what little warmth the shed held would leak out through the gaps in its walls or be sucked away by the tin roof. Eich lay down his book. It was time to douse the light and pull the covers to his chin, leaving to beard and cap the task of keeping his head warm until morning.

Still, he mused, there was much to celebrate in rain. There was comfort in its murmurs, companionship in its many voices. Nature's blood, that's how he thought of it. After trudging through miles of parched desert and brown prairie grass he'd found the lush green of the Willamette Valley inexpressibly beautiful. He particularly liked the fall season when spinning maple seeds, tossed into the promise of future life by the gusting winds, found their way to shelter and nourishment beneath the colorful mounds of fallen leaves.

He smiled at his romantic fancies. Reality was closer to hand in the form of drips pinging into the tin cans he'd positioned across the rough plank floor. His widowed landlady was not to blame for the sieve-like roof. She barely charged him for this space and was pitifully grateful when he'd taken it. His few dollars in monthly rent bought food for her two children. Her tiny two-room house, his shed a leaky adjunct, perched on the edge of the Marquam Ravine. One block to the east was the north end of the only bridge spanning the 150-foot deep ravine. Tonight, the roaring stream at the ravine's bottom was so loud that it drowned out any street traffic. As was his practice when readying to sleep, Eich began mentally tracing the stream's transformation from a trickle seeping from beneath rocks just below the western ridge, into a roaring torrent that fattened with every foot it traveled.

What a contrast was this winter crescendo to the summertime stream, when poor children played beside its quiet trickle in the mess of broken glass and jagged metal that people tossed off bank and bridge. Summertime was when the ravine rang with children's chatter and the shouted cautions of their mothers.

Eich reached out his gloved hand to twist down the wick. The last splutter of light caught on the decorated porcelain handbasin he was repairing for a young woman who worked as a maid in the prestigious Portland Hotel. A slight crack in the rim made it unacceptable for use by the hotel's upscale clientele. Once mended, however, the basin would be the poor woman's treasure and he'd be a few cents richer. Other damaged porcelain objects crowded his workbench top. Nothing to make him rich but, along with the proceeds of his ragpicking, enough work to keep him fed and housed.

On the other side of the Marquam Ravine, just a few hundred yards as the crow flies, Clarisa Brown blinked sleepily in the light of the flaring match. She lit the candle before bending over to lift the wailing infant from his crib. "Shush, little Daniel, Daddy's sleeping." She kept her voice soft and loving even though a part of her was irritated and impatient. She was so bone weary, wanting silence and to creep back into the warmth of her bed. She thought of her husband down below them on the first floor.

Poor Daniel. Driven from her side by his namesake's crying, he'd stumbled down the narrow stairs to try sleeping on their short parlor sofa. He was such a good man her Daniel.

She moved over to the rocker, taking the candle with her and placing it on the small table beneath the window. Lifting her breast from the warmth of her flannel nightgown, she gave it to her son. For a few moments, she gazed at her reflection in the black mirror of the rain-spattered window—the edges of the filmy curtains framed the tableau. Baby Daniel in her arms, like that picture in the church—another cradling mother, just like mothers through all time. Ah mercy, she was tired, so head-hanging tired. Clarisa buried her nose in the sweet fragrance of baby hair. In seconds, the gentle suckling carried her into deep sleep. Not even the candle's bright flaring penetrated her heavy eyelids.

❀ ❀ ❀

At first, Eich didn't know what woke him. Only that an unusual noise had set his heart to pounding. He sat up, ears straining, turning his head this way and that. Had the sound come from his dream or the waking world? Seconds later, the answer came in the form of a shrill scream of animal agony. Eich threw his covers back. He began yanking canvas trousers over baggy long johns even as his stockinged feet felt for his boots. The screams came from somewhere outside. He heard his landlady stirring, crying out in alarm on the other side of their shared wall. When the animal screamed again, his more alert mind honed in on its location. It came from near the bridge, yet somehow muffled.

Eich banged open the shed's door and stepped out to look along the side of the house toward the bridge. Its dense structure stood disfigured against the lighter black of sky—the familiar geometry of its supporting beams broken into jagged ends, dangling all catawampis. "Dear God, in heaven," he breathed, "the bridge has collapsed with someone on it." He began running toward the disaster as the horse screamed again, its agonized cry followed by the faint shouts of panicked men.

He cleared the stand of fir trees at the ravine's edge to obtain a clear view across it to the other side. Near the end of the bridge, across the ravine, a house was on fire. Flames were shooting out its upstairs windows. The competing horrors momentarily froze Eich's steps until the sight of a black figure, leaping like a frenzied marionette before the flaming house, spurred Eich back into action.

A horse's scream soared up from deep within the ravine, followed by fainter human cries. A wagon, carrying men, had fallen through the bridge. The wreckage was down there, the men maybe lying in freezing water. And a house was ablaze. Unsure which disaster to address, Eich snatched up a tin pail and a length of rope from beneath the overhang of his landlady's house and started running.

Eich reached the bridge and saw that the choice was out of his hands. The structure canted perilously downstream. Just before mid-span, a black hole gaped, planks tilted waist high. On the other side of that chaos the man at the fire raced to the bridge only to whirl back toward the burning house, his arms raised to the dark sky in supplication. There was no way to reach the frantic man. The bridge looked impassable. A sudden roaring swoosh rolled across the ravine. The house tumbled inward, sending flaming embers spurting into the night sky.

As if witnessing that explosive conflagration, the horse below screamed again, its terror rising up from the blackness like a scream out of hell. Eich took one last agonized look at the burning house and sent a pessimistic prayer skyward that fire had trapped no souls inside that inferno. He dropped the pail and plunged over the steep bank, rope in hand, toward the streambed below. As he slid and staggered downward, with tendrils of vines grabbing at his ankles, he heard a pistol pop once above the stream's roar and the animal screams ceased. Dread at what he was going to find overtook him even as he fought his way toward the creek bank.

Midpoint down the slope the outlines of a hulking mass started to emerge. It hung half in and half out of the stream. Twisting as it fell, the wagon lay in bits and pieces nearly parallel to the water's course. Eich squinted, trying to see the wagon's contours. He saw a collage of wooden wheels, a large copper tank and a long sinuous hose trailing upslope. In the stream's edge, a high-crowned, stiff leather helmet lay upside down until the water swirled it away. He was looking at a fire wagon, scattered in pieces across the hillside. The men who'd fallen with the wagon also lay strewn about. Some groaning softly, sprawled against the muddy slope, others lay crumpled, still as death. Eich dropped down beside a man to lever a splintered bridge timber from off his chest. Even as he frantically tossed the wood aside, Eich became aware of three things. More rescuers were sliding down the bank toward him. The fiery glow lighting the sky above the ravine was dimming to a faint rosy hue. And, the rain had stopped.

FOUR

It was the silence outside that woke Sage. Rain no longer splatted against the window and it was still too early for the drays to rattle down the wood-block street below. A soft rustle drew his eyes to where Fong was laying out the soiled but dry "Sam" clothes. Incipient dawn light caught the flash of the Chinese man's smile when he looked in Sage's direction.

"Time you rise up Mr. Sage." Only Fong, St. Alban and his mother called him "Sage," the diminutive of his middle name. "Sagacity" was an old family name on his mother's side. Family legend held that the first Sagacity served as tactical advisor to a vanquished Irish chieftain. Given the outcome of his advice, Sage wondered why the family held the name in such high esteem.

Fong looked in Sage's direction, mild impatience taking over his expression when Sage didn't move. "It is early. Still, best to rise now. Because of newspaper story," he said. He bent to light a lamp and, for a minute, Sage contemplated the Chinese man's aesthetic profile with its broad forehead and sharp cheekbones. A northern Chinese face, according to Fong, although he'd been born near Shanghai where faces tended toward being round and soft featured.

Newspaper story? Sage's sleepy mind caught up with Fong's words. Right, his visit to *The Journal* the day before. "Ben Johnston came through for us?" He flung the covers aside and reached for his clothes. No need to explain further. Fong knew exactly what he meant because, over the last two years, Fong had evolved into being a partner, a teacher and, more recently, his closest friend. The three of them, Fong Kam Tong, Sage and Sage's mother, Mae Clemens, were a team fighting for economic justice.

"Yes, Mr. Sage. Mr. Johnston came through for us, I think. So does your mother. Eat now," Fong gestured to a tray of bread, cheese, meat and coffee on the table beside the morning's newspaper.

Sage ate as he read the story positioned just below the fold on *The Journal*'s front page. "*Labor Dispute Turns Deadly*" announced the headline while a subtitle continued, "*Unarmed strikers attacked by thugs.*" Sage's submission of the previous day, with minor changes, was below the fold.

"The front page positioning is good," he said. He flipped the paper over to see what lead story pre-empted the strike news. A blurry picture, obviously taken using flash powder at night, showed a hodgepodge of timbers, a wagon wheel jutting high in the air and maybe the haunch of a downed horse. The headline just above the picture stated, "*Bridge Collapse Destroys Fire Wagon.*" Sage scanned the story. The trestle bridge over the Marquam Ravine collapsed during the night, just as a fire wagon was crossing it on the way to a fire. One horse died. Six firemen injured, two seriously. The story's final paragraph noted that the house burned to the ground, killing a mother and baby. The father had survived.

He shuddered, imagining that poor woman's last, terrified moments. "Wonder why that bridge failed?" he asked aloud.

"Maybe all the rainwater washed out bridge," Fong replied as he began loading the dishes back onto the tray, preparatory to returning downstairs.

"Mr. Fong," Sage called out to halt Fong's exit. "Your cousins find out anything about Abner Mackey or his son, Earl?"

"No information yet. Mackeys never hire China men. Not to work in kitchens or wash laundry—so no information comes from that way. I will keep asking," he promised as he closed the door softly behind him.

That was discouraging news. Often, Fong's "cousins," members of his fraternal society, his "tong," ferreted out information that was inaccessible to the city's Occidentals. This was because, like most servants, the Chinese laboring in the white man's world performed their tasks virtually unnoticed by those they served once familiarity set in. Sage smiled ruefully to himself. He was guilty of that arrogance as well. He'd been oblivious of Fong's keen interest in their goings-on until the night Fong rescued him from a savage beating. That was the night that Fong shed his own false persona and became their partner in all things.

Sage finished drinking his coffee while he mulled over the strike situation. The persistent lack of information about the Mackeys was yet another frustration in a litany of frustrations. Was this job for St. Alban jinxed? Not one single thing seemed to be going in the strikers' favor. To turn the situation around, they needed to discover a crack in the Mackeys' public facade and figure out how to use it. The Mackeys hid a secret of some sort—most rich men did.

When he was a wealthy mine owner's foster son, Sage rubbed elbows with many of the country's robber barons. One nefarious scheme or another usually accounted for their obscene worldly wealth. Greed begat greed—since they grew more rapacious the wealthier they became. It was almost as if they believed God blessed their undertakings and, therefore, only God himself was entitled to set their limitations. By the time the year 1900 arrived, the rich were in a frenzy of capital consolidation and corporate expansion. Daily, these corporate masters gained in power as they seized control and formed trusts to govern utilities, railroads, timber, banks, meat packing, and almost every other essential of life. It seemed more than ironic that, even as the newspapers shrilled about the anarchists, they remained deathly silent about the devastation corporate greed was wrecking on the lives of most Americans.

The only effective opposition to this limitless greed came from organized labor, citizen groups like the Consumers League, and a smattering of progressive groups agitating at the state and local levels. Despite being underfunded and outfoxed, these citizen led groups had forced progressive ideas front and center in the 1900 presidential election. Sage allowed himself a rueful grimace. Given the corporations' power over both houses of Congress and Teddy Roosevelt's own privileged background, it seemed unlikely that the people's sentiments would get the upper hand. Those who worked in Washington seemed to be the obedient thralls of corporate power, despite their populist vote-getting promises to the people. Still, following McKinley's assassination and shortly after assuming the presidency, Roosevelt took on E. H. Harriman, the nation's most powerful railroad trust baron.

A swath of rain slamming against the window stopped his woolgathering, reminding him that Leo's nephew, Sam, needed to make an appearance. Sighing, Sage pulled on his canvas coveralls, wool coat and felt-lined cloth cap. He departed Mozart's through the secret stairway that descended from the third floor into the cellar, shuffling along the concealed brick-lined tunnel until he reached the trap door that lifted into the adjoining alley. Although there was little fear of discovery on a day like this, Sage carefully studied the street at the alley's end. The few people hurrying by had their chins tucked and their thoughts focused on finding a dry haven, so he was unnoticed when he lifted the trap door and clambered up into the alley.

About ten policemen stood at the head of the cul de sac. Given the consequences of their absence yesterday, Sage figured that they were under orders to present a show of force today. Surprisingly, a large number of strangers also milled about. In fact, warmly-dressed men and women crowded the bottom of the cul de sac, many of them holding placards, while they sang and chattered despite the rain. He moved closer to read the placards. The newcomers represented a panoply of unions: "Butchers," "Bricklayers," "Iron Workers," "Cannery Workers," "Boiler Makers," "Tailors," "Barbers," proclaimed the placards they waved in the chill air. Apparently, *The Journal*'s story about

Rufus had brought the city's other unions out in a show of support for the Mackey strikers.

Leo was easy to spot. He stood atop his trusty soapbox—his jowls jiggling with indignation as he exhorted the group, his finger jabbing the air. To one side, a small fire warmed the coffee pots nestled in its midst. Women in walking skirts and high-top boots distributed steaming tin cups among the crowd. All in all, a markedly different scene from the last few weeks. Sage sidled up to one of the strikers. "So what's the commotion about?" he asked.

The man said excitedly, "Sam, glad you're here! Somehow *The Journal* found out about what happened yesterday and printed a real good article. All morning long, we seen folks coming down the road to join us." He gestured toward a coffee tin standing on the corner of a small table. "They been dropping money in that coffee can and some of the unions are promising they'll take up regular collections for us as long as we're on strike. It's wonderful." The man's grin gave his face more furrows than a cornfield.

"Wonderful," Sage echoed. It was an encouraging development. Yet, he knew from experience that this big turnout was likely to be short-lived. These supporters might show up for a few more days before dwindling away, returning to their own tough lives, leaving the strikers to stand a lonely vigil once again.

"I tole the foreman that damn bridge wasn't safe." The words caught Sage's ear as he moved past three men standing close together.

"Don't matter none to the Mackeys, long as they make their off-the-books money. It probably only costs them what little bit they give to the city engineer," came the grim rejoinder.

Sage froze in his tracks. He looked toward the three men who he knew to be level-headed stalwarts walking the strike line.

"Are you saying that the Mackeys might be responsible for that bridge collapse last night?" Sage asked as he stepped toward them, keeping his voice low and calm.

For a moment, the three men said nothing, looking uncertainly at this nephew of their leader—he was an outsider, after all. Finally, one of them said, "Guess its all right to tell you, Sam," he said, "seeing as how you saved Jimmy's life yesterday. Elmer here worked that Marquam bridge job. Let him tell you."

The man called Elmer cleared his throat and darted a glance around before speaking in a low voice. "When we worked on that bridge, I feared whether it would hold up. I suspicioned that punk riddled the timber that got left in place. And them rough slabs Mackey gave us to nail over the weak spots in the roadbed weighed too much for the sagging supports underneath. When we raised a fuss over it, Mackey moved us to another job and replaced us with day laborers. Those monkeys finished the job so quick I wondered whether they'd just slapped a coat of creosote over it. I was planning on taking a look but the strike happened and I forgot all about it. If all they used was creosote, it were only a matter of time before that bridge collapsed."

"Punk?" Sage asked.

"Rot," explained the third man who'd remained silent until that point. "It's possible for bridge timbers to be full of rot and still look good on the outside. If you dig into them with something sharp, though, you'll find them all acrumble inside. We call it 'punk,' most other folks call it 'dry rot.'"

"Why didn't the Mackeys just replace the rotten timbers?"

"Well, I hold my own ideas on that," said Elmer his eyes flicking around and stepping closer. "Problem is, there's no proof."

"What ideas are those, Elmer?"

"Let's put it this way, if a fella charged for timber that wasn't used, well, a fella might sell the same timber a second time, or even a third time, mightn't he now? And there'd be the labor costs. Suppose the city pays a construction contractor for labor costs on work that ain't never done . . . what happens to that money, do you suppose?"

"How did such thievery come about? Doesn't someone inspect the work?" Sage felt outrage but no surprise. Over the years, he'd seen plenty of laziness and corruption in municipal matters.

The three men exchanged glances and Elmer again took the lead. "Well, a fellow might say 'there's inspection, and then, there's inspection.'" Sage looked around in time to see Leo dismount his soapbox and talk quietly with a few men. Sage nodded at the three and headed in Leo's direction. When Sage appeared at his side, Leo looked up and grinned. "Hey, Sam, how about the turnout today?"

"It's heartening, Leo, that's for sure. What's the word on Rufus?"

The other man's face sobered. "No word yet. He's the same. They don't hold out much hope," he said.

"Police doing anything to catch the man who rode him down?"

"Nope, they never asked nobody nothin' as near as I saw." Leo changed the subject, "Looks like *The Journal* got the jump on the competition, even shamed the *Portland Gazette* into sending that reporter down here." His hand gestured toward the bowler-hatted man questioning the strikers, pencil and notebook in his hand.

"Don't be too quick to celebrate." Sage cautioned. "The day *The Gazette* prints a story favorable to labor I'll eat my cap."

Leo laughed. "Well, I guess that means that cap of yours is safe."

Sage lowered his voice, "Leo, may I speak a moment with you in private?"

Leo dipped his head and the two of them moved closer to the road's edge. The roaring stream at their backs provided cover for their words. Sage quickly told Leo what the three strikers said about the Marquam Ravine's trestle timbers.

"Do you see? Maybe if we figure out how to lay the collapse at the Mackeys' door, folks won't be so sympathetic to them. One thing I've learned about Portland's money men is that they make themselves scarce whenever disapproving fingers point toward one of their own. They don't want their own doings scrutinized," Sage said.

Leo rubbed his chin and nodded saying, "Well, the men's word alone won't mean all that much against the Mackeys' claims. Maybe let's start by checking out Elmer's information. One of my right-hand guys, Chester, knows everything when it comes to bridge construction. He started out building rail-road trestles here in the West. Can't get no more specialized or dangerous than that job. Lots of those fellas died. How's about you and him go take a look under that trestle bridge?"

"Sounds like a good plan," Sage agreed, feeling a wisp of hope rise. He looked away from Leo toward Chester, thinking, "If only we can discover something to use—some kind of edge."

Sage and Chester set off together a few minutes later, with Sage hurrying to keep up with the other man's stride since Chester was at least three inches taller than Sage's six-foot height. The bridge carpenter was gangly and sported a rough, beaky nose extending out beyond the shelter of his hat brim. He began Sage's education by gesturing toward a nearby elevated roadway where it crossed an extensive marshland adjacent to the river. Pointing at the bridge he asked, "Now, from the looks of those heavy timbers, I expect you think that marsh trestle there stands all right and regular."

Sage nodded in agreement since he saw nothing unsound about the structure.

Chester, however, shook his head. "Fact of the matter is, you can't say that it's sound and neither can I. A bridge might look just fine from a distance, especially if it's wearing a new coat of creosote. So, that bridge you're looking at might be unsound, but a fella won't know for sure unless he crawls down under and pokes into its timbers."

"So, you are saying that particular trestle over there might be ready to fall down even though it looks fine?" Sage asked.

"That's right," Chester said, "Can't tell since I ain't drilled into its posts with an auger yet. Point is, there's no telling just from looking, 'specially if someone's hid the wood under fresh creosote. For certain, rotten trestles ain't gonna hold up under all this water we've been getting."

Chester's prediction struck Sage like a unexpected clout on the ear. Miles of elevated roadways and trestles dotted Portland's landscape. They spanned gullies, gulches, ravines, and large expanses of marsh. Chester said there were forty trestle bridges at least. How many of them hid dangerous rot under a fresh coat of creosote? What if the fall and winter rains caused more of them to collapse? If that started happening, other houses might burn to the ground because fire wagons couldn't reach them. Lord, imagine the chaos. People having trouble reaching work, shops, doctors or wherever they needed to be.

The two men reached the north end of the bridge that crossed the Marquam Ravine. Watery sunlight streamed from between sullen gray clouds. Curious onlookers, the sun having pulled them out of their houses, stood along the northern edge of the ravine pointing and jawing. Farther south, a storm's towering edge sent a dark curtain slanting downward as the weather front came rolling inexorably north. The sun break was going to be damn short. Sage buttoned up his coat and pulled his cap snug. At least that oncoming rain wouldn't be so cold. Nothing like when rain came from the north or roared out of the Columbia River Gorge to the east. Of course, the warmer southern rains brought their own unique difficulties. This early in the winter, they melted new snow and set the rivers rampaging. "Hope we finish this inspection before that storm hits," he said to Chester.

"Hmm" was all Chester said. For a man who always worked outdoors, the weather was likely too commonplace to discuss. He stopped, studied the bridge and said to Sage, "Looks to me like the decking broke under a slab patch. The falling wagon tore loose the stringers underneath on her way down." Chester shook his head and said, mostly to himself, "Hell of a repair job ahead."

Sage studied the bridge and thought he understood. About fifty feet from where they stood, a jagged hole punctured the trestle's roadbed. Before and past the hole, the roadbed's planks jutted into the air, as if some giant had slammed his fist down onto the bridge. Also taken out was the sidewalk running along the west side. On the eastside, only a foot's width of sidewalk atop a narrow stringer and a sagging wooden railing connected the two ends of the trestle. Fragments of road planking dangled from the stringer, tilting the whole length of broken sidewalk boards toward the hole in the trestle's middle. Sage tried to sight down that one remaining railing and saw that the bridge tilted sharply to one side. The entire structure looked on the verge of collapse. "And it's a hell of a long way down," Sage said softly, paraphrasing Chester's last words.

Three boys, one a few years older than the other two, appeared at the bridge's other end. They stepped out onto the bridge and began to cross. Reaching the gaping hole, the leader gripped the railing and started sliding his feet along the narrow stringer. Reaching the middle of the gap, his face took on the rictus grin of forced bravado as the tilted sidewalk and stringer swayed under his light weight. He slowed and began placing each foot carefully, moving an inch at a time. The two smaller boys, maybe eight years old, trailed close behind with fear widening their eyes and compressing their lips. All three whooped when they finally reached the solid planks at the trestle's north end. They thudded past Chester and Sage and up the street.

Chester stepped to the side railing to study the ravine's depths. "Looks like they're fixing to hoist up the dead horse and wagon," he said over his shoulder. Sage joined him at the railing. Sure enough, far below, a hive of men were hauling on ropes and shouting directions to each other. Peering down through the leafless tree branches, Sage made out the undercarriage of the fire wagon.

"Damn lucky that wagon weren't at the middle of the span when that roadbed broke loose," Chester commented, "Looks like the wagon slid through tail end first, hit the bank high up and rolled to the bottom. Gave the men time to jump clear." He snugged his cap down tighter on his head and headed toward the middle of the bridge. "Too much activity down there. Someone's going to notice if we go down on this side. We'll need to go at it from the south end."

Sage thought he'd misheard until Chester started edging along the tilted sidewalk just traversed by the three boys. "You ain't afraid of heights, are you, Sam?" Chester called back.

"No, not much," Sage said, sweat instantly beading under his cap band and his response a squeak as it caught in his suddenly dry throat. Chester twisted around to grin back at him, flashing a set of horsey-yellow chompers, his bright blue eyes teasing.

One look at the chasm beneath the shaking bridge and Sage ordered himself not to look down again until they'd crossed the damnable thing. Either the entire structure actually swayed under their weight or else his imagination played tricks on him. Regardless, it seemed to take forever to reach safety at the trestle's southern end.

There, the house fire's pungent stink saturated the cold air. Sage paused to look at the charred rubble, a pang of sorrow hitting him when he thought again of the young mother and child who'd died in the inferno. Were their two deaths needless? Would the fire wagon, with its long ladders, water tank and trained men have saved them? Sage heaved a sigh, knowing that question would remain forever unanswered. The muttered curses accompanying his companion's slithering descent sounded clearly in the dead, cold air. Sage turned and also plunged over the ravine's muddy edge.

FIVE

THE MARQUAM RAVINE WAS DEEPER and steeper than yesterday's gully where he and Jimmy got dunked. "Lucky there's more bushes here or I'd be sliding straight to the bottom," Sage thought as he clutched at one wet branch after another in an effort to control his descent down the hillside's muddy runnels.

"Take care, this bank here is slick as a crooked politician," Chester called over his shoulder.

Fifty feet downslope, on either side of the bridge span, small abandoned huts dotted a narrow hillside bench. They were dilapidated, sporting roofs peppered with holes, glassless windows, gaping entrances and siding boards hanging loose. Once a community of squatters had lived here, out of the sight and mind of those traversing the bridge overhead. Now their abandoned abodes were collapsing, soon to become indistinguishable from those bits and pieces of junk people tossed off the bridge and over the bank's edge. Trash lay scattered everywhere, like ugly confetti. Even the trees sported wads of garbage wedged into their branches. Downslope, shrubs and vines anchored knee-deep piles of tin cans, broken cutlery, legless chairs, rusted bedsprings and the tattered remnants of fabric. The city campaigned to stop people from dumping garbage into the ravines and gullies. If the volume of trash scattered around him was any measure of success, it was a failed campaign.

At last they reached a second narrow bench halfway to the bottom. Sage was feeling the strain of staying upright on the muddy slope. Acting before Chester shot him another amused look, Sage sucked in a breath and quickly side-stepped over to stand by the trestle timbers. Once there, he noticed that halfway under the bridge, a single ramshackle hut clung to the hillside, its door and window glass long gone. Still it was marginally more intact than the others farther up the slope because its roof looked relatively sound. Likely because of the sheltering bridge overhead. Sage studied the hut. When was the last time someone lived in it? Where had they gone? Up out of the ravine and into a better life, he hoped.

An onslaught of sheeting rain lashing into the ravine with a ferocity that made the naked branches tremble cut off that thought. He and Chester quickly crab-stepped deeper beneath the bridge, seeking a spot sheltered from the water streaming down from the sieve-like roadbed. The driest spot they found was next to a piling that sported a plywood patch overhead.

Heaps of garbage, tossed from above, lay here too, mounded against the creosoted pilings by gusting winds. Chester kicked the garbage away from the nearest piling until he'd exposed its base where wood met earth. He reached into his pocket for a sharp metal rod with a wooden handle. Crouching down, he jabbed the rod into the post, meeting resistance at less than an eighth of an inch.

He stood up. "This piling seems to be solid enough, though it won't be for long if they don't clear away this mess," he said gesturing at the garbage. "This stuff holds water against the wood and that causes rot. Bad enough that this ravine is so damn deep no sun ever reaches down here to dry it out. All this trash makes it ten times worse."

Chester moved downhill to the next post, ignoring the rainwater streaming onto him. Sage slid behind. This time, Chester's jabbing blade easily slid into the wood at least two inches. Chester shook his head. "This one's decayed bad." The next piling let him sink his blade all the way to its hilt. Once the bridge carpenter finished inspection down near the creek bed some minutes later, they climbed back up to stand under the plywood patch near the shack that sat lowest on the hill.

Raising his voice over the sound of the driving rain and the noise of the swollen stream, Chester summed up the results of his jabbing. "There's bad decay riddling a number of the substructure pilings. You look careful, you'll see that the bridge has settled uneven because of the rot in so many posts. That high water down there, shoving against pilings weakened by dry rot, torqued the whole kit-and-caboodle past its ability to carry a load. Likely that's why the planking gave way up above. The nail spikes worked loose. Probably pushed the underlying stringers so out of kilter they tore loose when the wagon broke through."

Chester shook his head, his weathered face grim. "Even without inspecting it, we know that the bridge's north end is in the same or worse shape since that's where the wagon broke through." He nodded toward the men across the ravine who were struggling to rig a block and tackle around the fire wagon so they could winch it uphill. A wide swath of snapped bushes leading from the wagon to the gully rim meant the horse's carcass was already on its way to the rendering shed.

"Hard to believe anyone survived that fall," Chester said. He pulled a brightly patterned blue bandanna from his pocket and wiped the rainwater off his face.

Sage studied the crosshatched timbers far above his head. "What about all that wood way up there? What determines whether those timbers are in good shape or not?" he asked, pointing and hoping Chester wasn't planning on their climbing up the structure.

"Don't matter too much about them girders if these support pilings are rotten," Chester responded. "Especially since the road planking overhead is so bad. Look," he pointed upward too, "See how there's so much light coming through in some places? That's where the plank patches are near to hanging free in the air." Chester shook his head. "It's a wonder the whole damn thing hasn't collapsed long before now."

"But I thought the Mackeys supposedly repaired this bridge not that long ago?" Sage said.

"Yup, not more than six months ago." Chester's lips twisted. "There is no way on God's green earth that all this decay happened in such a short time. I'd guess the Mackeys just painted the old timbers black with creosote so they'd look new. Look up there." Again he pointed, "You see, they stopped creosoting once they reached the point where a man might not notice if he looked at the bridge from the edge of the ravine. Even so, this mess might have held up under that fire wagon except for the high water down there." He pointed to where the creek bed was overflowing its banks and pushing against the bridge pilings. Unlike the stream where Sage fought to save Jimmy, the one flowing below was shallower and narrower—no more than six feet across. But the steeper incline sent the water racing downhill with tremendous force.

"Like I said, just too much strain for the bridge to hold," Chester continued. "Pilings probably shifted under the water's push and with things already so rickety everywhere else . . . ." He shrugged his shoulders, leaving Sage to provide the inevitable conclusion.

"The whole structure was loose as a goose and failed under the fire wagon's heavy weight," Sage supplied and Chester nodded grimly. Overhead, the rain began to drum ferociously on the bridge planking.

"Isn't the city engineer supposed to inspect repair work?" Sage asked, raising his voice above the din. It seemed impossible that some bureaucratic functionary decided to risk people's lives that way.

Chester's lips twisted with disgust before he shouted back, "Now, that there's a good question. Before you and I set off, I spoke to a couple of the men who worked on this bridge. They said that, before Mackey moved them to another job, the city engineer showed up a few times. They all say he stayed on the bridge jawing with Mackey before the two of them ambled off together, likely heading for their favorite watering hole. For certain, if a man was serious about inspecting, he'd come down here where we are. When a substructure's no good, like this one, any fool who took the time to look would know that the whole trestle structure is rickety. 'Course, that's the problem. A fellow first needs to see it to know that. The men told me that city engineer never climbed down off that damn trestle roadway. They said he hates getting his shoes dirty. Can you imagine such gol darn laziness?"

An inarticulate cry at their backs made them both jump and whirl around. The scarecrow figure of a man leapt out the open doorway of the nearby hut that Sage had studied earlier. Within seconds, the man scrambled up the hill and disappeared behind the shrubs crowding the bank edge.

"A hobo," Chester commented. "And likely a bit demented if he's living down here. He probably thought the police had come to round him up. They've been cracking down lately. Some of our so-called 'better' citizens don't appreciate seeing homeless folk on their streets."

Sage shuddered. What is it like, living down here in these huts, in this sunless, bone-chilling damp? Some kind of hell to his mind. No thanks. He'd rather curl up in a doorway or under a fir tree.

Chester's brow furrowed making Sage wonder whether the other man was pondering his own uncertain future in light of their seemingly futile strike against the Mackeys.

The two men returned to the strike line late in the day to find the men's spirits still high even though some of their newfound union supporters had drifted away up the road. A laughing audience stood around one newcomer in particular. He appeared to be regaling them with a story. They stood in a warming sun break, their heads bare, their sodden coats open. Sage smiled at the sound of their laughter. He and Chester sidled up to Leo. "How's it going?" Sage asked.

Leo grinned in response. "Ah now, the men's spirits are perking right up." Leo took his elbow and they stepped aside. "You and Chester find anything helpful?"

"The whole Marquam trestle is rotten through. Chester here thinks the Mackeys replaced a few timbers to keep that bridge standing a bit longer and painted creosote over the rest so they'd look new. He thinks all the rain is what caused it to collapse last night. That collapse was inevitable, though, even without the rain."

Leo nodded slowly, "That fits with what I've heard. I questioned some of the men after you and Chester headed off to inspect the bridge. They agreed it was commonplace for Mackey to tell them to replace some of the bad timber low down on a trestle only to find themselves transferred to another job before they finished repairing the whole bridge. Said Mackey always seemed to finish up his bridge jobs with a maverick crew, using the most worthless kind of unskilled day laborers, fellas who are desperate and drunk. Usually both at the same time."

"How certain are you that the Mackeys used day laborers like that on other bridges beside that one over the Marquam Ravine?" Sage asked.

"Pretty certain. They win the construction contracts for most of the city's bridge work since Mackey Sr. is exceedingly tight with the powers that be. He's on the board of directors of some big banks and a trustee of that highfalutin' golf club down there south of the city."

Chester rubbed the whisker stubble on his chin, pondering the situation. "Thinking back on it, those jobs kinda smelled like five-day-old fish. They'd send a crew out with their tools, keep them busy for a few days on the lower part of the trestle and then move them on to another bridge. Since we were working so Godawful many hours, I don't think none us really thought about what was happening to the bridge repairs we didn't finish.

"I guess, if you asked me back then, I might have told you that we expected Mackey'd send us back to finish them off. But, according to the fellas, I reckon that none of us ever was." Chester stopped speaking and stared up into the sullen sky that for the moment was again allowing the sun to break through. Regret was heavy in his features. "I'm mighty sorry now that we didn't think to ask. I'd like to think at least one of us would have said something about how unsafe the darn thing was."

"Do you think the city commissioners know that the city engineer is not inspecting the work on the trestles like he should?"

"There's no telling. From what I've seen the last few years, City Hall seems to run its contracting business with a wink and a nod," Leo answered.

The strikers' laughter erupted again. The storyteller punched the air with a fist and the group roared. Sage studied the man who wore canvas trousers with a dingy union suit showing above the open collar of a wool plaid shirt. His only distinguishing garment was a tan water-repellant duck coat adorned with a bright orange corduroy collar. The bill of the man's fifty-cent cap was too narrow to offer much protection when rain fell. Now, however, it allowed sunlight to strike blue eyes bright with humor and flashing white teeth midst a neat blond beard. The man looked to be somewhere in his mid thirties and accustomed to working outdoors.

A striker approached them, chuckling. "Say, Leo," he said, "You oughta come hear the stories O'Reilly's telling us. He's just come down from the Idaho mines. Said his boss acted just like Mackey until somebody sent a barrel of lit dynamite slid'n down the water flume into the stamp mill! 'Course, after that, the Dickensen detectives landed on the scene 'thick as flies on a fresh cow pie.' His words. So O'Reilly headed on down here. Sez the pot's boiling a mite too hot for him up north." The man chuckled before hurrying back to take his place among O'Reilly's audience.

Sage again studied the newcomer. The man intercepted the look and smiled widely before returning his gaze to those gathered around him.

Hmm. Had the Saint sent this O'Reilly fellow to help out? He knew that St. Alban sometimes sent in reinforcements. He hoped that was the case here. They could definitely use the help. Especially from someone as cheerful as the Irishman. Laughter was always good. Still, he didn't think it like St. Alban to send in someone without giving Sage notice. Well, maybe it's some other labor leader whose lending a hand by sending in O'Reilly to raise the men's spirits. Regardless, there was no cause, as of yet, to look this particular gift horse in the mouth.

Sage was at Mozart's in time to step in as its supper hour host. Business was slow. The gas lit dining room, elegant with its damask-covered tables and sparkling silver cutlery, was nearly empty. Outside, rain poured down, undoubtedly keeping Mozart's regular customers snugged close to their warm hearths. Fine with him. He needed the time to think. His thoughts bounced around like a rock tumbling down a streambed. He tried to impose order on his thoughts. First, there was the Mackey bridge repair scheme. How to use that fact and was there time to use it? It also meant that more was now at stake than just winning the strike. That woman and her baby might still be alive if that fire truck had reached them in time. What about other fires? Even without the strike, the idea of bridges falling and more people dying was reason enough to take immediate action.

He'd worked it out by the end of the supper hour. Not a complete plan—just a place to start. The first step, find Ben Johnston. As a journalist, Johnston was familiar with City Hall because that was his job.

"Sage," his mother said with asperity, as she entered his third floor room and found him dressing in his warm street suit of herringbone tweed, "Do you think you might trouble yourself to spare a moment to tell me what happened today? I don't mind managing the restaurant all by myself. That said, I'd at least like to be kept in the know about what is going on down at the strike line."

He sighed, pulled off his hat and sat on a chair. Her point was valid. Without her, Mozart's doors couldn't stay open and they'd lose the most important prop in their entire subterfuge. Besides, over these past two years, she and Fong proved irreplaceable comrades in their secret endeavors for the labor movement.

He quickly told her about the rotten bridges.

"My Lord, Son" she breathed. "That's so dangerous. That poor woman and her baby son. Is there no act so low that those greedy scallywags won't stoop to doing it?"

"Chester tells me most of the trestle bridges are over twenty years old, built when thousands of newcomers started moving into Portland. The land developers needed the trestle bridges built to give prospective home buyers easy access to the newly platted lots. They pushed for city-wide taxes to build the ravine trestles. Once their lots all sold, though, those same developers sang a different tune because they'd moved their money on to other interests. In the years since, they have vehemently fought any taxation for trestle repair. So the city has been repairing the bridges on a shoestring. Which brings us to the Mackey's little scam. The way they work it is to bid low and short the job every which way possible to make a profit. Looks like they grease the skids with a few bribes here and there."

She shook her head. "So what about that poor dead woman and her baby? You want to bet that the Mackeys will never be forced to answer for those two deaths?"

"I'd lose that bet, I'm afraid." Sage said. "Still, I refuse to accept the fact that it's just fine and dandy if a rich man makes decisions that kill people, just so he can parade around in three carriages instead of two. The excuse is that he's just using shrewd business practices, like anyone would. Yet, if a man steals to feed his family, he's sent to jail as a criminal."

A bitter fury welled up but Sage restrained himself from expressing it. Mae Clemens didn't abide hateful talk. More than once she'd lectured that hate, and the violence it bred, was too easy an answer and doomed to failure. She'd lived smack in the middle of a war between the Dickensen agents hired by the mine owners and the Molly Maguires who fought for the miners. Her world flipped upside down when her father and brother joined the Mollies. Company thugs murdered them both, the ambush made possible by inside information. Worst of all, his mother's own husband—Sage's Welsh father—was the Judas who marked them for death. Although she hadn't killed John Adair, Sr., Sage figured it was basic decency rather than a lack of desire that had stopped her. Sage had never met his father, which was just fine with him.

His mother put her arm around his shoulders and squeezed hard before she departed.

Sage stayed seated for a while longer, staring at the pencil his fingers had just snapped in half.

SIX

Sage found Ben Johnston in the hotel lobby, his long legs sticking out from beneath an open newspaper. The middle class hotel served as Johnston's temporary residence. He'd told Sage his plan was to move his family over from the eastern Oregon town of Pendleton once *The Journal's* future seemed certain. Until that happened, the hotel lobby served as his evening parlor whenever he was in residence. Pleasantries completed, Sage began querying the newspaper man about the functioning of the city's common council. After answering a few questions, Johnston raised a palm to forestall any more, saying, "Wait just a minute now, John. I'd be both inaccurate and incomplete in my explanation if I tried to tell you how City Hall really operates in this town. I am too new here and certainly no insider. I'd rather you hear the information straight from the horse's mouth. Meet me here tomorrow at 8:00 a.m. and we'll go over to the Stumptown Café. I'll introduce you to a man much more knowledgeable about City Hall's inner workings than I am."

❀ ❀ ❀

The next morning found the two of them striding down Portland streets beneath a steady drizzle. The clang of horse-drawn trolleys mixed with the shouts of men wrestling heavy wooden freight boxes on and off wagons. Women wearing ankle-high walking skirts carefully wove through the bustle on their way to the public market, willow baskets dangling from their arms, gloved hands holding furled umbrellas aloft. Despite the rain and significant poverty in this western town, the people on its streets had a brisk vitality that said they had plans and the will to achieve them.

"The man I want you to meet is Mr. Fred T. Merrill. He's the city's 'bicycle king.' And, he is also a city councilman," Johnston explained, his voice raised above the rumble of wagon wheels over the uneven street.

"I've heard of him," Sage said. "Isn't he something of a crackpot who uses his political office to sell his bicycles?" Merrill's *Bicycle Emporium* was where Sage purchased a bicycle for Matthew, Ida's nephew, in an attempt to jolt the boy out of his despair over his brother's brutal murder. The strategy had worked, sort of. The new bicycle definitely distracted the boy. Unfortunately, that bicycle also led him into being shanghaied and nearly shipped out on a rotted-out whaling ship. These days, Ida watched the boy like a mother hawk.

Sage had never met Merrill, however. What little he knew about the bicycle merchant came from the pages of the *Portland Gazette*. Oddly, Merrill never ate at Mozart's. For most men of Merrill's social status, Mozart's was a frequent stop because it was one of the best places to see, or be seen by "those who mattered." It and the Portland Hotel dining room were rivals for the reputation of Portland's most top-notch eatery.

Johnston's laugh intruded on Sage's ruminations. "Now there you go! That's exactly what *The Gazette* wants you to think when it ridicules Merrill's marketing antics. Sure Merrill uses loony publicity stunts to draw attention to his business. That's why he's successful. Personally, I like his bicycle stunts. They draw a lot of spectators for good, clean fun. But no, those marketing ploys are not what rankles our respectable establishment types and spurs *The Gazette* into jeering. What they flat don't like are the stands Merrill takes as a member of City Council. He stirs up more trouble for the rich men of this city than ten other men put together. He knows how to get their dander up and keep it there."

"Like how? And when?" Sage asked.

"Well, this ought to interest you, given your set-to with the shanghaiers this past summer. Just before your efforts sent that shanghaier Mordaunt off to jail, some council members planned to grant him an exclusive franchise to haul city garbage. Merrill raised a stink about Mordaunt's sweetheart relationship with some of the councilmen. He forced them to back off that idea. A couple of months ago, he made them even madder. Standard Oil wanted to install huge storage tanks on the east side of the river, right across from downtown. Merrill's followers pitched such fits at the council meetings that the oil company dropped the idea. Now it's eyeing parcels of land farther downriver, near the town of Linnton."

Johnston chuckled and responded to Sage's sideways glance with a grin but then the newspaperman sobered. "The Standard Oil fight riled up the bigger businesses and Merrill's fellow councilmen went past hopping mad to apoplectic. Supposedly, the plan was for our councilmen and their esteemed pals, the near eastside landowners, to make packets of money selling the land to the oil company. At least that was their intention before ol' Fred's rabble rousing squashed the project.

"They are determined to get Merrill booted off the council, come hell or high water. Every election they hunt for a candidate to oppose him. Since councilmen are elected by district, rather than citywide, they're just spitting into the wind. Merrill's constituency remains intensely loyal to him. Still, I don't think the money men will ever stop trying to kill his political career."

When they reached the Stumptown's fogged-up glass door, Johnston paused to warn Sage, "Once Fred starts talking you'll not be able to drop in a word. Keep in mind that's not necessarily a bad thing. Despite his love for telling stories, most of what Merrill says is reliable. Just sit back, relax, and let him roll."

Winter's ubiquitous wet-wool smell hit their noses as they stepped into the warm café. Edging between tables crowded with working-class men, Sage and Johnston reached the rearmost table. There Merrill sat, a copy of *The Journal* spread across the table before him.

"I see that you are a man of refined journalistic taste," Johnston greeted Merrill who watched their approach. Beneath a full head of curly gray hair, Merrill's face was strong, rather handsome, with a prominent nose, deep-set, piercing brown eyes and bushy brows. "Well, if it isn't the publisher of this fine rag himself. Sit down, sit down," Merrill said, folding the newspaper and gesturing toward the booth bench opposite him. The man vibrated energy. He stood and gave Sage a firm, friendly handshake across the scarred wooden table.

Johnston wasted no time. "My friend, John Adair here, is the proprietor of that fine restaurant, Mozart's Table. He came to me with questions about how the City Council hands out construction contracts . . . for jobs like the trestle spans across gullies, ravines and swampy ground. He's most interested in why the Marquam Ravine bridge collapsed the other night."

Merrill's face lost some of its geniality and his eyes narrowed. "Suppose you tell me just where your interest lies, Mr. Adair."

Sage shot a quick look toward Johnston and received a nod in return. He took up an explanation he thought meshed with his role as a prosperous restauranteur. "I spoke with a man who told me that he'd worked on that trestle. He said the contractor who repaired it deliberately shorted the job. I'm a businessman. And, I started thinking that if this contractor does shoddy work and has performed other city work, there might be any number of trestles falling down around town with all this heavy rain. That's bad for business. I figure someone needs to say something about it. Still, I don't want to fly off like a loose axe head. It occurred to me that, before I raise a ruckus, I need to learn something about how things work at City Hall when it comes to public works contracting."

Merrill nodded, signaled for a coffee refill and settled back against the wooden booth. "That'd be Mackey, Abner Mackey," he said with a sigh. "He's awarded all the city's bridge repair contracts. Never has to face any competition. Me, I squawk about it every time." He shook his head ruefully, "And, they also out-vote me every time. I don't make more of a stink because I can't provide a solid reason for objecting. I just think it's better if we spread the work around—keep it competitive. So, you saying his company might be doing shoddy repair work interests me. I'd like to see somebody prove it. That'd jab a big ol' stick between their spokes."

"How so?" Sage asked.

Merrill leaned forward over the table. "I hope you don't mind if I give you a little civics lesson, Mr. Adair. Not telling you about how things are supposed to work but telling you how they really work.

"That's what I'm here for." Sage grinned and scooted closer to the table.

"I hear a hint of the back East in your words, Adair. You once live back there somewhere?"

"Yes, Pennsylvania and later on, New Jersey," Sage answered truthfully, omitting the particulars—like how he'd been born into a coal mining family only to become the foster son of a rich mine owner. That background he always kept secret. Only three Portlanders knew about it—his mother, Fong and a certain brothel madam.

Merrill looked at Sage who said nothing more. After wait-ing a beat, Merrill said, "Well, you probably saw instances of bla-tant graft, back there in the East,"

At Sage's nod, he continued, "Out here in Portland town, the rich boys tend more toward engaging in what I'll call 'honest graft' for lack of a better term."

"'Honest graft?' That seems a contradiction in terms, Merrill," Johnston spoke up.

Merrill nodded slowly, "Most folks consider a distinction between 'honest' and 'dishonest' graft to be a distinction without meaning. I'm one of them. Yet, that distinction makes one hell of a difference when you try to stop it."

Merrill took a sip of coffee, twisted his lips, set down the cup and started speaking again, "Dishonest graft is when the politicians and civil servants demand secret bribes, like from the prostitutes, saloon owners, gamblers, and in exchange they promise to look the other way or do them one favor or another. That kind of lawlessness makes for real rowdiness. Makes the streets unsafe. Dishonest graft like that is why I keep fighting for an ordinance legalizing prostitution. That way, we tax the business—keep it clean—if you'll pardon the unsavory pun."

Merrill shook his head ruefully. "I'm losing that battle though," he added. "Those prostitution grafters are crafty. Anytime I bring up licensing, they just mention 'God' and the air steams up with cries of moral outrage. Waving that red flag steers most folks straight past reason right into blind opposition. Happens every time. Come voting day, on their way to bank their prostitution booty, the hypocrites cynically tip their top hats to the fools they've deluded."

He paused to give another rueful shake of his head before adding, "Some of their wives are clamoring for an ordinance requiring a posting of the building owner's name on those buildings that house operations of ill repute. My, my. Aren't those righteous ladies going to be mighty shocked when their own last names are mounted up there for all the world to see?" Merrill's eyes danced at the thought.

Then he sobered, saying, "Honest graft, now that is more pernicious because it's harder to fight. Let me give you an example. The council authorizes certain public improvements. Say, one of the council members learns, in advance of the rest of us, where a particular improvement is to take place. What he does, he has friends buy up all the land in that location while the price is still low. Next, that friend sells the land to the City at a much higher price. The councilman's friend makes a neat little profit, some of it eventually landing, in one form or another, in the friendly councilman's pocket. Guess who foots the bill for that little excess profit? You do, and Johnston does, and all the rest of us poor saps who pay our taxes faithfully."

Merrill thoughtfully sipped his coffee before continuing, "And, your so-called 'honest' grafter's payoff isn't always money. Instead of directly receiving some of the profit from the deal, it's understood that the friend now owes the councilman. A little later on down the road, the friend's councilman might receive a little gift or special treatment for one of his children or maybe the opportunity to participate in some sweetheart side deal. 'Course, your typical 'honest' grafter tells himself that it's merely a matter of taking advantage of 'opportunities.'" Merrill used two bent fingers on either hand to demonstrate the quotation marks. "So what if the taxpayer ends up paying for all that sweetening that's been spread around like manure in a farmer's garden?"

Merrill didn't wait for an answer. "That's what every smart businessman does," he said, his tone now bitter. "They talk endlessly about such 'opportunities' while standing around in their silly golfing pantaloons or sitting on their well-clad butts in the Cabot Club's leather armchairs. Bottom line, they make certain sure everyone of them benefits. You try to confront them and what you hear is, 'Just sharing information' about 'opportunities'—that's their explanation. 'Nothing wrong with that,' is what they'll tell you." Merrill's lips pursed in disgust. "I see them as a pack of sharks circling a leaky lifeboat full of taxpayers and telling each other, 'Oh, my, looky there! Another opportunity, snark, snark.'"

All three of them laughed at Merrill's fanciful picture.

Merrill paused to sip his coffee before moving on to specifics. "Talking about Mackey," he continued, "some people claim that Mackey's been unusually lucky when it comes to public works projects. That idea of luck is suspect once you know that Mackey's built houses for some of the men sitting on the City Council. You gotta wonder if he's given them real good deals on their lumber and labor. Is there a way to prove it? No, of course not. The Mackeys also sit on various company boards with some of the councilmen or on boards with the councilmen's close business associates. Who knows what 'opportunities' they cook up when they're together? One way or another, they make sure that all those juicy 'opportunities' stay right within their tight little circle."

Merrill studied Sage before asking, "Have you listened to enough of my griping or are you ready for the rest?" Sage nodded for him to continue, so Merrill bent forward and said in a lower voice, "Rumor has it Mackey also employs people on his payroll who exist nowhere except on his books. Where those phantom workers' wages go is anybody's guess. 'Course, if it goes to some of my fellow council members, that'd be dishonest graft. Still, there'd be no way to prove our theory without a full-fledged investigation, and the district attorney won't authorize that look-see because he'd be investigating the same men he breaks bread with." Merrill sat back in his chair, laced his fingers across his flat belly and looked inquiringly from Johnston to Sage.

"Whew," Sage said, momentarily taken aback by the idea of such a complex fight in the middle of the strike. Fighting the Mackeys over their bridge contracts would be like fighting the city's entire upper class. Not an easy task because that class always covers over its shenanigans with an oh-so-respectable veneer.

"So, how can we taxpayers stop the so-called 'honest graft'?" he asked Merrill.

"Can't hardly," Merrill responded, "Their scheming is slipperier than live eels in a barrel of oil. Unless and, until, someone acts so greedy that it becomes obvious. If what you suspicion about the repair work is true, the Mackey's plain ol' greed's going to bring the city's trestle bridges crashing down."

For awhile, the three of them sat without talking, letting the hubbub of patrons and the clatter of cutlery fill the silence. Merrill leaned forward across the table as if to share a secret. "Fact is, the challenge facing our honest citizen reminds me of a bicycle race I won in 1898," he said.

Next to Sage, Johnston reacted to Merrill's statement by relaxing back against the booth's back, evidently readying himself for a lengthy exposition. Taking Johnston's cue, Sage also relaxed. This quirky fellow was definitely entertaining.

Merrill remained leaning forward, intent on telling his story. "I'm not talking about an ordinary race. No, siree. I matched my bicycle against horse flesh. It was my nickel-plated safety bicycle against sixteen of the best horses in Cook's livery stable. Safety bicycles became the new rage in 1898 because their same-size wheels make them safer and more practical for everybody. I wanted to publicize that fact. Of course, nowadays, a safety bicycle is all that anybody buys. No one wants a high wheeler any more."

Merrill took a breath and another swallow of coffee. "So, the first step I took, I announced the contest in the paper. We scheduled it to take place over six days, eight hours each day, up there at the Multnomah Athletic Club field."

Sage shifted uneasily. Surely this bicycle salesman wasn't going to regale them with a minute-by-minute account of his six-day, horse-bicycle race.

Merrill evidently noticed Sage's impatient twitch because his steady brown eyes looked into Sage's appraisingly, even while his magpie chatter continued flowing, "So anyway, we started out with a pretty big crowd, and, as I stuck with it, that crowd grew in size each day of the race. Every thirty minutes they traded out the horses. Me, I just kept pedaling. Sometimes, I pedaled so slow that I nearly lost my balance. Other times, I'd manage to pump up into a sprint. The point is, I never stopped. They declared me the winner at the end of those six days. The horses got too pooped to come out of their stalls."

He ceased talking and in the ensuing silence Sage struggled to make the connection. How in the world did wanting to stop honest graft relate to Merrill's story?

"The point is," Merrill supplied, with an air of patient indulgence, "these grafters and rich ne'er-do-wells are like those sixteen horses. They'll prance in all full of confidence and sometimes it'll seem like they are leaving you in the dust. Give them steady, unrelenting opposition, though, stay the course, and they'll tucker out eventually. They're used to having others haul their water for them. Just keep on pedaling down the track and you'll end up wining the race, no matter how bleak the outlook might seem at times."

Sage raised a skeptical eyebrow as he asked, "Do you think, with this bridge deal, that the city engineer is one of those hauling water for them?"

"Now there's a good question." Merrill's eyes glinted with merriment. "Might be worth your while to determine which councilmen recommended our city engineer for his position. There's rumors about that the engineer did not inspect that new sewer pipe laid in the Guild's Lake area up north of the city. It's already leaking like a sieve. Phewee—I can tell you that sure doesn't make the neighbors' noses happy. Maybe he used the same blind eye when he inspected work on the elevated roadways. He's always struck me as a lazy, self-important old boy. Yet, certain council members won't hear a word against him. I know, I've tried." With that Merrill stood, clapping a hat onto his thick gray hair, saying, "Well, fellas, I've stocked some bicycles that need selling, so I best return to work."

Sage and Johnston also stood and thanked Merrill for his time. As he shook their hands, Merrill said, "The thanks I want, Adair, is proof that Mackey and that nasty piece of work he calls his son are dirty with graft. Between me squawking at council and Ben here lambasting them in his newspaper, we might be able to send some of their horses back to the stables for good. That'd be loads of fun," he said, leaving them with an exaggerated wink.

SEVEN

INSIDE MOZART'S KITCHEN, THE STAFF bustled about preparing for the dinner hour. Sage thought his mother absent until a burst of laughter sounded outside the kitchen door. He looked out the kitchen door window and saw his mother and Fong standing in the alley talking with that ragpicker, Herman Eich. The talk stopped the moment Sage opened the door and stepped onto the small porch.

"So, ah, how is everybody?" Sage asked, his question sounding stilted to his ears.

After a hesitation, his mother spoke, "We are fine, Mr. Adair. Just having a few words with Mr. Eich here. We'll be in shortly."

Right. She was doing exactly as she was supposed to around a stranger—carrying on with the pretense of their being merely employer and employee. So Sage said, "That's quite fine, Mrs. Clemens. There's still some time before dinner starts." He felt rooted to the porch floor, having nothing to say, yet reluctant to leave without knowing why.

Mae Clemens and Fong KamTong, however, merely smiled at him politely, which left him with no choice. His need to flee the awkwardness of the situation won out. Sage reentered the kitchen, closing the door softly behind him. Through its glass, he heard Eich's low rumble and they laughed again. Sage felt a nip of irritation, only to regret it immediately. "Feeling a bit excluded are we?" he chided himself. "Can't be in the center of things all of the time, fella." He poured himself a cup of coffee, opened the day's *Journal* and waited for the alley conversation to end.

The dinner hour concluded and the patrons sent on their way, Sage and Fong climbed the stairs to face each other in the attic, preparing to train in a fighting style that Fong called the "snake and crane." Weak sunlight filtering down through the rooftop skylight, onto the space's lacquered wood floors and whitewashed walls. With an intense yet distant gaze, Fong stepped one foot forward and raised his right arm across his chest. In response, Sage raised his right arm until their wrists touched, back to back and push hands began.

Many moves later, muscles wobbly and body sweat-drenched, Sage called a halt. Any more and he might upchuck. While Sage paced to cool down, Fong began a round of movements he called "temple exercises," starting with the gentle rocking movement of the "prayer wheel."

Once his heartbeat slowed to normal, Sage ventured a question, keeping his voice soft to fit the peacefulness of the attic. "So what are your thoughts about him, Mr. Fong?"

"Who is that, Mr. Sage?" Fong's flowing movements didn't pause in their expression of elegant, focused power.

"That ragpicker, Mr. Eich."

"I think he is a most interesting man," Fong answered, his breath steady. Fong often found people "interesting." It made him seem like a friendly Asian anthropologist meticulously studying the peculiarities of the European-based cultures.

"And just how is it that you find this Eich person interesting?" Sage asked.

"Well, for one thing, Mr. Eich say he admires Chinese because we are different from Americans because we honor wilderness and not fear it. After thinking on this observation, I believe he is correct. I never notice difference before he say it."

Insight fizzed briefly in Sage's mind like a newly-opened sarsaparilla. Come to think of it, that children's story about Hansel and Gretel was all about being afraid in the woods. Fact of the matter, the first few times Sage was alone when night crept beneath the towering evergreens, he'd even thought of that fairy tale. Later, when he came to know the forest better, he'd become no more than reasonably afraid of its actual dangers—falling limbs, bears, cougars, wolves, sasquatches, and the stray crazy man or two.

Sage sighed, saying, "Great. Another one of you is on the loose."

"What does that mean, 'another one' of me?"

"You know, fond of those little sayings that roll about in the head like a ball of string with no end to catch hold of."

"No string in my head," Fong said before bending to "grind corn," his hands moving in flat circles about a foot above the floor.

Over late afternoon coffee in his third floor room, Sage told Mae and Fong what Merrill had said about the city's letting of bridge contracts. "If Chester is right and the bridges are in bad condition, we might be able to use that to bring a little suffering to the Mackeys," he said.

Mae protested, "Surely, Sage, it is much more important to make sure no more bridges fall down than to make another human being suffer."

"Yah, yah. Tell that to Rufus's wife," Sage started to say as he lifted a hand to wave her words away only to catch himself just in time. It was dangerous to denigrate Mae Clemen's opinions. First, because she usually made good points and, second, it made her madder than a poked hornet.

Clearing his throat he said instead, "It's just that I am so damned angry. Why is it that the rich always escape the consequences of their immoral acts? Mackey squeezes his workers out of decent pay and hours, he squeezes the city taxpayer by doing shoddy jobs, and now it looks like his greed has even squeezed the life out of innocent people like Rufus, as well as that poor mother and child who died in that house fire."

Mae Clemens was nodding as he spoke. "Yes, Mr. Eich talked to us about that fire today," she said.

"Really? What did he say about it?"

"Turns out, he stays beside the Markham ravine. He saw that awful fire. When he tried to go help he couldn't get across the wrecked bridge. He says that poor woman's husband has gone right out of his mind. Mr. Eich is worried about him. We talked some about what to do for him."

Sage raised an admonishing palm, "Please, no more projects. We're up to our ears in problems already. If we take on one more thing, I think my head will explode just trying to sort it all out. Let Mr. Eich handle the problem of the widower by himself. You are right. Figuring out how to prevent more trestle bridge collapses will be our contribution to easing that man's sorrow and saving lives. Imagine what will happen in this city if all the bridges start falling down. If we can prevent that, we must. We also need to stop this strike from petering out. The way it's going, the effort is staggering around on its last leg. I don't relish telling St. Alban that we've failed—not when there's so much at stake."

Mae Clemens stood. "Sometimes, Sage, we're not always the ones picking out what lands up on our plate," she commented mildly as she headed off to start supper preparations. Once the sound of her footsteps faded away, Fong returned to Mae's earlier point. "Your lady mother is right. Hatred destroys man who hates. 'No evil is equal to hate, no virtue is greater than compassion!'"

"Your Mr. Lao again? That is easier to say than it is to practice."

"Just old Buddhist saying. Yes, you make good point. It is true, some days, it is hard to feel what words mean," Fong said quietly before falling silent. The air thickened with their shared memory of a few months back when hate gripped Fong's thoughts to the exclusion of everything else, even his friendship with Sage and their work for St. Alban.

Shaking his head free of those sidetracking thoughts, Sage asked, "So what is the solution here? Is there a way to rescue this strike? By all that is supposed to be just in this world, these men do not deserve to lose their fight against the Mackeys."

Fong's eyes took on a faraway look, signaling that yet another dose of Oriental wisdom was in the offing. Sage readied himself for the mental challenge.

Sure enough, Fong drew a deep breath and launched into a story. "Lao Tzu see man digging valley through mountain. When he ask man why he undertake such hard task, man say he want to make it easier for visitors to reach house."

"And, of course, the estimable Mr. Lao set the man straight?"

Fong nodded. "Lao Tzu tell him it better to move house than the mountain."

Sage laughed. "And what was Mr. Lao's point, other than that the man was an idiot?"

"His point," Fong said, "is sometimes when you face problem, it better to reject obvious solution and look for simplest."

Sage said nothing because he was intent on catching hold of the will-o-wisp of an idea that flitted through his thoughts. It vanished, though, before he captured it. So, his attention returned to Fong's last words. Maybe that Lao fellow was right. Were they missing a simple solution to the strike deadlock? At times like this, he silently reminded himself, waiting is the best approach. Somewhere deep within the recesses of his mind, a solution was likely fermenting. Eventually it would surface, complete and exactly right. The wait-and-see technique had worked so often for him in the past that he'd come to rely on it.

Despite a determination to push it aside, Fong's mountain-moving story niggled at Sage as he headed toward the strike line. He strode along secure in his disguise, knowing that to passersby he looked like a poor working man in his sensible if tattered clothes, trudging through the day. Nothing about him hinted that he owned and operated one of the city's finest restaurants or, stranger still, that he was strolling along, preoccupied with the trying to understand the cryptic sayings of his ostensible Chinese manservant. Sage snorted at the absurdity of the situation, only to notice that his noise attracted a few bemused looks from those around him.

He made an effort to return to the present by studying the faces of the people he passed. Once he engaged in that exercise, it was irrefutable that each one of their faces was unique. He felt a dash of shame for his arrogant assumptions. Who knew, really, where they originally came from? What equally unique ideas occupied their thoughts or directed their steps?

Sage's speculations ceased when he reached the muddy road leading down to the strike line. Although more men than usual picketed before the construction shack, the brusqueness of their gestures, the shaking of their heads and the tightness in their faces telegraphed that something bad had occurred. In a quiet voice, one of the strikers told him that Rufus had died in the early morning hours.

Emotion swirled through the air, passing between men like electric arcs off one of those Tesla coils. For once, Earl Mackey wasn't smirking from behind the window glass. Instead, a drawn curtain covered that window and Mackey was nowhere in sight.

The newcomer, O'Reilly, was orating from atop Leo's soapbox. Although Leo often allowed men to sound off from atop his box, the union president's wrinkled brow suggested he'd just as soon O'Reilly shut up. Sage sidled up to him.

"What's the new man talking about?" Sage asked Leo, nodding in O'Reilly's direction.

"I'm not too sure," Leo replied, the worry crease in his forehead deepening. "That O'Reilly, he's talking up violence and the men are already hopping mad. You heard about Rufus dying?"

"Yah, just now." Leo was right. The wet air sizzled with fury. "If the men jump the gun and act stupid, they'll hurt their own cause. Public anger over Rufus's death will turn against us," Sage said.

"Yup. That's exactly what I'm thinking," Leo agreed. "There's a few hotheads that are always a chore to hold back. Now that O'Reilly's stirring them up even more. I better cut him off." Leo moved from Sage's side and began elbowing his way to the center of the group. He placed his foot atop the soapbox.

This action halted O'Reilly's rant, since courtesy required that the newcomer make way for the union president.

Leo mounted the box and raised his voice so that it carried as far as the construction shack's veranda where Earl Mackey now stood, arms folded across his chest. Leo turned his back on his boss and began speaking low and slow to those gathered around him, "Men, I promise you that the Mackeys will receive their comeuppance, and soon. Until then, we cannot give in to anger because it just plays into their hands. This morning we need to hold thoughts of our brother Rufus and his sacrifice foremost in our hearts. Rufus lived life as a good man. He deserves our prayers and thoughts today. He always found the funny in a bad situation and kindness in everyone. Even in the Mackeys. Remember how he'd always talk about when old man Mackey gave Rufus's family that Christmas turkey and all the fixings when Rufus's daughter took sick?"

The men murmured in agreement and some smiled. Leo continued, "We'll all miss Rufus. A bright, sweet light has departed our world. Let's each of us take a moment to pray for Rufus and his family." Leo lowered his head and the others lowered theirs. Sage snicked a look toward O'Reilly and watched the other man's face change from mulish to somber before he too bowed his head. Yet, despite O'Reilly's outward compliance, Sage thought he'd glimpsed glittering in the other man's eyes.

The squeak and squish of trundling wagon wheels interrupted Sage's contemplation of the stranger. Huge Belgian draft horses were hauling a plank-sided wagon around the corner and down the muddy road toward them. A dozen or so rough dressed men filled the wagon bed. Although they appeared to be unarmed as they peered out from between the side slats, their faces showed a battlefield mix of fear and defiance.

"Strikebreakers," a voice next to Sage growled and the man spat into the mud before adding, "Scabbing strikebreakers."

The strikers began jeering, their voices hoarse with the cold and emotion, as the horses clomped past and into the lumber mill yard. Once the wagon was safely inside the gate, the strikebreakers dismounted. This was the signal for Mackey's scrawny-necked clerk to throw open the construction shack door. He wore a bowler hat and minced his way onto the veranda between two burly bodyguards. The clerk moved to a small table and wooden chair on the covered porch, picked up his pencil and gestured for the men from the wagon to line up before him.

"Sign up right here, men," he shouted even as the quaver in his voice undercut his attempted bravado. "There's work for each of you, provided you'll accept $4 a day for a ten-hour day, six-day workweek," he declared in an unnecessarily loud voice. As the men shuffled into line, the clerk cast nervous looks over his shoulder toward the striking men.

"Yah, you tell 'em, you cowardly runt. You tell those scabs to go right ahead and take the food off my family's table! I hope you choke on it, you sons of bitches!" yelled O'Reilly, his shouted words spurring others into raising their voices.

"You fools. You'll be working three weeks a month just to keep a roof over your head. You'll never feed and house your family on the remaining ten dollars a month!" shouted one of the strikers.

"I sure the hell can't feed them on no money at all—like I'm trying to now. I take this job, they're going to eat something besides bread and milk for a change!" shouted back one of the braver scabs.

"Fine looking crew, Mackey!" shouted another striker, "What North End saloon floor did you scrape them off of? You sure they know the difference between a hammer and a mallet?"

As the din increased, Sage once again studied O'Reilly. He was pretty sure that O'Reilly had no family near to hand and everyone knew he'd never worked for Mackey. This strike wasn't O'Reilly's fight. Yet, he seemed intent on inserting himself right into the thick of things.

The police, who'd taken up post halfway up the mud road ever since the day of their conspicuous absence, started shuffling toward the strikers, batons raised across their chests. At this sight, the strikers' shouts quieted to angry mutters.

Shooting a worried glance in Sage's direction, Leo stepped up onto the soapbox, calling out, "Can't you see Mackey's trying to goad you into rash action? Don't give him the satisfaction. Don't let him divert our attention away from the loss of our brother, Rufus." Leo lowered his voice and told them, "As I started to say, before that despicable interruption, Rufus's widow asked that we all stop by their home today. She's grateful for all the food and comfort your wives have given her. She wants to thank everyone personally before she packs up their house. Right after tomorrow's funeral, she and the kids are heading back East to live with her kinfolk."

Leo's words calmed the men. They said nothing more, standing silent, as the scabs lined up on the porch in front of the clerk, who made a show of writing their names down, carefully licking his pencil tip as each new man approached. Sage fought an almost overwhelming urge to stride onto the porch and smack the clerk across the back of his head. Leo, however, pointedly ignored the scene and headed up the road. The rest of the strikers followed.

As he sloughed up the muddy road with the strikers to pay collective respects to the widow, Sage discovered that O'Reilly was walking beside him. Not wanting to waste the opportunity, Sage said, "I understand you are down from Idaho. You worked as a miner there?"

"Aye, that's for sure that I did," said O'Reilly, his words laced with a hint of the old country's brogue. Mingled scents of tobacco and whiskey wafted toward Sage. "Hmm," Sage thought, "that might explain the fella's fervor. O'Reilly wasn't the first man to waltz with stupidity after draining a bottle dry."

O'Reilly interrupted this rumination. "So, you're the son of Leo's brother I hear."

"No, his sister is my mother," Sage answered. At that moment, a passing man asked O'Reilly a question and the pair moved off, leaving Sage wondering whether O'Reilly's question was a mistake or a test. Leo had no brothers—just the one sister.

EIGHT

IN THE DARKEST HOUR, WIND GUSTS slammed sheet rain against the window glass, jolting Sage awake. He lay staring up at the ceiling for as long as it took the rain to settle down into a steady patter. Its rhythm made him drowsy enough that he rolled over, snugged deeper into his warm blankets and returned to sleep.

A mile away, the watery deluge fell on the Mackey Construction shack. Inside, fire crept up a wall at one end of the shack, gaining in size, until it flowed across the exposed rafters and began charring the underside of the cedar roof shingles. Breaking through to the outside the furious flames met drenching water and shrank back, their yellow heat doused, leaving only wispy gray smoke to twist upward through the rain.

Sage opened the kitchen door and paused on the threshold, taken aback by the scene confronting his eyes. For the third time, in less than a week, he was looking at Herman Eich. This time, the ragpicker was inside Mozart's, seated at the kitchen table. A skeletal man, all thin sharp angles, sat across from him. The man's short black hair grew in a rounded peak above a face bent so low over the table that Sage saw only the ridge of his dark eyebrows and the side of his clean-shaven face. Eich pointedly cleared his throat and the stranger glanced up, causing Sage to take an involuntary step back. The man's eyes shone like smoldering coals deep in the dark hollows made by sleepless nights. He said nothing, merely nodded before returning his eyes to the table's surface. For a fraction of an instant, the man seemed somehow familiar. Sage immediately dismissed that idea. He was certain that he'd never seen him before. Definitely a stranger.

Sage's mother entered the kitchen and crossed to the stove. She pulled two plates from the warming oven and piled them high with food from the pots that simmered on the stove. Ignoring Sage, she set the two plates before the men at the table, poured two cups of steaming coffee, set those before them and urged them to "fill yourselves up. There's plenty more where that came from." Turning toward Sage, she ordered him into the adjoining dining room with a sideways snick of her eyes.

"I know, I know," she said before Sage said anything. "Having the city ragpicker and a homeless man in Mozart's kitchen is not exactly the image we hope to project to our exclusive clientele. What else could I do? Mr. Eich showed up this morning with Daniel in tow. He's the poor man whose wife and baby just died in that fire. Apparently he's been wandering the streets in a daze ever since. Finally, this morning, Mr. Eich was able to corral him and herd him into the public baths for a scrub. Afterwards, he said he brought Daniel here to eat because that's the best idea he had. He says Daniel's still too agitated to go anywhere public or to be by himself. Sage, I couldn't turn them away." Compassion warmed her dark blue eyes.

He reached out and squeezed her shoulder. "No, I don't think you had any choice about that," Sage said, earning a grateful smile.

Ida, Mozart's cook, poked her head out the swinging doors, a worried crease beween her eyebrows. "Mr. Adair. There's a young boy at the alley door. He says he needs to speak with you. He says it's real important. He looks scared out of his wits."

Sage exchanged worried looks with his mother. On his way to the back porch, through the kitchen, he saw the two men still eating breakfast in companionable silence.

Outside, a young boy of no more than eleven years of age stood at the bottom of the porch steps. Although he wore the cap and half-pants common among the city's lower class, the presence of the father's square jaw and agate brown eyes in the young face made the boy instantly recognizable as Leo Lockwood's eldest son, Bobby. Once, while strolling the downtown streets in his uptown John Adair clothes, Sage came face to face with Leo and his son and noticed how the boy admired his father.

Today, fright widened the boy's eyes and knotted his jaw. "Bobby, is something the matter with your father?" Sage asked, his mind leaping ahead to injury by assault or accident.

Relief at Sage's recognition swept across the boy's face as he snatched off his cap. "Yes, sir. My pa said to come here to the kitchen door and ask for Mr. Adair, ah, you sir, if there be any serious trouble."

"Serious trouble. What's happened, son? What serious trouble?"

"Trouble at the strike, sir. The police arrested my pa." At this, the boy's chin wobbled and he blinked rapidly to hold tears in check.

"Arrested him, whatever for?" Sage asked, though he figured O'Reilly's rabble-rousing finally triggered a fight and, consequently, Leo's arrest. Sage's thoughts raced through the mechanics of bailing the union leader out of jail.

Tears flooded the agate brown eyes in earnest, spilling onto the boy's cheeks. "They say he killed the boss man."

"Killed the boss man—you mean Abner Mackey?" The boy nodded. Sage's mind flashed over half a dozen potential scenarios where Leo might raise his hand against the elder Mackey. Each one of them involved self-defense, not murder. Leo was a peaceful man. More important, he was also a smart man. Without a doubt, Leo knew that strike violence would only strengthen Earl Mackey's hand.

"What are you talking about, 'killed' him? What happened?"

When the boy only dumbly shook his head, Sage patted his shoulder and told him to return home and tell his mother not to worry—Sage was going to hire a lawyer. He watched the boy turn the corner into the street before returning to the kitchen where the two men were digging into their food with suspicious gusto. In his haste, he'd left the door ajar. Likely they'd listened to the exchange. Sage shook loose of that thought, setting it aside for later consideration. Right now, it was time for him to transform into Sam, Leo's nephew, and get down to the strike line. Someone there would know why Leo was under arrest for killing Mackey.

Chester stood with a few glum strikers at the top of the road leading into the cul de sac. When Sage looked beyond them to where the construction office stood, he noticed something amiss with the building. Half of it looked normal. From the other half, however, a sinew of gray smoke curled upward to mingle with the morning mist. Jagged black holes punctured that burnt half's roof, while sooty tendrils trailed up the outside walls from around glassless window openings.

"Good Lord, what happened down there?" Sage asked Chester.

"Last night, someone set the place on fire. The night watchman discovered the fire, called the brigade and with the help of the rain, they doused it before the whole thing burnt down. When they broke inside, they found Abner Mackey, dead. Someone had tied him to a chair. Least that's what I overheard one of the coppers saying."

Sage's mind raced. Was it possible one of the hotheaded strikers decided to take matters into his own hands? What with O'Reilly stirring the pot, the scabs, and Rufus dying—maybe one of them liquored-up and took action.

Still, it made no sense. Luring Mackey to the shack, tying him to a chair and setting fire to the building, that indicated a deliberately cruel attack, one that did not fit the character of anyone he'd come to know on the strike line. It would take a snoot full of liquor before they'd go that extra step of even starting a fistfight with Earl Mackey. The cruelty needed to tie old Abner Mackey up and burn him to death wasn't in any of the men he'd come to know and respect. Besides, the son was, by far, the more obnoxious Mackey. If it was revenge someone wanted, Earl was the one hated by the strikers—not the old man. They spoke fondly of Abner, most thinking him a puppet of his son. "Where's Leo?" Sage asked Chester even though he already knew the answer.

"Leo came here this morning with the rest of us and found the police waiting for him. They arrested him on the spot," Chester answered. "They kept mum about why. We figure it's because of old man Mackey being murdered. I sent a man around to Leo's house to let Mrs. Lockwood know." The man's voice was thick with despair as he asked, "What in God's name are we going to do now? This damn strike keeps going from bad to worse."

Sage took a deep breath before saying in a deliberately reassuring voice, "Try not to worry about it, Chester. Leo's always known that, because he's our leader, they might arrest him. So we planned for it. Your vice president, Homer, knows what to do. He'll keep things on track here. Since you let Leo's wife know about the arrest, I am sure that everything that needs doing is being done." Thanks to Fong, he was certain Leo was already in the very capable hands of the lawyer, Philander Gray. Although sometimes irascible, lawyer Gray displayed unsurpassable zeal and skill when it came to defending his clients. He was probably already blistering the ears of whatever police sergeant had the unfortunate luck to pull jail duty this day.

Chester wandered off, leaving Sage quietly considering the gloomy men milling around him. Just yesterday these same men felt somber yet still hopeful. Abner Mackey's murder was a terrible blow. Certainly the public wouldn't scrutinize any case the police made against Leo, no matter what the strikers said in Leo's defense. Over the years, *The Gazette* was eternally unrelenting in its effort to gin up public antipathy against unions and union men. Newspapers, *The Journal* excepted, seemed the same everywhere. The labor movement incessantly struggled against the twin foes of public indifference and hostility created by lopsided newspaper reporting. The sad truth was that too many people swallowed newspaper sloganeering whole rather than thinking for themselves.

Sage anticipated Earl Mackey using his father's death to strengthen his war against the union. Mackey the younger inherited all of his father's stubbornness, in addition to possessing a streak of meanness all his own—or maybe that came from his mother. From what Sage observed as a rich mine owner's foster child, there seemed to be two different outcomes from inherited wealth. Either the new generation struggled to renounce the self-serving amoral values of the old or it strove to outdo them in the callous greed department. Earl Mackey fell squarely into the latter category. He was greedy, arrogant and seemed without a lick of compassion.

Sage gave a mental shrug and tried to focus on what was important. For example, these men needed Leo back on his wooden soap box leading them, with his name cleared. That required Lawyer Gray quickly straightening out the situation. Otherwise, this strike was lost. As if to underscore that grim prognosis, fat, cold, raindrops began streaming down onto saturated ground, creating puddles for the unwary to splash through. Sage scurried, alongside the others, to find shelter beneath the wide eaves of the dilapidated warehouse at the head of the road.

For a while, Sage simply listened as the men's quiet talk ranged from bewilderment over Mackey's death, to worry over Leo's arrest, to despair about the eventual outcome of the strike. Beneath the thrum of rain hitting overhead, Sage started wondering whether Abner Mackey's murder was a death blow to the strike.

Sage shifted his feet, only to feel water squish up into his socks. Pulling his coat collar tight, he signaled for Chester to step out into the rain, away from the other men. Sage didn't consider himself a patient man. For him, doing something, anything, was always better than doing nothing. He and Chester might as well continue with the bridge inspection plan although there was no guarantee there'd be an opportunity to use the information. He spoke quietly into the foreman's ear, "Chester, did Leo talk to you yesterday about maybe helping me out today?"

"Yah, he said he wanted me and you to survey some other trestle bridges and elevated roadways. He didn't give me no names of particular bridges to inspect though."

"That's all right. I know the trestles we need to inspect," Sage said, patting a sheet of folded paper in his breast pocket. The list was waiting for him, propped against the coffee pot, when he woke up that morning. For a man of words, Johnston didn't waste them. The note simply said, "Here are the locations of most of the city's recent bridge repair contracts. They'll give you a place to start." The names of ten cross-street locations followed this missive.

Chester looked at the list, "Yah, I know where these trestles are. Closest one to us is on Front Street, between Porter and Gibbs. What about Leo, though?" he asked.

"Don't worry about Leo. A good lawyer is already taking care of the situation. Believe me, if Leo stood right here, he'd tell us to go on ahead with these inspections. He's really given his heart to this strike and just maybe, our inspection will be helpful. You know, Leo wouldn't want us to stand around and mope over something we can do nothing about."

The crease between Chester's eyebrows said he felt dubious about inspecting bridges while his strike leader sat in jail. Apparently Sage's blood ties to Leo prevailed, because Chester finally sighed, shrugged and said, "I guess you'd know him best." He shoved the list into a side pocket, buttoned his collar tight and led the way toward the first bridge.

Preoccupied with bracing against the downpour, their mission and gloomy thoughts, neither man noticed when another man stepped away from the group to trail them. He kept well back, ducking into alley openings and shop doors whenever he thought they might look back. Such precaution was unnecessary. Intent on reaching the first bridge, neither man thought to check whether anyone followed.

❀ ❀ ❀

Six hours later, Sage ached everywhere. His filthy, sopping woolens felt icy cold where they hadn't rubbed his skin raw. Scrambling up and down the muddy slopes of ravines and wading in muck was hard work. He gulped more hot coffee and pushed aside his discomfort in order to write down every discovery before he forgot it. His pen raced across the paper, even as he snuffled with the beginning of what he feared was an attack catarrh or something worse.

1. Alder Street bridge near Chapman, sidewalk, roadway planking and stringers in dangerous condition due to decay.

2. East Alder near East 3rd, punk riddles all the substructure, especially the pilings. Water pushing against pilings, making the bridge shake.

3. Belmont at East 9th, underlying decking missing in places, leaving small sections of roadway suspended in midair without support.

"Mister Sage," Fong's soft voice made Sage jump. "Mr. Philander Gray is downstairs in the restaurant dining room. He said to tell you he is here."

"He just walk in the door?" Sage asked. When Fong nodded in the affirmative, Sage asked the determining question, "Is he staying to eat supper, Mr. Fong?" Fong's answer would tell him how long it would be before he needed to go downstairs. Philander Gray was a tall, string-bean of a man who remained thin despite packing in more food than a cookhouse full of loggers. Equally misleading was his long, doleful face which concealed a lively, aggressive mind. More than once, Sage saw the lawyer use this visual misdirection to his advantage in the courtroom.

Fong, understanding the import of the question, smiled. "Yes, of that I am certain."

Sage nodded and continued writing no faster than before. If Gray intended to eat, plenty of time remained to complete his notes and to change his clothes. Fong returned to the restaurant. Alone again, Sage continued writing:

4. East 8th near Washington Street dumping of dirt and debris off bridge has pushed the piling substructure from underneath the caps . . . Structure unsteady

The clang of mental alarm bells mounted steadily as Sage listed the structural problems their quick inspection uncovered. The ten bridge trestles they inspected represented just a few of the ones recently repaired by the Mackey company. Yet, more than five were clearly in dangerous condition. How many bridges and elevated roadways existed in the city anyway? Everywhere you looked, water poured downhill. That meant gullies, ravines and swamps that people needed to cross, by horseback, buggy, wagon, carriage, as well as on foot. This early winter's ceaseless rain made the situation dire as it swelled trickles into raging streams and small ponds into large lakes. How many more days of rain until another bridge collapsed? Would a man, woman or child be crossing it when the road bed shuddered, dipped and fell? How many more might die?

Sage's thoughts hopped in another direction. What use was this information now that Leo was in jail? For that matter, without Leo's steady hand on the reins, how long before the strike petered out? Or, worse, how long before the men's pent-up frustration spun out of control and Mackey obtained the overt violence he was hoping for?

Sage called a halt to his worrying. The best he could do was trust that the way forward would unwind like a forest trail in fog, one cautious step at a time. Right now, that approach required finishing the list. After that, he'd see what Gray had to say.

NINE

THE EARLY MORNING LIGHT FOUND Herman Eich hunched over his repair bench, a fragile teacup cradled in his hand, paintbrush bristles poised to stroke delicate pink across the smoothed surface of the repair clay. "Lindy Ann might actually smile when she holds this little beauty in her hand," he muttered to himself. "If so, that smile will be my payment—a sight welcome as a fire in winter, glorious as sunlight on snow."

Hearing a noise outside, he held his breath, listening. No, not Daniel. Probably just that cream and ginger cat, finding a marginally drier route home beneath the shed's narrow overhang. He glanced at the pallet he'd made for Daniel on the floor beside the crackling stove. Not genteel, perhaps. Still, it was dry and warm compared to that shanty where he'd finally found Daniel shivering. God's pity on the poor man. Home, wife and son all gone up in flames. He accepted the comfort of food and warmth but Eich's kindly words failed to ease the young man's crazed grief. Eich sighed. "Silly old, fool," he chided himself. Overwhelming grief took its own time to work its way out of a spirit—just like a blood spot from under a fingernail.

Still, Eich did what he could—making room in his shed and his life for the young man and his grief, keeping him company throughout the night once exhaustion and hunger drove Daniel off the streets. Last night he had not returned until dawn started cracking behind the eastern mountains. Two hours later he was up and out the door again.

Eich forced his attention back onto the teacup. Its sprinkle of blue flower petals reminded him of that interesting woman, Mae Clemens. Her eyes shone with the same deep blue intensity of the petals. A curious situation, that fancy restaurant. Mae was an employee. Yet, what sort of employee invites beggars into a kitchen with no rebuke from the boss? And that owner. Curiosity he evinced, yes. But no hostility, no repulsion and little surprise. And then there was that Chinese man, Mr. Fong. In the normal course, Chinese servants slid around the edges of things, careful not to draw attention. Mr. Fong, however, stood beside the woman and conversed as though her equal. As a vagabond for many years, Eich moved about in the eddies created by numerous other peoples' lives. In all that time, he'd never encountered such an odd group of people. Curious, most curious.

He set the teacup down and took up its saucer. The saucer also sported a chip in need of filling. Even mended, such a damaged cup and saucer would never be found in his mother's good china cabinet. But neither would Sophia Eich, ever mindful of harsher days, toss a cup with such minor damage into the dustbin. Instead, she would consign it to the kitchen cupboard as being perfectly suitable for everyday use.

Eich carefully sanded the clay patch on the saucer. Oy vay, such long ago days. Years before he'd traveled West, hoping to create a communal utopia. Now, that had been one grand adventure. And rewarding too because, for a brief few years, life's potential bloomed gloriously in that southern Oregon commune. That is, until the gossamer strands of moral compromise, self-interest and mutual disappointment layered up until the dream lay smothered beneath their weight.

Eich sighed again, rolling his shoulders free from the pain of hunching in one position too long and from the memory. He flipped the saucer over to read of its origin. An English ceramics factory. So delicate and yet it traveled such a long journey to this bench, all the way across sea and continent to reach that fine

Portland house. A dab of paint and off it goes once again, its life journey renewed and changed.

Maybe this little cup and saucer is destined to serve its time in a better place, Eich mused. Truly treasured, instead of being just one more acquisition among so many others. Lindy Ann's wan face appeared in his mind's eye. She was growing old before her time, working for Alma Mackey. Now there was a human being who passed her days far removed from her own humanity. Alma Mackey, benevolent woman in public, tyrannical witch in private.

He could hear his mother's chiding voice asking, "And who do you think you are, stepping into shoes bigger than your own to pass judgment? There was an easy answer to that question, "Just a judgmental old curmudgeon, wallowing in memories and imaginings."

He raised the teacup up to the window, turning it, admiring the pearly luminescence of the thin porcelain. Yes, it was ready for the sad-faced Lindy Ann. And, in return, he hoped to see her smile. A rare sight, indeed.

❁ ❁ ❁

By the time Eich's cart wheels rattled down the alley behind the Abner Mackey mansion, weak sunlight was coaxing mist from the cobblestones. He settled the cart shafts onto the ground and slowly pushed the gate open, peering about to make certain that no one stood within the yard. The only sound was the dry rasp of wind-driven leaves across the brick pathway. He followed that path alongside the house, bending his knees just a little so that the top of his head stayed below the window sills.

Ragpickers were a common sight in this city overflowing, as it was, with the homeless and hungry. It was his practice to follow the same routine from day to day so that most of the household servants knew when to expect his appearance. Many watched for him whenever they needed his skill to mend discarded tableware or when they wanted to purchase, for themselves, one of the inexpensive reusable objects he recovered from dustbins, spruced up and sold from his cart.

Today, he saw that the window above the dustbin was cracked open a few inches. Lindy Ann once told him that Alma Mackey forbid cigar smells in the house. That prohibition forced her men folks to always raised a window whenever they smoked. Of course, they always forgot to close it, letting in puddles of water for the servants to wipe up.

Yes, he smelled it now—the pungent odor of cigar smoke growing stronger the closer he moved toward the window. He slowed, stepping carefully. No need to draw attention to himself. Of course, householders usually chased him off. One was so used to being shooed away that it was nothing more than a momentary annoyance—like summer flies or a rat scurrying across his boot. Still, given a choice, he preferred to avoid confrontation.

When he reached the overflowing dustbin, Eich paused to contemplate its fullness and to plan his stealthy exploration of its contents.

"There's nothing to worry about, I tell you," a churlish voice came sailing out the slightly open window.

"So what? There's no proving we knew," said the same voice.

It was a one-sided conversation. Evidently, the answering party was situated too far inside the room for his words to carry outside. Eich froze, straining to hear more. In earlier days, he never eavesdropped because it felt like trespassing. Over the years, though, he found that his yearning to know more about his fellow humans, and less about himself, had grown. Nowadays his ears drank in other people's words, as he gently tested their perceptions of the world against his own. He'd come to view it as a harmless educational exercise since he never took advantage of what he overheard and never passed it on. Instead, strangers' words melded into that chorus of voices singing from his poems. Or so he hoped.

"Hell, no, they won't look at the other bridges. Why should they go to all that trouble? We'll say all the water running down the Marquam Ravine caused the problem! People will believe that since the damn rain hasn't let up for over three weeks."

Another pause.

"Well, let me know if we need to encourage them to turn their attention elsewhere." The voice rose in volume, irritation giving it bite as the speaker continued, "Jesus, man! Today is not the time to make me listen to you whine. I told you not to worry, God damn it! Now clear out of here and make sure nobody sees you leaving. Damn stupid for you to come here."

Silence. Because he sensed that the speaker remained inside the room, Eich didn't move. Sure enough, a minute later the man spoke again, this time his voice sounded calm and amenable.

"You can come on out now. He's gone."

For a panicky instant, Eich thought his presence had been discovered. Somehow, the man in the room, Mackey in all likelihood, had realized that the ragpicker was lurking beneath his window. The urge to flee was on the verge of overcoming Eich's paralysis when the man barked out a mirthless laugh.

"Yes, he is a fool. This world is full of fools like him. It is my misfortune that I am forced to continually deal with them, one bribe at a time. That one may find himself in serious trouble if he doesn't pull himself together. We can't afford to be associating with someone unreliable and so easily spooked." The speaker's tone switched to hearty, "Here, try one of these fine Cuban cigars."

The room above Eich again fell silent, presumably as the new man took Mackey up on his offer. Next came a question that perked up Eich's ears. "So, my man, what are they saying about the fire?"

As before, Eich only heard one side of the conversation. "He's still jailed? How is that affecting the men?"

Once again, Eich heard only one side of the conversation.

"Great. At least in that regard, our situation couldn't be better. Come on, let's move into my father's library. I've put your money in there."

Eich waited until he heard a door shut and no further sounds came from the room above him. Movements deliberate, his gloved hands began quietly burrowing into the dustbin. By the time the screen door on the back porch screeched open, a number of reusable items lay piled at his feet. He looked up to see Lindy Ann standing there, her face more morose than usual. She gave him a watery smile and he noticed that one side of her mouth was red and puffy.

"Child, what has happened to your lip?" he asked.

She flushed and ducked her head. Speaking into her chest she said, "Mrs. Mackey backhanded me when I brought her the wrong dress."

"It's not right to stay where they hit you, girl," he told her softly.

"What choice is there? Where on earth can I go? I've no home, no friends except for you." She kept her voice low, glancing fearfully toward the kitchen door.

She spoke the truth, of course. If she quit the Mackeys, she'd never find work in another fine house. Mrs. Abner Mackey was an influential woman whose reputation for vindictiveness meant none thwarted her wishes. Her negative reference would doom Lindy Ann to barroom work or worse, just like the other country girls lured off the farm by phoney advertisements for housemaids. Arriving in the city, friendless and nearly destitute, many found themselves manipulated into a life of prostitution. Compared to those other farm girls, Lindy Ann was lucky. She held a reputable position, no matter how abusive her employer.

The girl hurried to excuse her mistress. "She's awful upset today. Somebody murdered her husband the night before last, poor lady. Just tied him up and burnt him to death." Lindy Ann's thin frame shuddered and her pale eyes brimmed with tears. "Old Mr. Mackey, he weren't really all that bad. Better than her." She sniffed.

"Murdered? Burnt him to death?" Whose voice was it that he heard speaking inside the house if Mr. Mackey was dead?

As if divining his thoughts, Lindy Ann supplied the answer. "Mr. Mackey Junior is here, helping his mama and taking care of his daddy's business."

"Lindy Ann! Where in heaven's name did you disappear to? Come here right now!" The screeching command came from inside the kitchen. After throwing him an apologetic half-smile, the girl hurried into the house without another word.

Once back in the alley, Eich realized that he still carried the cloth-wrapped teacup and saucer in his pocket. He'd forgotten to give them to Lindy Ann. As he stood, indecisive about whether to knock on the Mackey's back door or return the next day, a man barreled out the yard gate, nearly knocking him over.

"What the hell!" the man exclaimed, giving Eich's arm a push with both hands, more from the irritation of being startled than from any need to clear a path.

Eich looked briefly into a pair of flat staring eyes before the man shoved on past and disappeared around the corner into the street. After his departure, a question teased Eich's mind. "Why was such a well-dressed man leaving the Mackey house through its back door and in such a temper?"

Eich shrugged. It mattered not to him. He picked up the cart shafts and trudged down the alley, a vague unease tensing his shoulders. "'To work! To work! In heaven's name! The wolf is at the door!'" he quoted to himself, a little louder than he'd intended.

TEN

DISTRACTED BY LINGERING DREAM images—a hodgepodge of screaming horses, broken bodies and smouldering oil-soaked torches—Sage failed to see the man sitting on the top stair tread. Sage's foot slammed into the other's hip and only a grab at the bannister saved him from tumbling down the staircase. "What the hell?" he exclaimed.

The man looked up. It was Daniel—the fellow Herman Eich had brought into the kitchen the day before. The homeless man was gripping a bucket of white paint in one hand and a small paint brush in the other.

"Sorry," Sage said. "No one told me you'd be here. Are you hurt?" Daniel shook his head while saying nothing, his lips pressed closed.

Sage paused until he realized that the other man did not intend to speak. Then Sage added reassuringly, "Ah, painting the balusters, I see. Good. They've needed it for some time now."

At Sage's friendly tone, the other man seemed to relax a bit. A quick dip of his head signaled his agreement with Sage's observation. Sage still waited on the top step, thinking the man might now speak. But, Daniel remained silent and his brush began applying white paint onto the baluster spindle. Lacking anything more to say, Sage smiled and silently stepped around him to continue down the stairs. He found his mother sitting at the kitchen table reading the newspaper while Ida and a covey of kitchen staff bustled about cutting up vegetables, stirring pots and sudsing dishes in the sink. Sage glanced over his mother's shoulder to see a full page of advertisements offering, among other things, "Swamp Root Kidney, Bladder and Liver Cure" and "Syrup of Figs Is the Best Used Laxative."

"Feeling poorly, Mrs. Clemens?" He spoke softly, right next to her ear, making her start before she slapped the newspaper shut. He pressed on, "I see that you are still performing good works on behalf of Mozart's. I stumbled over that Daniel fellow at the top of the stairs."

Her response was uncharacteristically tentative. "Well . . . yes, well . . . I wasn't too sure what to do with Daniel when Mr. Eich brought him this morning."

"Hmm. Mr. Eich again? How is it, you suppose, that your ragpicker friend has come to believe Mozart's runs a private charity out of its kitchen door?"

"Mr. Eich is doing the best he can," she said, her customary asperity snapping back into place. "He's been housing poor Daniel while he tries to find him some steady work. He says he's afraid to leave him alone just yet. Daniel's been wandering the streets and Herman's afraid he'll land himself in trouble or die from exposure."

"Herman?" Sage asked. She flushed.

"So now we are to pay Daniel to paint our stairway?" Sage asked.

"Mr. Eich actually offered to pay us to let him paint for awhile."

"Why didn't Mr. Eich pay to have Daniel paint Eich's house? Why Mozart's?" Sage felt suspicion grab hold.

Mae looked uncomfortable. "Well, Mr. Eich says he lives in a one-room, lean-to shed that would be kind of silly to paint and, he says he likes the look of naked wood."

Sage looked at her closely. Was that a blush creeping up her neck? He arched an eyebrow to let her know he'd noticed her discomfort but merely said, "Ah well, as Mr. Sherlock Holmes might say, 'we end where we began.'" Like most of the reading public, Sage was a devotee of Conan Doyle's serial detective so he struck a pose, rubbed his chin and continued, "The town rag-picker wants to pay for a another man to paint the town's most elite restaurant. Now there's a twisty group of facts worthy of Sherlock's consideration."

Mae said nothing, merely rolling her eyes before snapping the newspaper open once again.

Sage took a clean mug from the wall shelf above the table. "Maybe I better drink some coffee. It's like I'm still asleep and dreaming all of this. I hope you informed your mister 'Herman' that we would pay for the paint job ourselves."

Mae pushed back her chair, grabbed the mug from him, filled it with coffee and sat it down on the table none too gently as she said with exasperation, "Of course I said we'd pay. Like I told you, Mr. Eich is worried about the fellow and it seemed the right thing to do. Agreeing to let Daniel paint a bit around here, I mean," she clarified once she'd taken her seat again, adding, "And, he's not 'my' Herman!"

The coffee tasted perfect. Sage relented. "Of course we'll pay Daniel ourselves. It looks like he is being careful with the paint. Still, I don't like it. It's damned uncomfortable having strangers around when we are in the middle of a job for the Saint."

She nodded. "Unsettles me a bit, too. No matter, Daniel's not involved with the strike and the poor man is really beside himself with grief. I don't think he knows what's going on around him half the time. He's a painter by profession, so it's good for him to work. Anyways, we've needed that grimy stair rail painted. So, it's not like it's charity. In a day or so he'll be painting lower down and be out of our way more or less."

Sage raised a hand to halt her rush of words, "Maybe. Still, though, I can't help but worry whether this is just the beginning where Mr. Eich, oops, I mean Herman's, charitable impulses are concerned," he said, grinning widely at her blushing discomfort.

※ ※ ※

Sage exited Mozart's using the hidden staircase, descending from the third floor into the cellar and passing through the tunnel to reach the trap door that opened into the alley. It had been tricky to slip noiselessly behind a tapestry hanging less than ten feet from the stairs where Daniel was painting. The man's persistently silent presence was unnerving. Fong's task was to signal Sage that the hallway was clear and then to remain puttering about in case the strange painter decided to wander about the third floor. Not that Sage was really worried about that happening. Daniel seemed too far sunk into the depths of his own despair to have much curiosity.

Dressed as "Sam," Sage trudged down the street beneath a downpour as random thoughts pelted him with equal ferocity. He replayed his last night's discussion with Philander Gray. As usual, the lawyer shoveled in the food like a starving logger, his unsuccessful efforts on Leo's behalf apparently working no ill effect on his appetite. That was good news, Sage told himself. When Philander lost interest in food, the outcome was looking bleak. As it was, Gray parsed out his information without slowing his intake.

Once he'd stowed his first fork of beef roast, Philander spoke, "Shortly after twelve midnight, the watchman employed to keep things secure at the Mackey lumber mill observed red flaring behind the construction office's windows. He looked in the window, saw the flames and raised alarm with the fire company."

A fork piled high with mashed potatoes followed the roast. "Ordinarily, a fire consumes a building like that within minutes. However, not surprisingly, it was raining hard. Quite hard, they tell me. That downpour greatly assisted the fire company in its efforts to extinguish the blaze."

Gray swallowed wine and continued, "A creek also flowed handily nearby so there was no lack of water for the fire hoses." A fork-load of green beans, another of mashed potato and a large bite of biscuit followed this morsel of information.

"Once they extinguished the fire, they discovered Mackey the Senior. Apparently the evidence showed whomever was responsible neither burned nor bludgeoned Mackey to death. It is the fire chief's expert opinion that Mr. Mackey died of breathing smoke or perhaps his heart gave out from the terror of his perilous situation."

Sage felt real regret as he recalled the rather benign and befuddled face of Abner Mackey. The men on the strike line believed that the elder Mackey functioned as a brake on the more brutal excesses of his son. From Sage's perspective, if a Mackey was going to die, fate had chosen the wrong one.

Gray's empty fork stabbed the air before him for emphasis. "Two circumstances led to the inevitable conclusion of murder. Foremost is the fact that they found Mackey securely tied to a wooden desk chair. The location of the knots in the rope mean it is impossible that Mackey tied himself up. Secondly, someone flung kerosene all over the office and, while some of it caught and burned, generous amounts of it remained pooled about. One of the company's kerosene cans is missing. The fire chief's report states that there is no way a falling lamp started the fire accidentally. It was deliberately set." Gray began eating again.

During the relative silence of Philander's mastication, Sage ventured a question. "Even if they murdered Mackey, why do the police think Leo is responsible? I mean, other than the fact Leo was in a dispute with the Mackey Company over the men's wages and hours of work?"

Philander leaned back with a heavy sigh. His doing so was not a sign of satiation since his plate remained a third full. "There's where I encountered a problem. Quite a serious problem, I am afraid."

Philander leaned forward, his face grave. "Before I arrived at police headquarters, the police questioned Leo. I protested, of course. Too late. The damage was already done. He told the police that he departed the strike line that afternoon and that he thereafter remained in the loving bosom of his family until the next morning."

"So what's the problem with that explanation?" Sage asked.

"Unfortunately, he lied," Philander said. "At least two individuals came forward to swear to the fact that, about the time of the fire's outbreak, they'd seen Leo in the vicinity of the road leading down to the construction shack."

Sage protested. "Wait a minute, Philander. You know from our experiences together that there are witnesses who'll swear to anything."

Philander dipped his head to one side signifying only partial agreement. "Ah, yes. That is true. The problem John, is that once they confronted Leo with the claims of these two witnesses, he confessed that, yes indeed, not only had he been in the vicinity of the construction office but that he was going there to meet with Mackey, only to reverse direction when he caught sight of the construction shack in flames and the fire wagons clanging down the road toward it. He claimed this sight sent him home at a sprightly pace. He feared he'd be accused of setting the fire."

"That doesn't make sense! Why was Leo meeting Mackey that late at night? The whole scenario unwinds like one of those penny dreadful stories."

Philander smiled faintly. "Does it not? Leo says Mackey set the time and place. He claimed that about 10:00 o'clock, a bicycle messenger delivered a verbal message from Mackey requesting a private meeting. Not only is there no written note, but Leo can't even provide an identifiable description of the messenger boy." With that, Philander finished up, wiping his plate clean with the basket's last biscuit before pulling his napkin from his collar and tossing it onto the table.

Following the lawyer's departure, Sage decided one piece of Philander's information needed immediate follow-up. He'd summoned Matthew, Ida's nephew, to his room. The boy appeared with alacrity. As usual, the sixteen-year-old's red hair, freckles and earnest, blue eyes brightened the room like a rainbow.

"Matthew, take a seat, please." As the boy moved awkwardly into a chair at the table, Sage studied the boy's open, earnest face and thought that while it might be possible to take a boy out of the country, it was a lot harder to take the country out of the boy. Not a bad thing, all in all, although it made city life a more dangerous proposition for the boy.

For a long moment, Sage said nothing, mentally wrestling with how to approach the situation. He needed to obtain Matthew's cooperation without giving him information that would spur him into finding trouble.

"I need you to find something out for me . . . ," " he began.

"I'm surely happy . . ."

"Wait a minute. Let me finish," Sage snapped. The boy looked abashed, immediately opening his mouth to apologize.

Sage cut him off. "Before I tell you what it is I need, promise me something. The boy nodded eagerly, his eyes bright with anticipation. Keeping his tone serious, Sage said, "Promise me Matthew, that you will do exactly what I ask and that you will not ask or try to find out why. If you won't give me your solemn promise on that I can't, and I won't, use your help."

Matthew blinked and the flush traveling up his face said he knew exactly why Sage was setting those conditions. The boy's curiosity about Sage's surreptitious activities a few months prior had led to Matthew being shanghaied. He'd triggered an elaborate rescue by Sage, Fong, Mrs. Clemens and a host of others. He clearly recalled that harrowing escapade and the dangers associated with being too inquisitive.

"Yes, sir," he said, his voice cracking. Clearing his throat, he continued, "You tell me what you want and that's exactly what I'll do. And, I promise you on my honor, I won't never, ever, even think of it again."

"All right, Matthew," Sage said, smiling gently. "The night before last, sometime after 9:30 p.m., a boy on a bicycle delivered a message to a man named Leo Lockwood, who resides at 425 Clay Street. Tomorrow, I need you to find the boy who carried that message and nothing more. Tell him there's money in it if he'll talk to me. Are you willing to undertake that task?"

"Yes, sir." Matthew's chair scraped backwards as he jumped to his feet. "Us bicycle errand boys fool around together sometimes, doing stunts and stuff. I bet one of those boys carried the message. I'll ask around."

"Don't bumble yourself into any fixes," Sage cautioned as the boy clumped from the room. It was for certain sure that

Ida would never forgive Sage if her only surviving nephew came to harm.

Sage's ruminations about his previous night's exchanges with Philander and Matthew abruptly halted. Less than five feet in front of him, Herman Eich was bent over the trash barrel that stood near the entrance of the dirt road leading down to the strike line. Before Sage had time to avert his face or change direction, Eich straightened and his penetrating brown eyes locked on Sage's. Then those eyes widened. Inexplicably, Eich whirled around and rapidly shuffled away from him. Sage only had an instant to puzzle over the ragpicker's strange behavior before being suddenly trapped, his arms pinned to his sides. Someone slapped a cold wet cloth across his nose and mouth. Startled, he gasped, started to jerk his arms free and then knew nothing.

ELEVEN

With a nauseating swoop Sage returned to consciousness. Fortunately, this time, no stabbing headache accompanied the swoop but an unmistakable medicinal smell wafted into his nostrils from his mustache hairs. That smell, coupled with the memory of cold wetness being slapped against his face, answered the "what happened?" question. Chloroform. He was face down, his nose squashed against rough flat planks. Cramps seized his arms and legs and as he muzzily tried to shift position, he found movement impossible. Cords held his wrists behind his back and tied his legs together from his ankles to his thighs. Splinters pricked his face everywhere the tight rag across his mouth didn't cover. He groaned. Not again. Someone had trussed him up like one of Ida's tightly rolled pork roasts.

He twisted onto his right side. The surface beneath his body felt uniformly flat down his whole length. He was lying on floor. Fortunately, it wasn't rolling like a ship's deck. And, he wasn't blindfolded. That last was maybe not a good sign. It meant that his captors weren't worried that he'd be around to describe either them or this place.

He craned his neck, trying to get a good look at his surroundings. Light glimmered between the horizontal planks of the wall before him. Even as he registered this fact, he also realized there was a distant rhythmic clang of metal hitting metal coming from beyond that wall. So this was not a ship nor an isolated hut. That noise meant he was some place where people worked. Maybe he was somewhere inside a factory? He relaxed his belly to quiet his breathing and felt his bonds loosen slightly as tension drained from his limbs—another of Fong's lessons. Of course, if he were Fong, he'd have escaped by now.

Sage's ears strained to pinpoint the direction of the clanging sound. It seemed to come from beyond the wall and somewhere to the side and below him, meaning that he was in a room above a factory floor. That question answered he rolled over to face the opposite direction. Another wall. This one was blank except for the outline of a door. He fish-wiggled over to that wall and listened. His heart stuttered when a voice suddenly started speaking from a point almost directly over his head. A frantic roll of his eyes established that he was still alone in the small space. The words were coming from other side of the wall.

"He still out you think?" a voice asked in a distinctive nasal whine. The voice was unknown to Sage.

The answer also came through the wall, "Hell, there was enough chloroform on that rag to bring down a moose. He'll be out till Sunday. Deal another hand." The second voice wheezed as if issuing from a chest overburdened by age, drink, fat, or all three.

Shuffling, the snick of playing cards slapping onto a hard surface and the faint swish of the deal told him how they were passing the time.

"Once we're done here, I don't intend to play cards for a week. We've been waiting here for hours," said Whiny.

"Stop complaining. It ain't like nuthin' better is out there waiting for you. He said we're supposed to wait until the operation shuts down and by gum, that's what we'll do." Wheezy's phlegmy chuckle carried a nasty edge that made Sage twitch despite his bindings. "You oughta be happy you won't be digging a hole with the damn mud up to your knees. Stuff 'em in, add some iron, down goes the lid and roll 'em off. It'll be easy as unloading beer kegs off the wagon. He'll bounce along the river bottom for a bit and be gone for good. Nothing easier."

"Yes siree, I know that's right." Whiny agreed. "That other guy, Chester, he's next, right?" The eagerness in Whiny's voice was as chilling as Wheezy's throaty cackle.

"Too bad we lost our chance to nail all three," Whiny said. "That means we ain't gonna get paid as much now. If old man Mackey hadn't turned stubborn after they run down that striker, we woulda taken out their leader too. Ah well, Lockwood is about to meet the hangman—too bad the boss won't pay us for him, 'specially since he's there 'cause of us. At least, now that the old man's out of the way, we got the go-ahead to scoop up this one. Piece a cake, doncha know."

Wheezy sounded his breathy cackle in response before saying, "Boss sez if we finish our job with that Chester guy tomorrow night, we leave the next day. Me, I'm looking forward to riding the cushions out of this God-awful damn dripping town. I'm sick of all this rain. Few days from now, I'll be holding a cigar in one mitt while a prissy black porter pours me a jigger of Kentucky bourbon for the other mitt. Heh, heh. 'Frisco here I come!"

Sage twisted against his cords. He planned to interrupt ol' Wheezy's travel plans, if given the chance. Sage understood Wheezy's references to rolling someone off a dock. Drop someone in the rain-swollen Willamette now and there was a good chance he'd never reappear. Or, days later and miles down stream, his decomposing body would bob to the surface and give some fisherman a scare.

Sage twisted around, searching for a way to cut the cords. No way he was going to lie here waiting for them to drown him like a kitten in a gunny sack.

The room was about ten by six feet. Stacked crates filled one end, otherwise it was empty. He stared at the opposite wall, the one separating this room from the factory floor. If those two in the next room needed the shop below to close down, that meant the men working on the other side of that wall offered his best hope for rescue. How to attract their attention with no window or door in that wall? He spotted a circular thread of light near the floor. It was a loose knot in a wall plank. Sage wriggled over, twisted around and used his elbow to jab at the knot until it broke free and fell away.

Swiveling, he pushed his face against the wall to look through the hole. His whole body twitched against the cords. So that's what Wheezy meant when he spoke of "stuffing him in," and "lids" and "rolling." Below him, a number of workmen engaged in constructing large, man-sized, wooden barrels. He was above a cooperage.

Sage surveyed the grimy workplace. The soot blackening the rafters and skylights high above the shop floor came from small fires smoking inside half-shaped barrels, the heat making the staves pliable. Freedom lay beyond a high, wide doorway opening onto the dock. Beyond the dock, the winter river glistened gray beneath a dim winter sun. Unless the chloroform was confusing his reasoning abilities, the river's debris flow meant the cooperage was on the river's west bank.

Below, the cooperage floor was a jumble of men, materials and equipment. Willamette Valley white oak staves lay stacked in neat rows, ten feet high, looking like a gigantic lattice. Piled against the far wall, metal barrel hoops were in staggered piles so that they looked like coins poking from between the knuckles of a closed fist.

Men bustled about the various work areas. On the wharf outside, a stooping man deftly wielded a short-handled axe, debarking and splitting rounds of white oak into bolts. A shop boy was pushing wheelbarrow loads of these wood bolts inside to tumble them off onto the floor. Another man was branding finished barrels with a hot iron, sending an aroma like baking spice cake drifting upward toward the tin roof. Meanwhile, a brawny fellow, his bare arm muscles bulging, augured tap and bung holes into the nearly finished barrels.

The fierce clanging began again as the master cooper placed a heavy chisel atop a hoop, and slammed the big-faced hammer down. He was efficient. With each blow, the hoop jumped further down the barrel, the barrel's hollowness amplifying the sound.

The high screech of metal on stone snapped Sage's attention in another direction. A young boy of twelve or so sat at a grinding wheel sharpening tools. He was evidently doing a good job because, when a knife fell from a nearby bench, the man using it sprang back, letting it clatter onto the concrete floor rather than try to catch it. Sage groaned aloud with frustration. Just two seconds with that knife and he'd be a free man.

Fruitless minutes passed as Sage rolled around the storeroom floor, searching for a way to free his hands or snag the gag off his mouth. His only accomplishment was the painful stabbing of more splinters into his face. As he rested from his exertions, he realized that he was hearing a counterpoint of snores and intermittent snorts from the adjoining room. Perfect time to try escaping if only he weren't tied hand and foot.

A new sound joined the cacophony below. A steam engine, near the open door to the wharf, rumbled into life. Within minutes, the boiler started hissing like a giant teakettle, powering the machine hooked to it into noisy action. As Sage watched through the knothole, unfinished staves began riding a leather belt into one end of the flat, rectanglar machine. When they exited the other end, they looked more like barrel staves—angled at their ends and somewhat bowed in the middle.

"Oh, damn it all to hell," Sage mumbled into the gag. That boiler and its attached stave-making machine were so loud that, even if he freed his mouth, the men below wouldn't hear his shouts before the yahoos in the next room burst in. He stopped struggling and dozed, pulled down into sleep by the muddling residuals of chloroform.

Consciousness returned, followed by sharp pains in his shoulders, wrists and ankles. Still his mind felt sharper, more alert. Over the metallic clangs coming from the factory floor, Whiny and Wheezy's voices sounded in the adjoining room. Now and again, a third voice also. That person's came through the wall muffled although something about that voice sounded familiar. Sage checked his memory for a face to attach to that particular cadence of speech. No one sprang to mind.

A door slammed in the distance and steps moved toward the door to the storeroom. Sage twisted into his original position, closed his eyes and slowed his breathing. When a heavy boot pushed at his butt, he relaxed his body, letting it flop in response. A man grunted, the footsteps departed. The storeroom door was slammed shut without a word having been spoken.

Sage lay with his cheek against the rough planks, his mind rebelling against the grim reality of his situation. The fading ribbons of light between the wall planks signaled the end of daylight. Within an hour, night would fall, making it too dark for the cooper and his assistants to see their work. The steam engine would fall silent, the clangs of barrel-making would cease and the men below would depart, heading home to their families. They'd never know of the murder taking place in their absence. He doubted they would even notice if a barrel was missing tomorrow morning.

He lay there, cheek pressed against the floor, while visions of his mother's glowing eyes, Fong's sly half-smile and the clatter and bustle of Mozart's kitchen flitted through his thoughts. Funny how such simple things summed up the meaning of "home."

Suddenly, the floor beneath him jolted and heaved upward as an explosive roar battered his ears.

TWELVE

Fine particles of drifting dirt sprinkled Sage's face as he lay momentarily stunned and unable to comprehend what had just happened. Shouted expletives sounded from the adjoining room, followed by the thud of boots as his captors seemingly fled. Sage frantically fish-flopped over to his knothole. Chaos reigned on the shop floor. While some workers raced to turn various valves, other workers gathered around a man, apparently the boiler tender. He sat holding his head with both hands. When the man raised his dazed face, he seemed unable to hear his co-workers' shouted questions. Shock and momentary deafness, Sage quickly concluded.

In the corner, the boiler hissed and thick steam billowed toward the rafters high above. A telltale trickle of water meandered from underneath the boiler tank, across the plank floor to disappear beneath the shop's outer wall. The boiler had run dry when the tender failed to see the leak. A snick of movement along the wharf outside snagged Sage's attention. He strained to see what it was. His eye stared until dryness forced him to blink. Nothing moved out on the wharf other than the sundown glint atop the river flow.

Sage rolled away from the knothole, listening closely for sounds in the adjoining room. He heard distant shouts, seeming to come from somewhere outside, then the pop-pop of revolver fire followed by silence. Seconds later, his straining ears caught the soft pad of footsteps moving toward the storeroom door.

The man who slowly pushed the door open held a wooden staff in one hand and a short bladed knife in the other. Seconds later that knife sliced the cords binding Sage's wrists. With numb hands throbbing painfully from the rush of blood, Sage yanked the soggy rag from his mouth and spat, after which he asked with a wry smile, "What took you so darn long?"

"Wanted to make sure you appreciate our effort," Fong answered with a wide and toothy grin. He led Sage through the cooperage's empty second floor office to reach a door that opened onto an outside staircase. As they descended down to the dock, Sage saw nothing of his captors.

"You blew the boiler?" Sage asked as the two of them moved swiftly off the dock and into the surrounding neighborhood.

"Yes. First we twisted the screw near bottom of the boiler tank so the water dribbled out. We watch gauge from out in the dark on dock. At the right time, we made noise, like hurt dog, to lure boiler man away. He is not hurt, I think."

"Yes, I saw that. Gave him a helluva scare though. Where are we anyway?"

"Cooperage shares the same dock with the Mackey lumber mill."

Sage, mind racing, vigorously rubbed the stinging tingle from wrists and arms as they strode along. "I want to hear how you found me. First, though, we need to reach Chester's house as soon as possible," he said. "Those men plan to kill him, just like they intended to kill me. Where are they now? How'd you chase them off?"

"Myself and cousins hide on the dock, behind barrels and piles of wood. When the two men stumble down stairs we keep them going by throwing hatchets at them. They never see us. Still, they shoot bullets into the air. When they reach dock, they so scared each run away in different direction."

Sage laughed. "Good," he said, "That means they need to regroup. In the meantime, I better find Chester and convince him to hide out for awhile. They want to kill me, Chester and Leo—apparently that's how they plan to end the strike," he said.

They found Chester safe at home. He followed Sage out onto his covered front porch and the two men talked, the now heavy rain muting the sound of their voices. When told of his danger, Chester agreed to Sage's plans and quickly filled a duffle bag. When they set out, Fong trailed the two of them. Once certain no one followed, Fong melted into the night.

Half an hour later, Sage and Chester entered a building in the North End neighborhood where rent was cheap and the neighbors asked few questions. A weathered man with a ready grin answered Sage's knock on a second floor door. That grin widened at the sight of Sage. "Well, if you're not a sight for these sore eyes," Stuart Franklin declared, his clipped Bostonian accent seeming at odds with his shabby flannel shirt and denim trousers.

Sage spoke quickly. "Hey there, Stuart, this here is Chester. He's a friend of mine that needs somewhere safe to stay for awhile and I thought, 'Betcha my friend Stuart might help out his old pal, Sam Graham.'"

Franklin's face gave no indication he noted Sage's name change. He just continued to grin, opened his door wider and gestured for them to sit on the room's two chairs, saying, "You're right there, Sam. Anything you need, I'm delighted to help." They removed their wet coats and boots while Franklin hobbled over to make a pot of coffee on a paraffin stove. His movements remained painfully stiff from recently broken bones and torn muscles. Just a few months prior, Franklin nearly lost his life in their joint effort to stop the shanghaiing of men onto sailing ships. These days, the former sailor was convalescing and Sage was making sure Franklin wanted for nothing. He figured it was the least he could do.

Sage briefly explained the danger Chester was in. "Heck, he's more than welcome to bunk heah with me," Franklin said before Sage even asked for help. Franklin turned his smile on his other guest and said, "Chester, I'd be proud if you'd stay on heah with me. I admire what you and your union brothers are trying to accomplish. You'll be safe heah until Sam figures out how to throw those thugs behind bars. And he will, I promise you! Whatever Sam tackles, he conquers!"

Franklin's words, spoken with a fervent conviction, seemed to ease Chester's worries because the bridge carpenter's shoulders relaxed and the furrows in his forehead smoothed out. "Why, thank you most kindly, Mr. Franklin. I do appreciate the offer, " he said.

As Sage departed for Mozart's, he gave himself a mental pat on the back, certain that he'd guaranteed Chester's safety for the time being. Strolling along, there was finally time to mull over everything he'd heard coming through the wall during his captivity. They had said what? That's right—something about being responsible for Leo's jailing and also something about old man Mackey being 'out of the way.'

It sounded like Abner Mackey had resisted their plans to kill Lockwood, Chester and Sage. Was ol' Abner's resistence the reason someone got the old man out of the way? If so, who issued that order? Mackey's son? Who else, if not his son?

One thing was certain, Leo never harmed that old man. Leo wasn't a stupid man, far from it. He knew that such a heartless act would turn public opinion against the strikers. Nor was there a single cruel bone in his body. It was beyond Leo Lockwood's character to gin up enough hatred to burn an old man to death. Yet, is it possible for any son to order his father killed in such a cruel way? It was possible, Sage supposed, but highly unlikely.

Try as he might, not a single satisfactory answer as to who caused the old man's death came to mind so Sage let it go and simply walked, gazing at the storefronts and street activity and appreciating that there was no rain falling. Upon reaching Mozart's, he found his mother and Fong waiting for him in their third floor apartment.

"What? No customers needing attention downstairs? No staff to boss around?" Sage teased his mother, hoping to erase that deep vertical furrow between her brows.

She laughed and stood up quickly. "Hush! I'm going right back down. I just needed to see with my own eyes that you are still alive and wiggling," she said, giving him a none too gentle pat on his cheek. "And lather yourself up and shave before you come downstairs. You look like a wild boar with all them bristles and you smell ripe as one too," she threw over her shoulder as she headed out the door.

"You think she is a little sweet on that Eich fellow?" Sage asked, stripping quickly while Fong laid out restaurateur John Adair's starched snow-white shirt, black worsted suit with matching waistcoat and polished leather shoes.

"Maybe she is a little bit," Fong said.

"In that case, we've got ourselves a big problem because I think he helped those two galoots bushwhack me."

"I don't think so," said Fong.

"You weren't there. One minute Eich's staring me in the eyes. Next thing I know, they've got me trussed up in that dingy storeroom. I got to listen as they talked about barreling me like a pickling cucumber and dropping me in the river." Even though his tone was light, a shiver traveled up his back as he said the words.

Fong nodded. "Mr. Eich there and saw what happened that for sure. He only pretend to run away, Sage. He hide so he can follow those two bad men to see where they take you. He watch them carry you up the stairs into cooperage. After that, he came straight here. Without Mr. Eich, you still be in storeroom or maybe in barrel—one big, unhappy pickle." Fong displayed a toothy grin at his own witticism.

Before there was time to consider this unexpected bit of information, heavy boots thudded up the stairway. As both men looked toward the open door, a flushed Matthew appeared. "Mr. Adair, I found him! I found him! I pedaled to every place to find him and it turns out that, cat's whiskers, he's been home sick all this time and that's why I couldn't catch hold of him for such a long time. But, today, I peddled back to that corner near the market and there he was, the one boy I never talked to and sure enough he's the one. I found him!"

"Whoa, hold on there, Matthew. Exactly who was it that you found?" Sage asked, smiling at the young fellow's bristling excitement.

"Why, the boy who took that message to that Mr. Lockwood at the address you gave me."

Sage remembered then. Matthew was supposed to find the bicycle messenger who carried the message that lured Lockwood to Mackey's office just about the time the fire started. So, now they could prove that Lockwood was telling the truth. There'd been both message and messenger. With any luck, the boy might recollect who gave him that message to carry. "That's wonderful Matthew. Good work, really good work."

The boy flushed an even deeper red as he rushed back into speech. "His name is Thaddeus and he's downstairs right now. Not out front, of course, 'cause of the customers. I told him to wait around back." A sudden worry creased Matthew's forehead. "Umm, I, um hope you don't mind. I told him you'd give him a whole dollar if he'd come with me right off. I know you never said how much you'd pay him but I kinda figured it was important for you to talk to him otherwise you'd never bring me into it," he said, displaying an astuteness he'd frequently lacked in the past.

When the boy paused in his headlong dash of words to draw a breath, Sage spoke quickly, "Matthew, if this boy's the one we're looking for, his information is likely worth the dollar and more. Let's go see him."

The messenger, Thaddeus, stood leaning against the wall, partly sheltered by the back stoop's overhang. His face was thin and his skin pale except where a runny nose rimmed his nostrils red. He straightened when the back door opened, freeing his gloveless hands from the warmth of his armpits.

"Matthew here," Sage gestured to Matthew who'd followed him out the door, "said you carried a message to Mr. Lockwood a few nights back. Is that true?"

Thaddeus nodded vigorously. "Yup, I carried it I surely did. Last message I delivered that night and I think that's when this cold caught hold of me," he said, snuffling for emphasis.

"Do you remember the person who gave you the message?"

"He weren't nobody I know, that's for sure," said the boy.

"Tell me what his face looked like. Did he appear to be an older man?"

"Well, I didn't see much of his face. From the sound of his voice and how he walked I think maybe he was near to your age maybe, so I guess he was an older man."

"Did this fellow seem older or younger than me?"

"I'd say younger by a few years. That'd be my guess."

"Do you think you could identify him if you saw him again?"

The boy scrunched up his face in concentration before shaking his head regretfully, "Don't think so. He had his hat pulled low and a muffler wrapped over his mouth and he stopped me when I was out of the lamplight so it was real hard to see him. At first I thought he was aiming to steal my bicycle. The boy's eyes widened and he looked hopeful saying, "But I might recognize his voice if I heard it again."

"Was the message he gave you in writing?"

"Nope. He just said to tell Mr. Lockwood that Mr. Mackey wanted to see him at the construction office as soon as possible. At the time, I thought that Mr. Lockwood worked for the Mackey fellow who wanted him back to work for one reason or another. Didn't think all that much of it. You still gonna give me that dollar, mister?" His voice rose with the question, yearning widening the eyes he raised to Sage's.

"Yes, I most certainly will. Does Matthew know where you live, Thaddeus?"

The boy nodded. "I told him. He says he knows the place."

"If you come back tomorrow at dinner time, say at noon, to talk to Mr. Gray, he's a lawyer, we'll give you a good dinner and another dollar. Is that acceptable to you?"

"Oh, yes, sir!"

Sage put a hand on Thaddeus's shoulder, which was narrow and boney, most likely from lack of food. "Will you also tell a policeman about how you carried that message if I ask you to?" Sage asked him.

Fear flared in the boy's wide eyes but he said bravely, "Why, I guess I'd be willing to help out that way."

Sage fished in his trouser pocket and pulled out a shiny dollar coin. The boy's eyes focused on the money. He snatched it up before trotting down the stairs, the soles of his oversized boots kicking up water as he hopped onto his bicycle and pedaled furiously away.

THIRTEEN

WATER DROPS SLITHERED ALONG THE tin roof, seeking out unsealed seams and pinholes, spitting whenever they landed on the hot stove top. Herman Eich set aside the small porcelain bowl he'd been examining to check the bake oven. The oven temperature was nearly perfect for the first firing. Moving back to his workbench, Eich reached forward to tuck the calico curtain behind a nail, trying to capture all there was of morning's watery light. Just as he picked up his scoring knife, the shed door's rusted metal hinges screeched, causing him to turn from the bench.

Daniel entered the shed, holding his hat just outside the door to shake it free of rain before hanging it on a nail. Once fully inside, he halted, as if transfixed by sudden thought, unaware of the water dripping off his black slicker and pooling on the floor. Then his eyes seemed to focus. "Hello, Mr. Eich. I didn't figure you'd still be here this late in the morning," he said in a lifeless voice.

"Hello, Daniel." Eich held up the small bowl, "Since heaven saw fit to release so much of its blessings upon us, I thought to stay dry and mend this small bowl for Isabel. She works as a maid at the Portland Hotel."

Daniel shuffled closer to study the bowl.

"I don't know why you bother. They sell bowls everywhere for pennies. Can't she buy herself a bowl without a break in it?" he asked.

Eich gave a wry chuckle. "To be sure, there are many bowls made by hundreds of workers who are standing for hours in assembly lines doing just a little portion of the tasks needed to create a bowl. And, yes, it is true that Isabel could purchase one of those unflawed bowls for just a few pennies. This bowl," however," Eich held it up so that the window light bathed its translucent curves, "is unique. There is no other exactly like it in the world. It is the work of a skilled artisan who oversaw its creation from inception to completion. After being shaped from the finest porcelain clay and hand-decorated with these vibrant colors of red and blue, the piece was carried countless times to and from the kiln until each color, each glaze, shone bright. Once finished, it traveled all the way from France. A bowl like this can never be mass produced and bought for a few pennies. If fate is willing, this bowl will pass from Isabel to her daughter. And so that Frenchman's artistry lives on, delighting the eye for many years to come."

Daniel shrugged. "But it's broken. What good is a broken piece of pottery to anyone?"

Eich gently set the bowl down and swiveled atop his stool to speak directly into the bleak face of his lodger, "Everything in life is less than perfect, Daniel. Every thing, every person. No thing and no one person is absolutely perfect. And, although, I cannot make this bowl absolutely the same as it once was, it is possible to restore it to its former function and recover almost all of its beauty."

"Don't you think it's better to destroy broken things so that they don't have an opportunity to hurt you?"

"Hurt? I'm not sure that I. . . ." Eich fumbled in his effort to divine the meaning beneath Daniel's bitter words.

"That bowl, it might hurt someone. Cut em for instance."

Eich pondered Daniel's point. "No, Daniel, this bowl is unlikely to hurt anyone. With a little time and attention though, it will become close to what it once was. I will use clay to fill in the chip so there will be no sharp edges. In time, the mend will blend in, be less noticeable. It will not be perfect but sometimes it is the imperfections, in things and in people, that make them all the more precious to us."

"I just don't think like you do, Mr. Eich. If something's broken, throw it out—get rid of it. It's garbage—no good to anybody. If you keep it around everybody is in danger!" Agitation raised the volume of Daniel's voice. As Eich searched for a mollifying response to make, the other man snatched his hat from the nail and opened the door. "I gotta go out," he mumbled, banging the door shut behind him.

Eich was alone again, gazing after the departed man. "What was that exchange really about?" he wondered aloud. "Not you, my little beauty, not you," he assured the bowl, picking it up to cradle in his hand. He bent to his work, his mind snagging on the worry of Daniel's grief. It showed no signs of abating. If anything, its intensity had increased.

Comforted by the soft rain now pattering on his tin roof, Eich sighed and again raised the knife to score the edges of the break, making rough anchor points for the new clay to cling to. That task completed, he mixed the clay and water, stirring it into a creamy paste. Just as the mixture neared optimum consistency, a knock sounded at the door. "Come in," he shouted, unable to stop stirring because, if he did, the mixture would harden into an unusable lump.

He glanced over his shoulder to see the owner of Mozart's, John Adair, step across his threshold. On this occasion, Adair wore neither the suit of a prosperous entrepreneur nor the shabby work clothes that Eich last saw him wearing. Instead, Adair was clad in a nondescript suit and hat—garb that would allow him to travel unnoticed in the surrounding neighborhood.

"Come in, Mr. Adair. Please indulge me for just a minute. This wet clay hardens rapidly so I must smooth it quickly onto the piece."

"Certainly," Sage responded. He closed the door and crossed to stand next to the bench, watching silently as Eich scooped up the wet clay, smoothing it onto the bowl's edge with fingers as deft as a watchmaker's. Once he'd placed the bowl safely on the bench, Eich gave Sage his full attention.

"I am glad to see that you are well," he said.

"Every thanks to you I understand."

Eich stood up from his stool and gestured Sage toward it. "Only seat in the house, I am afraid. You rest there while I sit on the cot."

From his vantage point on the stool, Sage surveyed the shed. The blankets on Eich's cot were smooth and tucked neatly beneath the thin mattress. Underneath a small window stood the workbench cluttered with pottery, paint pots and small metal tools. A potbellied wood stove filled a corner, its top covered by a cast-iron bake oven—probably used as a poor man's kiln, Sage thought. Here and there, empty tin cans were pinging softly as water drips from above hit them square on. In the far corner, drab garments hung in neat rows from wall pegs. Below them, tidy bedding lay rolled out atop a rough wood plank floor.

Eich noticed Sage looking at the bedroll and said, "That's where Daniel is sleeping temporarily until he acquires a new home. Thank you for letting him paint at the restaurant. My hope is that working at what he does best will help him regain his footing."

Sage cleared his throat. "Actually, it looks like we're the ones benefitting. He's a skilled painter. Never uses a paint cloth, yet never spills a drop."

"I thought he might be. He has an air of persnickety in everything he does." Eich responded.

"I want to ask . . . I mean I'd appreciate it if you'd tell me what you saw when those men grabbed me yesterday."

Eich chuckled softly. "I confess it startled me to find myself staring straight into those eyes of your when I raised my head out of that dustbin. Those eyes are recognizable anywhere, no matter how you clothe yourself."

Sage shifted uncomfortably. He never considered his dark blue eyes to be particularly remarkable. If they somehow were, it could be a problem.

Eich seemed to read his thoughts. "Don't worry about other people recognizing you that way. I tend to look into the eyes of a person to the exclusion of everything else. I've always been that way. Unnerves some folks, I imagine.

"Those men that grabbed me, where did they come from?" Sage asked.

"They stepped out from between the buildings, moving so fast that I had no more warning than you did. One minute, I was staring into your face then there was a flurry of motion and next thing I knew two big men had their arms wrapped around you. I figured if they thought too long about me, I wouldn't be around to tell anybody what happened to you."

"So you took off?"

"Only until I was out of sight around a corner. I immediately doubled back and followed them. You hung limp as a rag doll so they had a hard time toting you and didn't look over their shoulders much. When I last saw them, they were lugging you up the outside stairs of that cooperage, so I figured they weren't planning on hauling you down again anytime soon. At least not until dark. That's when I hared off to tell Mae what happened to you."

Sage felt his face stiffen at the man's easy use of his mother's first name but gave himself a mental shake and pushed on. "Did you recognize the two men?" he managed to ask, trying to sound normal.

"Can't say that I've ever seen them before," Eich responded. "They wore big hats like farmhands and rubber slickers. I couldn't really see their faces or forms. I'm not even sure if I would recognize them if I saw them again. I was afraid to move too close because that dock was empty. So, I watched from a long ways up the riverbank."

Sage stirred on his stool. So far, Eich was not providing any useful information.

"Now the third man, I saw him better."

"What third man?"

"He climbed up the stairs of the cooperage a few minutes after your kidnappers. When he left a short time later, he moved like someone who had all the time in the world. There is no question. That man is a partner of the two kidnappers."

"Think you'd recognize this third man if you saw him again?"

"It's possible, although he didn't seem particularly remarkable in appearance. I never saw his eyes from where I stood.

Funny thing is, I had the distinct impression that I saw him before and not that long ago. The problem is remembering when or where. If I keep thinking on it, I am sure it will come to me. I usually remember things, although remembering takes me somewhat longer these days than when I was younger."

"If the memory comes back, let me know as soon as possible. I'd really appreciate it." Sage knew the edge in his voice wasn't going to help the other man remember. Memory was funny. Snatch at it and it moved farther away, let it be and it would unexpectedly tap you on the shoulder.

"Certainly, I will," Eich promised.

Sage entered Mozart's front door an hour before the restaurant was to open for the dinner hour. The smell of wet paint, not cooking food, assaulted his nose. Glancing around the foyer he discerned no change. A movement at the end of the narrow hallway caught his eye. Daniel stood back in the gloom, methodically brushing paint onto the wall.

Going through to the kitchen, Sage found his mother marshaling the dinner preparations. "You decided to ask Daniel to paint the downstairs foyer I see. Good idea. It needed it."

She paused in her glass polishing, her expression momentarily blank. "Me? I thought you told him to paint it."

"Nope, not me. Maybe Mr. Fong told him to?"

"I don't think so. Mr. Fong never issues an order like that without checking with us. Besides, he hasn't been in yet today."

A knock sounded at the back door cutting off their conversation. Sage opened the door to find the young messenger, Thaddeus, shivering on the doorstep, a hungry, hopeful look on his young face.

"Thaddeus!" Sage greeted him warmly. "Step inside out of the rain. You are just in time, the food is hot and ready to eat."

Thaddeus entered quickly and took a seat at the kitchen table. Mae took one look at the shivering boy frowned and reached for a dinner plate. Under his intent gaze, she heaped food onto a plate before sitting it and a glass of milk in front of him along with the admonition, "See that you eat it all up, boy. We don't want any of it going to waste." In the same stern tone, she continued. "There's more than enough waste taking place in that dining room out front there. You finish that plate, there'll be seconds and dessert."

Sage tried not to grin. Leaving Thaddeus to his task and certain Mae Clemens would stuff the boy until he was too full to wiggle, Sage retreated upstairs to change his clothes since it was nearing the time to assume his restaurant hosting duties. His mother hadn't complained, but she'd been doing more than her share when it came to keeping Mozart's running smoothly.

He was flipping the discrete sign to show "Open" when the lawyer, Philander Gray, came through the door.

"Adair. Glad you're here. Ida's young nephew said to come around noon, so here I am."

Sage took Gray's coat and hung it on the ornate hall tree. "How's Leo?" he asked.

"Things don't look good for him right now. The police are convinced Leo murdered old man Mackey. They aren't budging off that idea and far as I know, they aren't looking to find anyone else. Leo's feeling pretty grim about his family's future. I told him you'd make sure they wanted for nothing. Still, those assurances will be damn little comfort to him, or them, if he's hanged for this."

A clatter sounded in the dim back hallway. Sage saw Daniel hastily righting a knocked over empty paint bucket.

Sage took the lawyer's elbow and steered him through the dining room. "Come through to the kitchen, Philander. There's a young man I want you to talk to. He might provide you with some helpful information."

Soon the three of them sat at the kitchen table. Eating had brought a tinge of color to Thaddeus's pale cheeks and his big brown eyes sparkled with curiosity. Two empty plates and a drained glass of milk indicated the boy had faithfully followed Mae Clemens' orders.

Sage introduced the two. "It looks like Thaddeus here might be your rival when it comes to the quantity of food he tucks away," Sage teased, making the boy squirm in his chair. "I asked Thaddeus to talk to you about a message he delivered some nights back."

He spoke to the boy. "Thaddeus, suppose you tell Mr. Gray about that message."

The boy related receiving the message and delivering it to Leo. He remembered Leo's address and described the union leader accurately. His description of the message-giver was markedly less precise.

"His face was hidden because it was dark and his hat was pulled low and a scarf was up around his chin and mouth."

"Was he a big man? Was he breathing heavy?" Sage prodded, thinking of the voices he'd heard through the cooperage wall.

The boy shook his head. "Nah, he moved light on his feet. He was average-like."

"How about his eyes?" Sage asked thinking of Herman Eich's unique fixation.

The boy's face lightened as if he finally saw a way to be more helpful. "Yup. I saw his eyes all right. Pale blue and chilly-like," he said, a shudder seeming to travel through him.

FOURTEEN

SAGE WAS ONCE AGAIN HEADING TOWARD the strike line—for once, under a clear winter sky with the sun shining as bright as early November allowed. Admittedly, his lack of fear in taking this stroll was solely attributable to the presence of Fong's "cousins," trailing along on both flanks. Ahead a Chinese man stood gazing into a shop window while yet another sat on a porch step tying his boot laces. Sage found himself speculating whether some residents and shopkeepers in this neighborhood of small houses and stores wondered at such an influx of Oriental men into their otherwise Occidental neighborhood. A few widow women might bolt their doors and watch from behind partially pulled curtains. Most likely, though, the men and women who worked and lived along this particular street were too busy trying to keep warm, dry and reasonably fed to think much about the life passing by outside their walls.

Sage paused at the top of the cul de sac to study the strike line. Although he expected it, his heart sank at the sight of just a few strikers straggling back and forth in front of the construction office. What destruction time had wrought in the workers' optimism. Two months ago, exhilarated men walked off the job, confident that such a decisive action would improve all their lives. Their numbers clogged the road's end on that first day of the strike. Now, the remaining men numbered too few to even slow a lumber wagon, let alone block its passage. Sage straightened his shoulders and willed confidence into his step. Halfway down the nearby stream, a Chinese fisherman stood methodically dipping a net into the roiling waters. Fong was recognizable from his stance—anchored as securely to the earth as was the big willow at his side.

"Hey, Sam, heard anything about Leo?" a man asked as Sage neared.

"Yes. Leo now has the best lawyer in town working for him. I'd say things are looking as good as possible under the circumstances."

"Did his lawyer turn up a witness to clear him?" This question came from O'Reilly, his face as tense as everyone else's. Maybe O'Reilly was more than the fair weather rabble rouser Sage suspected him to be. Sage smiled, saying only, "Something like that. Anyway, Leo sends his best and asks that you men don't give up the fight."

Muttering stirred the group until one man spoke up. "What fight? Most everybody's abandoned the strike and the public thinks we're a bunch of murdering thugs. There ain't no 'fight' going on here." Murmured agreement followed this bitter declaration.

Sage raised a palm to halt their words. "Hold on, men. You ever heard the saying, 'It's always darkest before the dawn?' We're working on a little something that might turn things around. In the meantime, you need to help each other keep your spirits up for a few more days," Sage said, all the while hoping his bravado sounded more confident in their ears than it did in his own.

It evidently did, because a faint brightening of hope washed across their grim faces. No doubt, the grinding lack of progress made them ready to clutch at anything. Time had winnowed the strikers down to the diehards—men enduring the pain of the strike yet staying rock solid in their commitment to the effort. In the beginning, many abandoned their jobs without knowing how hard the struggle to win an eight-hour workday was going to be. By now, those who remained did so knowing the real stakes. They understood that the fight's outcome would impact many more people than just the Mackey Construction employees. A win here meant a rising of the wage floor for everyone who worked in Portland's construction trades. These few remaining men slogged through this mud knowing that the weight of many people's futures rested on their shoulders.

The sight of their tired, pinched faces was humbling. People might be unthinkingly or inescapably heroic. These men, however, were even braver because the choice they made was a calculated, deliberate choice with no guarantee of success and every likelihood of failure. Rufus made that same choice and, in a single terrifying moment, the result was death and an impoverished, fatherless family. And these men continued to make that choice every single day they trudged down that muddy track to stand in the drenching rain. Instead of shutting up or slinking away, they chose to fight with only an abiding faith in life's inherent justice keeping them at their post.

Sage clenched his fists, his anger toward the Mackeys and men of their ilk raging inside his head. Their fine dress and genteel demeanor concealed their true character. Just like the city's defective bridges, the world these powerful men controlled also needed rebuilding by honest, compassionate and caring hands.

A hesitant voice at his side intruded into his thoughts. "You think there's maybe still a chance, Sam?" asked one of the men.

Sage turned and rested a reassuring hand on the man's shoulder as he said, "Absolutely. We are going to win this one." Inexplicably Sage felt sure of what he said and was gratified to observe a few spines straightening at his words. We will win this strike or I'll die trying, he silently vowed.

Saying he needed to check on Leo's family, Sage headed back up the road. He trailed behind Fong who'd climbed out of the gully, a string of silvered fish dangling from one hand, dip net slung across his shoulder. Sage waited until they both reached the main road before catching up to the successful fisherman.

"I see that this morning's guard duty wasn't a total waste," Sage said, pointing to the fish, figuring it would look like he was initiating a commercial transaction.

Fong lifted the fish higher, the pale sunlight glinting on their scales, highlighting their worthiness. "Pretty good catch," he agreed. "I give to cousins for their assistance this day."

"Mr. Fong, can you deliver a message to the newspaperman, Ben Johnston?"

Fong nodded.

"Ask Johnston if he's able to meet me at the usual place in the farmers' market in one hour. If he can't make it, send word to me there. You know where."

"I understand," Fong replied.

Sage held up both hands as if cutting off further haggling over the fish and strolled ahead, his steps once again shadowed by meandering Chinese men.

❀ ❀ ❀

Two hours later, Sage was making his way toward Stuart Franklin's apartment in the North End. After making sure Mackey's men weren't tailing him, Sage sent his Chinese bodyguards home. At his meeting with Johnston, the newspaperman didn't sugarcoat his opinion of the city engineer, Horace Bittler. "He's a greedy, grasping, nincompoop who brags because he has to." Johnston also imparted the information that it was Bittler's habit to stop at the upscale Trade Exchange Saloon before heading home after work.

Sage's arrival at Franklin's apartment interrupted a lively checkers game between Chester and Stuart, each man sitting before an evenly matched stack of captured checkers. Their easy camaraderie gave Sage momentary pause. He envied them the time they were able to spend getting acquainted. Between Mozart's and St. Alban's missions, little time remained for him to cultivate new friendships

Chester stood up abruptly, leaving Stuart to steady the game board. "Is something wrong with my family? With the men?" Chester asked.

"No problems whatsoever, Chester," Sage assured him. "I came by to see if you'd like to go out for a bit. I'm going to have me a little face-to-face talk with that city engineer and need your bridge-building expertise. I don't want him knocking me off stride with technical references. With you there, that can't happen."

"I guess I might go along with you, although I promised Stuart that I'd buy him dinner from that café downstairs. He planned to go down and bring it up after I beat him at this here game of checkers."

"Don't worry none about that, and besides, buddy, you ain't that close to beating me," Franklin retorted. He looked hopefully toward Sage. "I don't suppose your little foray needs assistance from a busted up sailor?" he asked. "I'm mighty sick of these four walls, grateful as I am for them."

Sage squeezed the other man's shoulder. It was bony and bird-like, no longer the shoulders of the man who'd once braved the surging waters of the Columbia River bar in a rowboat just a few months back. "I know it's hard having to take it easy. But, you know as well as I that the doctor said you are still a ways from being healed and he doesn't want you taking any chances just yet," Sage said. "At least three ruffians might be lying in wait for Chester and me. And, the man we're going to confront might prove a little frisky. I'm not willing to risk you being hurt again so soon. Maybe there will be something for you to help with once I've arranged for some protection for the two of you. I promise to work on it."

The Trade Exchange Saloon offered the city's business elite an opportunity to rub shoulders with their own kind. Inside, an ornate mahogany bar with a polished brass foot rail stretched along one side of the square room. There was a scatter of marble-topped tables across a relatively clean, white ceramic tile floor unmarred by either the scrape of hobnailed boots or the smears of spat tobacco. Glass chandeliers, festooned with electric globes, kept winter's gloom firmly at bay. When Sage and Chester stepped inside, wearing their workingman's duds, the conversational hubbub muted as more than one pair of eyes widened with curiosity.

Johnston was right. Bittler was easily recognizable by his crimson bow tie and matching silk handkerchief. The city's engineer sat alone at a table against the far wall, sipping liquor from a shot glass while he idly flipped the newspaper pages before him. The bartender moved to lift the gate and step from behind the bar, obviously intent on intercepting these rough-dressed interlopers and sending them off. Sage, however, ignored this guardian of propriety and strolled confidently toward Bittler who looked up from his perusal of the newspaper when he realized that strangers approached. Sage thought the thin-faced man paled. Bittler's brow, however, started lowering so that his face was in full glower by the time they reached his table. The look was comical instead of threatening because his small dark eyes sat too close together underneath those beetling brows. That glower, the man's pointed nose and his pursed mouth with its slight overbite, all combined to give him the countenance of a dim-witted guinea pig.

"Mr. Bittler," Sage said, as he grabbed a chair and sat down before the other man could speak, "My name is Sam Graham and this is Chester." Recognition flickered in the other man's eyes before contempt hardened his gaze. The urge to slap the man silly came over Sage. He resisted. Instead, he said, "We need to talk to you about the Marquam Ravine bridge and other bridges about town." Bittler clamped his lips so tightly shut they blanched white.

Sage ignored the reaction and continued, "Chester and I looked at the bridges and we're here to tell you that we are concerned . . . ."

Bittler curtly interrupted, "Come see me at my office. I don't talk about work during my leisure time. This isn't some waterfront saloon."

Sage glanced around. Businessmen sat smoking their cigars, sipping their whiskies, talking with quiet intensity. "Right, it's no waterfront saloon. Too bad for that. Nevertheless, these men are working even as we speak. Besides, I'm not sure it's a good idea for us to meet in your workplace to talk about your receipt of bribes," Sage said.

With a loud screech of chair legs on tile, Bittler's chair scraped backward, riveting the room's attention on them. Shooting a quick glance at neighboring tables, Bittler hesitated. He leaned forward, bared his yellow teeth and hissed, "You better watch out. You besmirch my reputation and I'll sue you and end up owning whatever little hovel you call home."

Sage also kept his voice low. "I'm just telling you why we decided to talk to you away from the office. You and Mackey are endangering everyone's life with that substandard repair work you approve. Any more of those bridges collapse and it's you who'll be looking at losing your home, not to mention serving some prison time."

Bittler folded his newspaper with shaking fingers. "Listen you ignorant lout. I obtained my education in a well-known New York engineering school. The Mackey family is socially prominent and respectable. I do not intend to listen to any uneducated 'bridge monkey' . . . ," he hissed the insult, ". . . instructing me on how to perform my job. I vest my complete faith in Earl Mackey. He is not going to jeopardize the people of this city nor his own standing in it." He stood up. "Now, if you 'gentlemen' will excuse me, I am late for my supper. I trust you will not possess the temerity to intrude upon me again!" Bittler started to push past them.

Sage's hand shot out to grab the other man's forearm, squeezing until Bittler winced. Anger slowed Sage's words as he said, "At least one trestle bridge roadway has given way and many others are in danger of doing the same. You can't pretend it is not happening. This isn't a sewer failure where people's water closets are spewing crap all over their floors." Bittler's body twitched at the sewer reference. Sage squeezed the man's arm harder as he said, "Two people are already dead, firemen are in the hospital, and the city's fire wagon is a total loss. Another bridge collapses, you'll be the man Mackey throws to the wolves."

"Are you threatening me?" Bittler's question ended in a squeak that sounded like that of the rodent he resembled. Those sitting at the neighboring tables dropped all pretense of disinterest and stared openly. Across the room, the bartender again started to lift the bar gate, clearly intent on rescuing his regular customer.

Sage stepped away from Bittler saying, "Good God, man! Surely, you're not thinking that you are anything more than a pawn in Mackey's schemes."

Bittler stood up. "Earl Mackey is my friend. That is what I know and I refuse to listen any further to your impugning of his character." Bittler slapped a homburg onto his head and stepped around them heading toward the door. Sage and Chester trailed right behind, sidestepping the bartender. Outside, Bittler frantically signaled a hansom cab, clambered aboard and rode away.

Chester was glum. "Can't see how that conversation offered us much to go on. He told us not a single licking thing."

"Oh we learned something valuable from that exchange. Notice how Bittler's hands trembled when he folded that newspaper?" Sage asked. "And, he had the barrel of a six-gun shoved into his waistband. I saw it when he raised his arm to hail that cab. Bittler is terrified, and I very much doubt we're the ones he's afraid of. "

FIFTEEN

His eyelids snapped open. Not his usual nightmare. No reliving the climb up a narrow ventilator shaft, no longer the terrified nine-year-old boy escaping a collapsed mine. No, this nightmare was worse because of the self-revulsion that lingered once he'd opened his eyes.

Sage struck a match to light his bedside lamp, his hand trembling, hoping light would dispel the feel of revolver's heft and that unholy satisfaction of pulling the trigger and making Earl Mackey's face disappear. At least the dream ended before he'd shot that pencil-licking clerk cowering at the dream's fuzzy edges.

He pulled himself up until his back leaned against the wooden headboard. Questions prowled through his mind like restless cats in a cage. This was the first time during a mission for St. Alban that he'd dreamt of actually killing the opposition. That was understandable, given all the suffering Mackey's greed had inflicted on decent men who only wanted to provide for their families. No, what made him uneasy about the dream was that shooting Mackey had felt good. Too good. Was he turning into the kind of men he fought? Could hate-filled action spawn a better world? Was that the sacrifice people like him made? His own humanity worn away by continually warring and every chance for a contented life sacrificed? One thing he knew for sure, deep in his soul, was that the squeezing of the dream trigger should not have delivered so much satisfaction.

Water from an over-full roof gutter dripped onto the window, its steady rhythm summoning him back into the room, the building, his life and all the problems. It was 4:00 a.m., his customary hour for confronting demons. Sage sighed. He wasn't going to sleep so he might as well spend the time trying to think of solutions to those problems. .

One by one, he picked over all that he knew about old Mr. Mackey's death. From what he'd overheard those two in the cooperage saying, maybe Earl Mackey ordered the old man killed. But that wasn't exactly what they said. "Anyways," as his mother would say, was it possible that any son could be that cruel to his old man? And, poor Leo. Hopefully he was asleep and not staring out from between jail bars at that seeping basement wall. And the strike. That was on the brink of disaster. And the bridge calamity—the dire threat of splintered timbers at the bottom of countless ravines loomed over the entire city. What to tackle first? The questions swirled endlessly, without snagging any answers, until they pulled him down into sleep, like soapsuds down a drain.

The new day began with a breakfast meeting among Sage, Fong and his mother.

"I not believe that son Mackey ordered his father killed," Fong said after Sage finished laying out the various trails they needed to follow. "To kill one's father is too big a step."

Sage scrunched up his forehead. "But Leo did not kill Mackey, so all that remains is Mackey's son as a likely possibility, right? Besides, those two thugs I heard talking spoke as if Abner Mackey's death was a good thing. And, we know they work for Earl Mackey. So, I don't see any other conclusion. To free Leo, we must prove that someone else is responsible. Right now, that someone else seems to be Earl Mackey. We need to find those two men and twist their tails to make them talk," Sage said.

Fong raised his eyebrows even as he nodded assent. "Maybe two men know useful information. Still, I not sure they offer only direction to search," he said.

Mae spoke up, "I'm thinking that the best thing is for me to get hired on as a domestic in the Bittler household. Who knows, I might find evidence that Bittler is on the take."

"Whoa there, Mother. I don't want you in the middle of that rat's nest. Bittler's carrying a gun because he's afraid somebody's going to come after him."

At this protest, her brow furrowed, her bold cheekbones reddened and her blue eyes took on a steely glint. She opened her mouth to speak.

"I take it back. I take it back," Sage said hurriedly, realizing immediately that protest was fruitless. Experience taught him that Mae Clemens would do exactly whatever she decided to do, regardless of his objections. So wisdom dictated going along with her. At least that way, he'd know where she was and what she was up to. "I admit that's an excellent idea—provided Bittler has a job opening in his household," he went on to say.

"Humph," she responded. "There'll be a job. Folks like the Bittlers usually need household help because they think a few cast-offs or a 'thank you' now and again will somehow erase their meanness and pushy demands. You watch, I'll be working there within a few days."

Fong cleared his throat, saying, "For my job, I will find two bad men and make sure cousins protect you and Chester and Chester's family,"

"Okay, if you two take care of those things, all that remains for me are the teensy, minor tasks to accomplish—like proving Leo's innocence and winning the strike," Sage said, his rueful tone negating the sarcasm of his words. He stood up, plucked his bowler hat from a nearby chair and slapped it on his head. "Game's still afoot, damn it all."

※ ※ ※

When Sage reached the end of the block, he encountered Ben Johnston on his way to see him. "Glad to find you, Adair. Wish to heck you'd install a telephone, I really can't spare the time away from the newspaper except some things have come up and I needed to update you."

"What? Has something happened?"

"Since I knew of your interest, I told my police reporter to keep his ears fanned out for any information on the Mackey murder case. He tells me that the police found a witness who says he saw Leo Lockwood lugging a kerosene can, near the cul de sac, the night Mackey died.

"I don't believe that," Sage said.

Johnston nodded. "Well, from what the reporter said, the witness sounds a little suspicious to me. This witness is a stranger here in town, an itinerant. On the other hand, only the fire chief and a few others know kerosene fueled the Mackey fire. Anyway, I thought you better know. I figure you'll want to pass the information on to Gray, since I hear he's taken on the case."

It was one of the city's newer buildings, constructed after the disastrous 1894 spring that flooded many blocks west of the river. Philander Gray's two-room office was on the third floor. One look at the steam elevator's vibrating cage and Sage climbed the stairs. Since his secretary was absent, Philander shouted, "In here, come on in," from another room when Sage swung the outer door open. Seconds later, the lawyer's lanky frame popped into view from his inner office.

"Ah, John Adair, just the man I needed to see. Glad you hoofed it over. It just occurred to me that I needed to head over to sample some of Miz Ida's fine pie. I have some information for you and I'm afraid it's not good."

"You mean the witness turning up?"

"What witness? There's a witness of some kind?"

"Oh, dandy! I guess that means we both carry bad news. You first," Sage said, dropping into a well-worn leather chair across the desk from Gray.

"Well, there's two bits of bad news. The first is that, as it turns out, our messenger boy, Thaddeus, was not much help. Unfortunately, the way the police interpret his information is that Mackey sent the message by one of his men and that placed Leo right on the spot when the fire broke out. They figure Mackey wanted a peaceable meet and Lockwood took advantage of the situation by attacking him and setting the place on fire."

Sage's heart sank. "Damn, it's logical to figure it that way," he acknowledged. "Sometimes a person forgets there is more than one way to look at something. What's the other bad news?"

Gray's face became somber. "Those puppets on the grand jury indicted Leo for Mackey's murder. Of course, those grand juries always vote however the district attorney tells them. And our newly elected district attorney is quite eager to see Leo hanging from the courthouse yardarm. Probably a golfing or club buddy of Mackey's." Gray tossed his pencil on the desk with enough force that it rolled across his papers and off the side. His eyes followed the pencil's journey but he didn't pick it up. "So, what's your bad news, although I don't think it can top my bad news."

"It comes close," Sage said and related that a mysterious witness claimed he'd seen Leo toting a kerosene can in the vicinity about the time of the fire.

"That'll take some looking into. It's a bit peculiar—a stranger noticing and remembering something as common as a man toting kerosene. Let's hope someone's hired him to be helpful to the police and that we can figure out who that someone is. Was Johnston able to discover this fellow's name? We'll need to explore that angle further."

"Johnston told me his reporter is digging for the witness's name. So, how is Leo holding up?"

"He's looking mighty glum."

"Can you finagle me in to see him?"

Gray shrugged, stood up and pulled both hat and coat from the rack. "Can't hurt to give it a try. A friend's encouragement might be just what the poor fellow needs right about now."

The jail building stood taller than it was wide. Steep stairs ascended from the sidewalk to a small porch that seemed

overburdened by tall columns and an ornamental stone bal-
ustrade atop its roof. The ground floor of the building housed
police headquarters, the second floor the courtrooms for minor
infractions and, in the basement, was the jail. It wasn't Sage's first
visit to the building but as usual, he felt himself grow more tense
with each one of the steep steps he climbed. Gray, on the other
hand, strolled into the building like he owned the place.

"Good morning there, Finnegan, I'm here to visit with my
client if I may," Gray said to the sergeant who was manning the
front desk, his bony arms propped up on the counter with his
hands supporting his pointed chin and his bemused blue eyes
gazing upon the comings and goings of cop, citizen, counsel,
and criminal. Sage looked at him and wondered, as always when
looking at a cop, whether the jovial sergeant was on the take.

Finnegan stood upright and grinned. "Mister Philander
Gray, is it that I am dreaming here? I seem to recollect seeing
yourself here just yesterday. It's a wee bit surprising that this
Lockwood character can afford such special attention. Not only
that, you've even brought along a sidekick. And, just who might
he be?"

Gray chuckled like an indulgent uncle. "Well, Sergeant
Finnegan my boy, you insult me. My services are of the same
superior quality no matter what the pay. You just land yourself
in trouble and you shall find that out for yourself." The sergeant
smiled wide at this implicit promise. Gray elaborated no further
before returning to the goal at hand, "This gentleman is studying to be a lawyer. I thought I'd bring him along to observe how
a professional handles himself," Gray said, giving the policeman
a broad wink.

"Well, Mr. Gray, I'm supposing a wee visit from the two of
you carries no harm to speak of, especially seeings how the chief
constable's absent, you know. I doubt he'd be minding, anyway."
The man pulled a large key ring from beneath the counter, lifted
the gate and strode to a door across the lobby. Unlocking the
door, he led them down a narrow flight of wooden stairs. Ahead
stretched a long hallway, lit by bare bulbs and lined by barred
cells. The air was dank, chilled by seeping stone walls. A narrow

rivulet of water dribbled from the base of one wall to trickle down the hallway and disappear beneath a cell door.

"We're keeping him down here at the far end. His cell hasn't come on so wet as some others, I saw to that. I also fetched him extra blankets like you asked."

"Thank you, Finnegan," Gray said, as he slipped a few coins into the policeman's palm. "I appreciate you looking after him."

"It brought no trouble to me, Mr. Gray. Seems to be a nice enough fellow. Anyway, I can't help but like him, seeing as how he's a strong union man like my own self and all." He winked, picked up two straight-backed chairs and slung them into position before Leo's cell door. "Here's two chairs for you to sit yourselves on. I'm afraid you'll be talking to him through the bars being that we're a little short-handed and there be no one else to stand guard in our visiting room here."

"That's fine, Finnegan. Looks like he's all alone down here anyway."

"Nearly alone that be for sure, except for that cell two doors down. Ol' Rowdy Carter's in there sleeping off a drunk as usual. He won't be bothering you. And anyway, his mind is so gin-soaked he won't remember nothing even if you shouted into those cauliflower ears of his." With that, Finnegan departed, closing and locking the door behind him at the top of the stairs.

Sage turned to study a sleepy Leo who was slowly sitting up, taking a while to recognize Sage. Once he did, his brief smile was feeble.

"John, they are going to hang me," he said, his chin wobbling, as tears pooled in his eyes. "What on earth will become of my poor Betty and my little ones?"

SIXTEEN

As Sage laid cutlery in preparation for Mozart's dinner hour, his thoughts remained trapped in Leo's dank, gloomy jail cell. Mae Clemens was absent. He'd found a note propped up against his bureau mirror telling him that she'd taken a job in Bittler's household. Not exactly welcome news. Still, he might as well make the best of it since he knew from experience what he thought wouldn't change her mind. There was no stopping Mae from placing herself in danger short of locking her up.

A few feet away, Daniel stood atop a ladder, lightly sanding the foyer's pressed-tin plate ceiling, preparatory for painting. At Sage's query, the painter promised to tidy up the clutter before the doors opened for business. The man's curt response forestalled any further questions or social pleasantries.

Ida pushed open the dining room's swinging doors and called, "Mr. Adair, that rag man is at the kitchen door. He says he needs to see you right away."

"Be right there," Sage called, as he finished positioning a place setting atop its folded napkin.

Eich stood on the porch outside the kitchen door. Heavy rain streamed down from the porch roof, blurring the edges of Eich's tarpaulin-covered cart.

"Come in, come in," he said to Eich when the man hesitated.

The ragpicker stayed on the porch. "Maybe we'd better talk out here where we won't be overhead," he said softly.

Sage studied the rain-soaked man, who looked gray with cold standing in the wet, gusty wind. "No," he said, shaking his head. "It's too cold out here. The restaurant's not opening for business for a few minutes yet. We'll go on through to the dining room once I've poured you some hot coffee. It's not good for you to stand out in this."

Minutes later Sage and Eich sat at the small table beneath the musician's balcony. Sage saw that Daniel was true to his promise, there was no ladder in the foyer and no Daniel anywhere. Everything seemed cleaned up and put away.

Eich glanced around and shifted uncomfortably on his chair. "Mae's not here this morning?" he asked.

"No, she's away for few days visiting a friend. How about you talk to me instead?"

"Actually, you are the person I seek," Eich responded. "This morning I decided to conduct my rounds in that neighborhood directly south of the city—across the Marquam Ravine. It came to my attention that, with the bridge out, a number of the more prosperous householders in that area are changing abodes given the current difficulty they are having with ready access to downtown businesses. Others are moving because fire wagons can't reach their houses anymore. The terrible death of Daniel's wife and son . . . ." Eich paused, sighed heavily, and continued, "With so many people moving their households, it increases the likelihood of folks tossing useful objects into their refuse bins."

Eich smiled wryly before continuing, "So, there I am, examining the contents of a particularly bounteous barrel when two men lumber past engaged in heated conversation. One is castigating the other for letting 'Sam' escape and demanding to know when they are going to find someone named 'Chester.' Based on what has transpired in the past few days, I kept my head in the barrel, hoping they wouldn't recognize me by the attire adorning my nether region. After they traveled a sufficient distance, I took a look. From the back, I recognized one of them.

He helped carry you into the cooperage—I remembered his gait and torn yellow slicker."

"And the other man? Who was he? His accomplice?"

Eich shook his head emphatically. "No, not the accomplice, a different man. I only saw his backside too, but I am thinking that he might be that third man who visited later at the cooperage."

"That's right. You told me about the third man, someone you thought seemed familiar," Sage said.

"Unfortunately, my view of him this morning was of only his backside, which was no different than any other backside. So, I remain puzzled as to why he strikes me as someone familiar. One thing I know now, from listening to their exchange, is that the third man is definitely the other man's superior."

"Superior?"

"His boss in their endeavor. When he talked to the first man, it was with that degree of disdain common between hirelings and their bosses."

"Oh," Sage cast a glance around the dining room and saw the two waiters efficiently finishing the task of readying the remaining tables for business. Hopefully, their efficient diligence wasn't due to their desire to avoid his "degree of disdain."

When his gaze returned to Eich's face, he saw an amused glint in the man's deep-set brown eyes. Sage silently acknowledged Eich's perception with a quick smile before saying, "So, maybe this means the two of them might be staying somewhere south of the Marquam Ravine."

Eich laughed. "When you come to know me better, you will discover that curiosity is my greatest weakness," he said. For some reason, that implicit promise of a continuing relationship with this odd fellow gave Sage a buzz of pleasure. He found himself liking the idea that, someday, there would be an easy familiarity between the two of them. Making new friends was hard. His life was too complicated, with too many ways to slip up. Eich's stumble into the middle of Sage's adventures by-passed all the customary subterfuge. Sage studied the weathered face across from him and thought, "Maybe that is a damn good thing."

Eich continued talking, oblivious to the transformation taking place in Sage, "I followed them to a boarding house where

I suspect the two thugs are staying. Not the third man, though. I got the sense he stays somewhere separate from those two."

"What makes you think just the two of them are staying there and not all three?"

"The establishment is second rate and the third man remained inside only for a few minutes before he came out and headed back toward town. Gave me a bit of a startle. Caught me standing outside on the sidewalk looking up at the door when he opened it."

"Do you think he noticed you?"

Eich shrugged. "I turned away quick. Who notices a rag-picker, anyway? People tend to glance at me and quickly look somewhere else. They never allow themselves to really see my features nor meet my eye. After all, if they allowed themselves to see me, they might see someone like themselves and that might lead to self-questioning they don't wish to undertake."

Sage blinked. Eich's observation twanged home sure as an arrow hitting a bullseye. He quickly brushed that distracting thought aside until later. "That third man, were you able to get a good look at him?" he asked.

Eich shook his head. "Not really. I tried to catch a glimpse of his face by staying there and pretending to fuss with my cart. It was of no use. He ducked his head and looked away the minute he glimpsed me. Something about him rings a bell. I just cannot place that bell's location or its particular note."

"How was he dressed?"

"Like a typical working man. Soft, wide-brimmed hat, dirty brown canvas coat. Work gloves on his hands. Nothing about him really stood out. He looked like thousands of other itinerant working men in the city."

"What is the address of that boarding house where you saw them? Mr. Fong and his men are scouring the city for those two men. An address may help them."

Although Eich raised his eyebrows at this piece of information, he handed over the address, already written on a scrap of paper saying, "Thought you might be wanting it."

"Mr. Eich, please wait here. I need to get this address off to Mr. Fong and I want to talk to you a little more."

Eich assented and Sage started searching for Matthew and his bicycle before realizing that the boy might be in school where, according to the kitchen helpers, he in fact was. One of them, however, agreed to take Sage's note the few blocks to where the Fongs both lived and operated a small provision store. That task set in motion, Sage returned to the dining room where Mr. Eich waited.

"I am sure by now that you've figured out that I'm helping the strikers down at the Mackey Construction Company," Sage began. Eich smiled slightly, saying nothing.

That smile was disconcerting. Had Eich's curious nature already uncovered significantly more information? Sage decided to brazen it out. "Anyway, I'm working on the strike line to help a friend. For reasons that are not important, the men on strike line know me only as 'Sam Graham.' The thing is, the union president, Leo, is in jail. They've charged him with old man Mackey's murder. Leo did not murder that old man. I think those men you saw attack me are the ones who killed him."

Eich said nothing, merely waited, appearing totally receptive to whatever Sage said. Sage found this silent attentiveness unnerving but pushed on, saying, "Anyway, I mean, based on what I overheard them saying, I'm thinking that Abner Mackey knew nothing about his son's unethical bridge repair practices. So now, we're trying to find out whether only Earl Mackey was involved in bribing the city engineer, Horace Bittler. It was Bittler who approved Mackey's shoddy bridge repair jobs. Folks think maybe Earl Mackey charged the city full price for replacement lumber that he later sold to other people, making twice the profit. It's likely old man Mackey knew nothing about that swindle either. None of the bridge carpenters ever saw the city engineer meeting with the elder Mackey. He met only with the son. I'm also certain Earl deliberately kept Abner in the dark about the underhanded tactics Earl planned to use in handling the labor dispute. Those two at the cooperage made that clear. Apparently the older Mackey raised a fuss when those thugs on horseback rode down on the strikers. Maybe Mackey and his son had a falling out over Rufus's death. Maybe that's why they murdered him."

Skittering sounded overhead. Both men looked up and Sage felt his face burn hot, "Time for the rat man and his dog, I guess. Unfortunately, these buildings near the waterfront sometimes get infested when the rats start moving indoors for the winter."

Eich waved away Sage's discomfiture. "You are forgetting to whom you speak, Mr. Adair. I am quite familiar with, and not the least offended by, our smooth-tailed cohabitants. Generally, their behavior is eminently rational, and therefore less offensive, than that of our own species."

Sage laughed and stood to escort Eich to the kitchen's back door. Once there, he stepped out onto the back porch, watching as Eich hefted the shafts of his cart and slowly circled it around toward the street. "Watch out!" Sage called out after him, "Be careful."

Eich dipped his head in acknowledgment, reached the street and disappeared around the corner.

It was courtesy that inspired Sage's warning to the ragpicker rather than actual concern. After Eich disappeared from view, though, the thought flitted through Sage's mind that the ragpicker presented a markedly singular appearance to the world. He really looked like no one else on Portland's streets. A suspicious man, one engaged in nefarious activities, was likely to remember that tall, bearded figure with his knee-high leather boots and creaky wooden-wheeled cart. Sage shut the kitchen door thoughtfully.

Events, however, immediately pushed aside his half-formed worry over the ragpicker's safety. When he entered the dining room he found the gusting wind blowing through an open front door and rain soaking the foyer rug. He hurriedly mopped up the water and took away the rug, finishing up just as the day's first customers arrived at the door.

Hours later, Fong poked his head out the swinging kitchen door. It was the end of the supper sitting. Seeing him, Sage relinquished his hosting duties to one of the waiters. He headed toward the kitchen, pausing briefly here and there to shake a customer's hand and check on their satisfaction.

When he pushed through the doors, he found Fong at the kitchen table, his hands wrapped around a mug of hot tea. "We look everywhere for the two men and never found them," Fong reported. "So when your message come, we go to that address. We wait outside, watching boarding house for long time. They never come out. Younger cousin finally go to door and ask for the two men, saying he has message. Woman who answer door say that two men move away sudden in early afternoon. Landlady most angry. She say, just this morning, they promise to stay five more days so she turn away other boarders. She lose money."

Fong's information spurred an uneasiness in Sage. The sudden vacating by the kidnappers suggested something spooked them. Surely, moving wasn't part of their scheme to go after Chester. Sage thought it unlikely they knew where he had hidden Chester. Besides, an attack on Chester wouldn't require changing their residence. They weren't going to drag a captive back to the place where they slept. No, they'd use some isolated place to deal with their victim. Someplace like the cooperage.

As if slowly turning the pages of a picture book, scenes passed through Sage's mind—Eich looking up into the faces of Sage's captors just before they whisked Sage away. Eich looking up at the man coming out of the boarding house this morning. Eich seeing the same man somewhere before. Eich, a unique sight, trundling the streets between the shafts of his rattling cart. A most distinctive figure. In a flash of perfect clarity, Sage knew why the two men suddenly departed their boarding house. They had noticed and remembered Eich.

Sage looked into the dining room. Nearly empty. "Mr. Fong," he said, "I'm worried about Herman Eich. One of those men saw him today, right outside that boarding house. Maybe they recognized him from when they kidnapped me. We better go check on him."

Fong stood up, slapping his wet hat back onto his head. Sage slid his feet into a pair of rubber Wellingtons, stuffed his dress pants into the boot tops, grabbed a hat and jacket and they rushed out the back door. Striding down the alley they reached the street and turned southward toward the Marquam Ravine. Once there, they followed the ravine's edge westward, toward the hillside, until they came to the small house and Eich's shed. No light shone through the cracks in the shed's wall planks although Eich's cart stood with its tarpaulin thrown back, open to the rain, looking as if Eich had abandoned it while in the midst unloading.

Sage stepped cautiously toward the shed, taking care to skirt both puddles and sucking mud. Straining to hear, he heard only silence beneath the sound of the pelting rain and the ravine's rushing water. Fong waited in the darkness beneath a nearby low-hanging fir limb, monitoring Sage's advance. Reaching the shed's door, Sage knocked. When no one answered, he carefully edged the door open.

Inside, it was cave dark. Rain thrummed on the tin roof overhead, sounding like pebbles falling from on high. He heard nothing else. Stepping through the open doorway, he moved immediately to one side, since the outside gloom clearly outlined his form. Nothing happened. Sage took another cautious step and felt something hard give way beneath his feet. Another step yielded that same crunch underfoot. Pulling his match safe from a pocket, Sage struck a light, its yellow flare catching on porcelain slivers littering the floor. Pottery shards lay strewn everywhere, all of it smashed beyond repair. The glinting bits of a shattered oil lamp's chimney and base covered the middle of the room. Eich's cot sagged, one of its wooden legs snapped, his bedding spilling onto the floor in a twisted mound. The iron bake oven no longer sat atop the small, pot-bellied stove. Instead, its body rested on its side against a wall, while its lid lay upside down five feet away. A small wooden box sat safely against the wall, just inside the door. It was full of undisturbed teacups. The scene suggested that Eich had entered the shed, put the box down in order to light a lamp only to be ambushed by someone lurking inside.

Standing in the open door, Sage beckoned Fong forward. He lit a candle and held it aloft as both men grimly surveyed their surroundings.

"Someone waited for Mr. Herman to come back," Fong said, his voice quiet.

SEVENTEEN

SAGE GLANCED TOWARD HIS COMPANION. Fong looked strangely older, the lines bracketing his mouth deeper, his dark eyes dull and bleak.

"Shit," Sage said.

"Not good, I think." Fong nodded, his brow furrowed.

"We need to find them and quick. They're killers and Herman witnessed my kidnapping," Sage said.

"Hmm. They not want to take him far. Too many people live close around here. If they carry him far, everyone sees. Also, I think too many people know Mr. Eich and might step forward with questions."

"That means they hauled him off in a wagon or dragged him into the ravine."

"When I wait outside, I study ground. There are no wagon wheel marks other than his cart. That is certain. So I think they took him down into ravine.

"Jeez, how the hell can we find anyone down there in the dark? Every oil lamp in the place has been smashed and there's no moon," Sage said as panic surged through his body and seized his mind. He fought for control. This was the wrong time to lose his ability to reason.

Evidently Fong remained free of the same distraction because his tone was matter-of-fact as he said, "We need torches and many men. Maybe, I find torches and cousins while you locate helpful Sergeant Hanke and some of his men?" It was not surprising that Fong thought of Hanke. Although Fong might chide the big German policeman for being a noisy clod, Fong was also quick to seek him out whenever they found themselves in a pinch. Like now.

"Right. I'll go find Hanke and meet you back here in less than an hour. If I don't find him, I'll still be back here anyway."

They split up as each traveled north toward the city's center. Sage angled in the direction of the police station, hoping the big policeman was on duty. Fong headed northeast to secure the assistance of his "cousins." Not a hard task since, this time of night, they tended to stay within the confines of Chinatown's narrowly circumscribed locations.

Sage broke into a trot, spurred on by troubling thoughts. Was Eich being tortured or lying somewhere badly hurt? As he swiftly traveled the dark streets, Sage began muttering a prayer, over and over, in a chant that kept rhythm with his steps. "Please, don't let anything happen to that old man." At one point, a more detached part of Sage's mind wondered at his fervency given his short acquaintance with the ragpicker. The response sounded inside his head, speaking in his mother's voice, "Sometimes, a body can spot the gold glimmering in another person even when it's buried deep." In Eich case, that gold seemed to lie right atop the surface.

Sage was lucky. The big German sergeant was pushing out the police station door just as Sage reached the building. The man's pale eyebrows rose at the sight of Sage, who stood panting at the bottom of the stairs.

"Ahhhh," the Sergeant said, his hesitancy signaling his uncertainty as to how to address Sage in the midst of the passersby flowing in and out of the busy police station.

"Sergeant Hanke, might we confer briefly?" Sage asked, gesturing the man down the stairs and to one side.

When Hanke learned of the worrisome circumstances surrounding Eich's disappearance, he lumbered into immediate action. Although his pale blue eyes narrowed when he learned it was a ragpicker they were rescuing, he asked no questions. "Wait here," he commanded instead, before hustling back up the stairs and into the police station. Within minutes he returned with six other policemen, each one grasping the wire handle of an unlit tubular kerosene lantern favored for outside work because it resisted the extinguishing effects of rain and wind. Hanke handed Sage a spare lantern and the group headed south at a rapid pace.

They reached Eich's shed and found Fong and his cousins already there, sheltering beneath a fir tree's thick boughs. Surprise showed on every policeman's face except Hanke's. He grinned widely and his obvious pleasure at seeing Fong quickly communicated itself to his men, effectively unifying the group.

While they'd been waiting, Fong's men combed the ground for evidence of where Eich had gone. Boot tracks and two narrow, parallel gouges in the mud laid a clear trail to the ravine's precipice. Fong said a search at the base of the slope in that spot yielded nothing. They quickly split into two groups to search the ravine bank from top to bottom and along the streambed in both directions. They decided to search only the north bank since the raging stream guaranteed anyone crossing it a dunking or, at the very least, seriously soaked boots and trousers.

So the searchers fanned out along the bank, walking a horizontal track about ten paces apart. Each man crab-scrambled his way along the slope, keeping one boot on the uphill while his other sought purchase downhill. Their eyes strained to spot a human shape sprawled in the dark mud or rolled tight against the base of a leafless bush. Sage slid directly to the bottom and stumbled along the streambed, fearing that Eich's attackers had hit the ragpicker on the head and left him face down in the water. It seemed an ideal way to finish him off while suggesting an accidental death.

Two hours of slithering around on the steep hillside yielded nothing. No evidence of Eich or his fate. Sleet began riding the wind's edge and the searchers' teeth chattered. Finally, Sage halted the search until light. The cold men doused their lantern wicks and hurried off toward shelter and warmth. Fong and Sage stayed behind.

Inside Eich's shed, Sage started a fire in the potbellied stove and the two of them silently straightened the ragpicker's belongings. When the door swung inward, they both looked toward it with hope, only to see Daniel's suspicious face peering in at them from around its edge.

"What are you doing here? Where's Herman?" he demanded, stepping into the shed.

Sage explained and saw the news jolt Daniel out of his customary self-absorption. His face paled, he snatched up Sage's lantern and headed toward the door.

"Wait, Daniel!" Sage called. "We've searched every inch of the bank for at least half a mile on this side, up and down. Herman wasn't to be found,"

The young man paused, turning a bleak, desperate face in their direction. "We've gotta to find Herman," he said, his chest heaving, his eyes frantic. He yanked the door wide open.

"Wait. We're coming with you." Sage buttoned his coat and stepped toward the door. "Where are you going to look?" he asked.

"In those shacks, on the other side of the ravine. If they wanted to hurt Herman in private, out of the wet, that's where they'd take him."

Daniel led the two of them across the slick timbers of the collapsed bridge. In some ways, the dark made the bridge crossing easier because it prevented Sage from seeing the distance to the bottom. Reaching the other side, Daniel plunged over the edge, his lantern quickly disappearing behind the thick brush anchoring the slope.

Fong and Sage looked at one another, simultaneously shrugging their shoulders before they too plunged over the side to follow Daniel, their boots sliding uncontrollably down the muddy hillside. Seconds later, Sage glanced up just in time to see the lantern's light disappear behind a tumbled-down shack that Sage recognized. It was the same one he'd noticed the day he and Chester inspected the bridge. At the sight of it, a vague recollection tugged at his mind only to let go and slither away.

An agonized cry sounded and Sage's heart leapt. Either Daniel met with some misfortune or that cry signaled something else. It was difficult to hear over the splatting rain.

Sage and Fong plunged headlong down the hill, reckless in their effort to reach the structure. The inside was dense with the smell of damp earth. Daniel was kneeling on the dirt floor beside a still form. Lifting their lanterns, they saw it was Eich. He lay with his hands bound behind his back, his feet securely tied, a cloth gagging his mouth. He wore neither coat nor shoes. It looked like they'd hauled him through the creek to soak his clothes. The ragpicker's eyes remained closed despite their shouts in his ears.

Fong and Sage also dropped to their knees, assisting Daniel's frantic efforts to untie the knots. Sage rubbed Eich's unprotected hands, finding the ragpicker's bones hard and cold as icicles. His eyes still refused to open. Daniel whimpered like a terrified puppy even as he tried to rub warmth into the ragpicker's legs. Daniel's extreme distress made it easier for Sage to control his own fears.

"His blood still moves," said Fong from his place near Eich's head, his fingers tight against the side of the ragpicker's neck.

"He needs warmth, something hot in him," Sage replied, slipping an arm behind the ragpicker's back to raise him. When he did, the man's head lolled, and Sage saw a wet mass behind his ear. "Someone has conked him a good one. Treat him gentle. Let's carry him with his head up as best we can."

Daniel ran from the hut and returned immediately with an unpainted, planked door. They carefully laid Eich on the door, Daniel's coat pillowed under his head, Fong's and Sage's covering his body. Once set, the three of them stumbled up the muddy hillside for what seemed like an eternity. Uncontrolled backsliding canceled out nearly every other step. Their burden teetered precariously as they clung to the door edge with one hand and used their other hand to grab at bush branches and pull themselves upward. Once on top, they stood gasping until a wind gust slammed against them, spurring them into a jog toward the twisted wreckage of the bridge.

"Do you think that bridge is going to hold us if we cross it carrying him? That's a lot of weight all in one place," Sage said.

"No choice. We take him to one of these houses, it cause too many questions." Fong reasoned quickly.

Sage angled for a better grip on Eich's legs and gave the nod that sent them out onto the nearly collapsed bridge. Their feet shuffled across the slick boards like those of blind men feeling their way through untraveled terrain. Each froze mid-step whenever the bridge timbers dipped and swayed. Eventually they reached the other side and staggered the last three hundred or so feet to Eich's shed.

The fire was still burning so the shed was warm and became even warmer after Daniel frantically heaved more wood into the stove. Quickly they leveled the broken cot, using chunks of firewood. Fong gently removed Eich's wet clothes after which he and Daniel rubbed Eich's cold skin with a towel before wrapping him in blankets. Sage filled a pan with water and set it to heat upon the stove. Once it was hot, he cleaned the wound on Eich's head. The sight of color returning to the ragpicker's flesh rewarded their efforts. Still, despite his improved color and although his chest rose and fell rhythmically, Eich's eyes remained closed.

Daniel busied himself covering Eich with blankets and boiling water for coffee. That done, the three of them leaned against the drafty walls and watched the unconscious man until Sage's eyes blurred in sleep. Just as he started to contemplate sliding down the wall to sit on the floor, a groan sounded from the cot and all three watchers snapped wide awake.

Eich's eyes opened but remained unfocused. Daniel moved closer to him and at that movement the ragpicker's gaze landed on Daniel's face and seemed to sharpen.

"Daniel?" he asked, his voice thin and rising with the question.

Daniel grabbed the gnarled hand that lay upon the blanket and answered. "It's all right, Herman, you're safe now. We're here. Mr. Adair and Mr. Fong and me."

Eich smiled weakly and whispered, "Sorry that my humble abode is such a mess. My last visitors displayed considerable clumsiness in their effort to subdue me." He closed his eyes and lapsed into unconsciousness once again.

The three men conferred and eventually agreed that Eich wasn't safe remaining in the shed where he'd be vulnerable to a second attack, especially in his severely weakened state. He likely had a concussion. And, he was already sick from exposure which was exactly what they intended when they drug him through the creek to leave him wet and barely clothed in a place where no one would discover him until far too late.

"Let them think he is still in that shack for a few hours more," Sage said. "It's certain they won't check on him tonight and probably not first thing in the morning either. My guess is that they plan to untie him later, leaving the impression that he wandered out, fell down and the cold killed him. We've time to warm him up a bit before moving him to a safer place." Sage looked across the cot to where Fong leaned against the wall, his face shadowed.

Fong straightened and stepped forward. "He is safest if we hide him in Chinatown. No one look for him there," he said decisively. His lips stretched in that humorless expression that Sage thought of as Fong's "hatchet man" smile as he added, "They too afraid to look there, I think."

Sage gratefully agreed. He liked Fong's solution because he'd been unable to conceive of a way to slip an unconscious man into Mozart's this close to daylight.

"Best we unload Mr. Eich's cart, wrap him in blankets, cover him with tarpaulin and roll him to provision store," Fong suggested.

The decision made, the three quickly unloaded the cart and made a cushioned nest using Daniel's bedroll. Once they'd swaddled Eich in blankets and pillowed his bandaged head, they pulled the tarpaulin over him and tied it down. Daniel stepped between the shafts, angrily rebuffing Sage and Fong's offer of assistance.

"This is my job. I owe him," Daniel said, snatching up the shafts and charging forward, his body at a slant. The cart's wheels started creaking toward Chinatown just as dawn cracked over the mountains and the rain let up.

EIGHTEEN

SAGE STUMBLED UP THE TWO FLIGHTS of stairs to the top floor of Mozart's, his legs wobbly as a rubber stick from all those hours of sliding up and down muddy slopes. Sleep came instantly and so deeply that the sun was down to within a finger's width of the western ridge when he awoke.

Mae Clemens sat in the rocking chair beside his bed, mending in her lap, eyes closed, a gentle snore warbling in her throat. In repose, her strong profile always reminded him of a figurehead gracing a sailing ship prow. Her bones were hewn strong, not delicate, giving her face a powerful presence rarely displayed by other women. "Would she not have made an admirable queen?" he softly quoted Conan Doyle to himself.

Knowing she hated to wake and find him watching her, he reached out to jiggle her knee. She awoke instantly, grabbing her mending and feeling for her dropped needle even before her eyes opened completely.

"Keeping me company, Mother?" he asked.

She swiftly spooled her thread, tucking the needle into its wind. "Well, you seemed to be sleeping dead to this world and I wanted to talk to you as soon as possible," she said, her tone complacent, now that she had things under control. "I asked

Mrs. Bittler for time off to pick up my belongings. That nasty Mr. Bittler will complain if I take too long returning."

She moved her head and the white bandage plastered to the far side of her face so grabbed Sage's attention that he heard nothing more. He rolled out of bed and reached for the bandage.

Her hand flew up to knock his aside. "Don't be touching that bandage, it's not staying stuck on too good," she said.

Sage rocked back on his heels. "Well, tell me what happened," he demanded. "Why are you all plastered up? Take a tumble? Hit your own self out of pure contrariness?"

He was out of her reach and back sitting on the bed before her half-hearted swipe could connect with his ear.

"That's why I waited here for you to join the living," she said. "Someone took a shot at Horace Bittler yesterday evening— right through the dining room window. I was there, bringing dinner bowls to the table and a piece of flying glass hit me."

"Someone shot through the closed window? The bullet hit any piece of our Mr. Bittler?"

"Nope. The shot landed wide of its mark. Whoever that shooter was, he murdered a perfectly good French vase and drilled a big hole in the wall flocking. Bittler dove to the floor while his wife and daughters screamed and bolted out the room. Now, the entire household is acting crazy, just like bottled bees on a hot day. Forced me to think up an excuse so's I could clear out for a few minutes of peace and quiet."

"What kind of work are you doing for them?"

"I cook mostly and perform a little bit of hand holding. Bittler's wife is one of those nervy types trying to live above her background. Not a bad sort. She'd rather help me in the kitchen than sit in the parlor making polite conversation with gaggles of snooty callers."

Sage leaned back against the bed's headboard. "So, as I suspected, Bittler has reason to be worried that someone might try to kill him," he mused aloud.

"Well, Sage, if this nick on my face has any worth at all, it's to confirm that someone is inclined to shoot bullets in Bittler's direction."

"So what's he like?"

"It's no exaggeration to say that the man acts as though the sun comes up just to hear him crow. He's a darn bully too. You'd think there was strings fixed to his wife's and daughters' body parts the way they twitch whenever his royal highness is at home. I don't like being around the man, although he's not said more than a few words to me."

"He's not entirely stupid, then. Probably he daren't say 'boo' to you, for fear of how you'll react," Sage teased. "Sounds like a real likable fellow, though. I don't suppose you'd listen to reason and not return to his house?"

Mae gave an exaggerated smile and said with simpering ladylike sweetness, "Why, certainly I'll stay home. About the same time you start staying here at Mozart's to greet the customers instead of gallivanting around getting your head thumped and, I hear tell, stumbling around dark ravines."

"Mr. Eich's feelings are going to be hurt when he learns you think we should have left him to freeze in that shack—especially seeing as how he seems rather taken with you."

Color flooded her cheeks. "Hush. You won't tell Mr. Eich any such thing, if you know what's good for you. That's not what I meant and you know it!" She tossed her mending into a wicker basket, stood up quickly, heading for the door. "Oh, by-the-bye, Mr. Fong is out and, since I'll be returning to the Bittlers, you best plan to take yourself downstairs. You're in charge of the supper hour." The smile she tossed back at him was more in the nature of a smirk.

Sage groaned. Life would be so much easier if St. Alban didn't insist they operate an upper class restaurant as a way for him to insinuate himself into the ranks of the city's wealthy men. God knows, neither of them needed any more money. The interest alone on the investments of his Klondike gold strike yielded enough for them both to live most comfortably. Times like tonight, what he needed most was to talk to Fong but that was impossible if he was greeting patrons at the restaurant's front door. It was like being a juggler with one too many balls in the air. Leo was in jail for murdering Mackey. Three men were stalking Chester, Eich and himself—the very same men he believed killed old man Mackey. Bridge collapses were imminent. The strike was tottering on its last legs and new crises kept popping up like mushrooms in a Northwest rainforest.

Midway through the supper hour, Sage won partial deliverance from his frustration when Fred T. Merrill ambled through the door. The bicycle magnate paused in the archway between the foyer and the dining room, surveying the gas-lit elegance of Mozart's damask tablecloths, delicate glassware and gleaming silver. "Don't usually like to eat in places like this," he said to Sage by way of greeting. "My constituency is working class and they don't take kindly to the idea that I might be living high on the hog."

Sage laughed. "Well, if they are worried about you spending their tax dollars in Mozart's, I'd be delighted to provide you a meal on the house. I owe you that."

"Oh, Lord, no!" Merrill said, wagging an admonishing finger in the air. "That'd be even worse. As a matter of honor, I never take a cent from anyone. Take you for instance. You serve me a nice meal here in your fine restaurant free of charge, and I don't know but what next week, or next month, or next year, you'd be knocking at my door asking me to help with your business license or some such thing. Nope, Fred T. Merrill stands on his own two feet. He's beholden to no one. I intend to pay tonight." Here he leaned closer and lowered his voice, "But, really, I'm just here to talk to you, Adair. I've already eaten my supper, all I want is some coffee. Are you available to talk a bit?" he asked in a normal voice while straightening and raising an ironic eyebrow at the sight of the nearly empty dining room.

Sage laughed. "You're a perceptive man. It is a slow night. Let's find you a seat and I'll turn my greeting duties over to a waiter so we can sit and talk." He led Merrill toward the small table beneath the musician's balcony where the strains of a Mozart string piece would cover their conversation.

When Sage returned from appointing his replacement, he found Merrill sipping coffee from a china cup. "Fast service here, Adair. I hope you don't take offense at what I said. It's just that the people I represent suffer most from the lack of money. Truth be told, when I spend top dollar for a meal in a place like this, the darn stuff just sticks in my throat. Guess it's the sight of too many mothers touching opium-soaked rags to their babies' lips to stop hunger pangs. Can you imagine? That darn opium is cheaper than food!"

Sage merely nodded his understanding even though he wanted to confide that he'd seen more than one baby soothed with opium and more than his share of poverty's other equally appalling sights. He held his tongue because of Merrill's expansive personality. Merrill wasn't the kind of man able to hold onto a confidence. Not because Merrill was an idle or malicious gossip. It was more that Merrill's passionate pursuit of his own goals might render him careless with other people's secrets. He was a man who was likely to get so caught up in telling a story to make a point that he forgot he wasn't supposed to share certain aspects of that story.

Merrill didn't seem to sense Sage's reticence because he jumped quickly to the point of his visit. "After you and Johnston visited the other day, I started thinking about our city engineer. It occurred to me that this elevated road situation presents the opportune time to ask the council to reevaluate whether to continue Mr. Bittler's services.

"I thought you said that all of the council members supported his appointment?"

"Well, that's mostly true. You recall, I am sure, that Mayor Rowe lost his seat last July and so now there's a new mayor, George Williams. No question about it. Williams is a political machine man but, the important thing here is that the political machine Williams rides is a different one than Rowe's. And, none of my fellow commissioners will sacrifice himself for Bittler. 'Lily-livered' is too kind a description of their level of courage. We expose what Bittler's done to the public and I guarantee they'll keep their traps snapped shut."

"So how can a machine politician like Williams be of any help?"

"First, Williams is not beholden to the same group of thieves and grafters. Second, and more important, you recall that amendment to the Oregon Constitution that just passed? The one giving us the right to initiative and referendum? Well, it passed by 62,000 votes to less than 5,000 votes."

Sage nodded and Merrill continued, "The folks behind that little effort are the same ones who elected Williams, and those folks expect to see the City Hall swept clean. These falling bridges are a perfect opportunity for Williams to make them happy with a decisive hit 'hot from the bat.'"

"What is it that you want me to do?"

"Well, here's my thinking. You said that a bridge man inspected a few elevated roadways and compiled a list of those in bad repair. I'm thinking that if that same man inspects a good number of the city's bridge trestles, and if you give me a list of all the dangerous ones he finds, I'll make doubly darn sure Williams takes a gander at that list on the quiet."

"Just giving Williams the list is enough to spur him into acting against Bittler?"

"Naw, if he's going to step out and make a big fanfare of saving everybody's lives and rooting out the graft, he'll want some proof. My thinking is that we give him the list, we take him to one of the really bad bridges and show him the dry rot. He's older than Methuselah so we'll need to find a bridge that's easy to climb under. Anyway, if he's convinced there's a serious problem, he's in a position to make a big show of firing Bittler and hiring a new engineer who will confirm the rest of our findings."

"Sounds like a workable plan, provided Williams has the interest and guts to take on Mackey. Let me make arrangements with Chester, my bridge man. Can you get me a list of the recently repaired elevated trestles in the city? You do that and I'll see to it that they get inspected."

"I just happen to have a friend in the city contract office. So, I expect the list will be in your hand first thing tomorrow morning," Merrill promised.

"But who is going to pay for the repairs to the roadways?" Sage asked.

Merrill sighed. "That's a more ticklish problem. The city is in deep financial difficulty. Our budget's only $75,000 a year. That amounts to $23,000 less than it was eight years ago. Yet,

Portland's population has doubled in those same eight years. We're the third fastest growing city in the country. It's so bad that Williams is even talking about increasing the fines on the brothels and gaming houses, though why we just can't license them I don't know." Here Merrill's lips twisted ruefully. "Actually, I just told you a lie. We start licensing them and the whole bribery corruption schemes associated with those establishments will go away. Licenses or fines, though, we'll still be short. All thanks to the monied interests who don't want to see *their* taxes go up and to heck with the good of the city and everyone else. They want to reap the majority of benefits and none of the costs."

"I suppose, if Bittler admitted accepting bribes from building contractors, they'd be forced to pay a fine and fix the bridges or maybe even go to jail," Sage said.

"That outcome's as likely as a wax cat surviving hell. Even if the city fires Bittler, he'll be able to find a job pronto quick working for one of the companies that's been bribing him. That's the way the old boys work. Start out with one of the city bureaus, prove yourself helpful and you move up and out. Your next job, you're sitting pretty with one of the private firms, making more money, working a whole lot less and setting up city contracts for your new boss. Leaves you plenty of time for gentlemen's recreations, like golf or snooker at the Cabot Club. Anyway, there is no way that Bittler is going to turn on Earl Mackey, if that's what you're thinking." Merrill's mouth twisted as if the cream had soured in his coffee. "You ask me, the both of them are crooked as a barrel of fish hooks and twice as chummy," he said.

Sage persisted, the beginnings of an idea becoming a full-blown plan. "But, let's just say Bittler signed an affidavit admitting wrongdoing. Is that enough to force Mackey to fix the bridges?"

"An affidavit might be just the thing, depending on the judge and who he's beholden to. It's mighty hard to find justice in a town controlled by veteran hobnobbers." Merrill looked at Sage with narrowed eyes. "Adair, I see from the glint in your eyes that something's took hold of your mind. Don't think of using physical force to make Bittler confess to taking bribes. He'll just deny it once he's free of you."

"Physical force," Sage laughed, glee taking hold. "Nope, I hold no intention of using physical force. Quite the opposite in fact," he assured Merrill.

❀ ❀ ❀

Chester and Stuart greeted Sage with hearty backslaps when he appeared at their door. Obviously, their confinement was beginning to chafe. "Sam, I keep telling Stuart he needn't stay inside to keep me company," Chester said, "but the fool thinks I'm the type of guest he has to entertain. He won't even let me stay by myself."

"Aw, it's raining outside anyway. I don't need any more soaking, I had my share of that wet stuff when I was rowing the river," Stuart responded.

"Well, gentlemen, there may be a little chore for you to do, starting tomorrow afternoon, though I can't guarantee you, Stuart, that the rain won't soak you through and through," Sage said and saw their weathered faces brighten.

"Tomorrow, I'll send you a list of all of the recently repaired bridge trestles in the city, the ones over the ravines and marshes. Chester and I already inspected some of them. But the plan is to examine all of them.

Anticipation made their eyes dance. "By golly, it's about time we got a job to do!" Chester chortled with a gap-toothed grin that made a man grin right along with him.

"It's going to be a treat being outdoors and doing something worthwhile for a change. This sitting around heah in this small, stuffy box is getting mighty tiring," Stuart chimed in.

Sage fixed a stern eye on the semi-invalid. "Now, Stuart, you are not, under any circumstances, to climb down under those bridges because, if you re-injure yourself, your doctor will tar and feather me." Sage faced Chester, "You hear what I'm saying, Chester? You make sure that Stuart stays up top. His job is to write down everything you tell him about the bridge's problems."

Sage handed Stuart the umbrella he carried, saying, "Hold this over your head so you stay dry and the paper doesn't turn to mush while you're writing. Also, I'm arranging for a few men to guard the two of you. Don't take any mind of them and don't talk to them."

At their quizzical looks, he explained., "The men I'm having watch over you are Chinese. If other people realize you are out there with them, it will cause no end of speculation and we need to accomplish this job without attracting a lot of attention."

They eagerly agreed to his plan and conditions and he left the two of them in a jovial state of mind. He headed toward Mozart's, his own spirits rising even though the morning drizzle had become pelting rain. Still, he reminded himself, this path we follow is fainter than an old deer trail. No telling whether it's going to lead us to where we need to go.

NINETEEN

NEXT MORNING, DANIEL AGAIN STOOD atop a ladder in the foyer. this time loading up his brush with a light green paint and carefully spreading it across the bumpy swirls of the pressed-tin ceiling. Despite the difficulty of the angle, there was neither drop cloth nor paint drops on the floor below. "Mr. Eich says he needs to see you," he called down as Sage headed toward the kitchen for breakfast.

"How does Mother find the time to pick the paint colors?" Sage wondered as he pushed through into the kitchen where he found Ida vigorously flattening and rolling out pie dough, her pleasantly rounded face flushed from the exertion. "Have you seen Mrs. Clemens this morning?" he asked her, after they exchanged greetings.

Ida's response was mild, even though her answer meant she was coping with a lot more work. "Why, no, Mr. Adair. She stopped by our apartment yesterday afternoon for a short visit when she was here picking up her things. As far as I know, she's still taking care of her friend."

By consensus, they'd not burdened Ida with either the knowledge of Mae Clemens' relationship to Sage, or with the fact they worked for St. Alban. At times, this subterfuge seemed unnecessarily complicated since Ida, her husband Knute and her nephew, Matthew, all lived in the second floor apartment above Mozart's. Doubtless they knew of the strange goings-on taking place in the building. Despite this, they said nothing, keeping their inevitable speculations strictly to themselves.

"Tell me, how was it that Daniel gained entry to paint the foyer?"

"When I came down this morning, he was waiting on the back porch with his full paint bucket. I figured you'd want me to let him in to work. Was I wrong?" She paused in her rolling to look at him, using the back of her flour-dusted hand to brush a straying curl off her forehead. She looked tired. A feeling of guilt jabbed Sage. With neither himself nor Mae Clemens around, the burden of running Mozart's fell onto the shoulders of this already busy woman.

"No, that was the right thing to do, Ida. I'm just wondering who is giving Daniel his orders."

"Hmm, now there's a puzzle," she said, before resuming her baking. "All this time, I've thought that Daniel was painting under your orders, so I guess I don't know."

"It's probably Mrs. Clemens who is giving him instructions. In the meantime, I better shake a leg. I've got lots still to do." As an afterthought, he asked, "Everything going okay here?"

There was an ironic glint to the woman's bright blue eyes as she said, "Yes, the routine's the same. Long as I keep at it, we'll be all right" The loud thump of her rolling pin seeming to underscore both her resolve and, maybe, a touch of pique.

Sage was the only European-type walking Chinatown's crowded sidewalks. To his delight he saw that a sun break was pulling a few diminutive Chinese women from their cramped homes to step carefully about on wooden platform clogs. American immigration laws made sure their presence on the street remained a rare sight. Mostly it was Chinese men who filled these streets. Sage considered these industrious immigrants to be a cut above average. They'd braved a treacherous sea voyage to Mexico and a trek through the blazing desert into America, all the while knowing what lay ahead was the loneliness of many years' separation from their loved ones. Unlike European immigrants, the Chinese would always be a minority, each one an easy target for misplaced blame and violent race hatred. He sometimes wondered if immigrants, in general, weren't the best example of the country's founding spirit. Forever strangers in a strange land, they suffered, endured, adapted and succeeded.

Sage liked strolling through Portland's small Chinatown. These industrious foreigners had transformed the few buildings they were allowed to occupy. The elaborately carved entryways, wooden balconies and even round "moon windows," all lacquered red and added onto the otherwise staid brick fronts, made the street exciting and strange. The Asian culture's imprint was everywhere. Vibrant crimson signs sporting intricate gold characters swung outside cramped businesses. Summertime, woolen blankets flapped overhead and red paper globes jittered in the breeze, as if dancing to the eery wails of bamboo flutes that wafted out open windows. Today's rain guaranteed there were no flapping blankets or jittering paper globes. Instead, neighbors talking and laughing loudly crowded the streets, their slender hands gesturing excitedly as though they had not seen each other for a long while.

After the commotion outside, Fong's provision store was calm. Although, in here, it was the tumultuous combination of smells that demanded attention. Pungent ginger, garlic, incense and other indecipherable scents filled the air. Fong's wife, Kum Ho, came forward to smile at Sage and bow in greeting. Sage returned the courtesy before she led him to the back of the shop and into the couple's living quarters. The cloth slippers cladding her small feet let her move soundlessly across the room.

Herman Eich lay upon a cot that Fong likely set up in deference to the ragpicker's western bones. Sage took a seat in an ornately carved ebony chair next to the cot. Mrs. Fong silently retreated from the room, most certainly to brew the delicate tea she knew Sage liked.

A flush stained Eich's cheeks and his dark eyes glittered with fever. Still, he reached out a gnarled hand to touch Sage's.

"Thank you for mounting my rescue party. A few more hours and I would not be alive to receive the tender ministrations of the beautiful and gracious Mrs. Fong."

"Thank Daniel for that. Fong and I wanted to wait for daylight until Daniel insisted we search the other side of the ravine for you."

"I thanked Daniel for his persistence. He came by early this morning." Eich's broad forehead puckered and his lower lip jutted out. "That young man worries me."

"Well, rest easy on that account," Sage said, "Last I saw him, he was on top of a ladder painting the restaurant's ceiling. I expect he'll stay out of trouble there."

Eich's face didn't relax. "I remember myself when I was his age. I'm not sure whether I could have coped with a tragedy like his."

"Were you here in Portland, back then?" Sage asked. These last few days made him want to know more about this man who had somehow managed to captivate his pragmatic mother, Fong and even, he admitted ruefully, himself.

Eich's face relaxed as he lapsed into bemused recollection. "Such an idealist I was. I came to Oregon from New York in 1883 as part of a grand Jewish experiment. We trekked across the isthmus of Panama and caught a coastal steamer to Portland. We took the train south until its end. From there, we hiked many miles into a wooded valley. We called it New Odessa because many of my companions originated in Odessa in Russia. Not me though, I am a New York Jew, born and bred. Still, I reached these western shores all fired up with ideals, believing utopia possible provided we created an environment of intellectual stimulation and spiritual ecstacy." Eich paused, seemingly lost in his memories of twenty years ago.

"What happened to New Odessa? I don't remember hearing of an Oregon town with that name." Sage asked.

Eich's chuckle quickly became a deep cough that flamed his weathered face. Once he caught his breath he answered, "Oh, what usually happens over time whenever two or more human beings get together and attempt to manifest their dreams. Little disappointments, a few disasters, and finally the inevitable leave-takings as each made the decision to return to the wider world. For most, it became a journey back into practicality, their idealism tempered by their fear of the future—their own future—not humanity's." His smile was weary as he asked, "Have you ever noticed that it is usually our own aging that finally convinces us of our own mortality?"

"But not you. You didn't journey back into a traditional life," Sage said.

"No, I never did," Eich agreed, as he shook his head on the pillow. "For me, New Odessa was never a disappointment. For a few, brief, sunlit years, New Odessa was the dream made manifest, a sparkling gem of what is possible in the human heart."

"Yet, the experiment failed."

Eich's shoulders shrugged beneath his blanket. "What's failure? Sometimes I think that failure yields more authentic lessons than does success. If an experience leads to growth, is that more a failure than if you never sought the opportunity to change at all?" He smiled. "New Odessa is alive out there. In their hearts and in their stories and maybe living on in their children and their children's children."

Sage shifted uncomfortably. "Today you are a ragpicker. Why, Mr. Eich? You are an educated man, capable of becoming anything at all. Why a ragpicker?"

"Why not a ragpicker? Humanity engrosses me. There is much to learn from the detritus of other people's lives. Besides, the bits and pieces I restore allow me to lift the hearts of humble people. And, trundling from dustbin to dustbin, I enjoy the opportunity to gaze upon the verdant hills, the snow-topped mountains and to sometimes glimpse inexpressible beauty in the people I meet. Take you, Sage, for instance. And your lovely mother and," Eich's hand gestured at the room, "Mrs. Fong, who has graciously opened her home to a low-status, ragpicking Occidental."

"I notice you've called me 'Sage' twice now.'"

"Ah yes, a much more approachable name than John Sagacity Adair. No mystical powers required, though. In the excitement of your kidnapping, Mae and Mr. Fong let the name slip. I suspect that name is only one small secret among many bigger ones, is it not? Anyway, 'Sage' is a name that suits you, I think. Mae named you well at your birthing. A name to grow into one day, God willing."

Sage nodded saying nothing. Evidently Eich had figured out that Mae was his mother. Still, Sage remained uncertain what to tell this man and what not to reveal. Eich sensed his hesitation. "I know you are on the strike line. I know you are worried about the bridges. I know you want your friend, Leo Lockwood, to be freed from jail. Perhaps that is all I need to know because I am in sympathy with each of those concerns."

Sage sighed, "I appreciate your sympathy and your suggestions even more so."

Eich shifted on the cot and closed his eyes briefly, as if the movement exhausted him. Opening his eyes, he said, "It seems my fevered brain wants to mull over Mackey the elder's murder but, so far, an explanation eludes me.

"I actually received some information that might pertain to his death," Sage said and told Eich of the conversation he'd heard taking place on the other side of the cooperage wall.

Once again Eich's eyelids dropped briefly before he opened them to say, "Yes, that conversation is suggestive. Yet it fails, I think, to dispose of the question. I can't shake the feeling that how Mackey was murdered is as important as the fact he was murdered. Trussing him up like that tells us something about his killer's state of mind. Just what, I am not sure."

"What is it that you are thinking about the killer's state of mind?"

"Well, I subscribe to a theory about what motivates people. Some might automatically discount my theory as too simplistic. I keep testing it, though, and it's generally held true over the years."

"What's this theory?" Sage leaned closer, hoping to hear the words that would reveal the right path, steer him in the right direction.

Eich's voice diminished to a soft rumble. "Most animals make sounds that communicate their inner state of being. People sounds are more deceptive, more tricky, more complicated—so you need to listen carefully, beyond their words to hear their inner sound, the constant tone that runs beneath their life like an underground river."

The other man's face had turned scarlet, as if his fever was rising. Sage shifted uncomfortably in his chair. Eich was diving a little deep. Maybe his fever was affecting his thinking.

Despite his deteriorating condition, Eich's perceptions remained keen. "No, no. I see from your face you are thinking 'crazy old man,'" he said. "Let me give you an example. You understand and even accept, I am sure, that the sound of grief is a wail. Is that not true?"

Sage nodded cautiously. He wasn't sure whether he should stop the ill man from talking further. He didn't because some part of his mind was insisting that what Eich had to say might contain the answer to many nagging questions.

Eich didn't pause. "And, you know people whose grief consumes and directs their lives, is that not true? To the point where you might say their life is one long wail?"

Sage nodded again, thinking of a prostitute he'd once met in Seattle, the widow of a murdered union organizer. She'd abandoned all hope when her man died. A "continuous wail" would be a fair description of her alcohol-soaked life now.

Eich continued, "My opinion is that where the driving force of a life is hate, that life is experienced as a roar. Or how about a life of fear, can you see it as being a prolonged squeak? You'll agree, won't you, that those characterizations might sound a ring of truth?"

"Maybe. What about greed? What sound does a greedy man's life make?"

"I'd think you, in your authentic work whatever that work is, often hear the snarls of greedy men."

Sage laughed. "'Snarl' is the appropriate word all right, though I don't see how your analysis helps to identify Abner Mackey's killer."

"Yes, well, it is my thought that the man who killed Mackey, because of the method he chose, his sound was more like a roar, not the snarl you'd expect of a greedy man willing to kill his own father. A hate-filled man might tie someone up so he had to watch his death approach. A greedy man would simply knock him out because the victim's suffering was irrelevant to the killer's goals "

Sage shook his head even as he struggled to apply the theory. Eich's face was now deeply flushed. Sage knew the conversation had to end yet he didn't resist asking, "What sounds does my life or Mae's or Mr. Fong's make?"

Eich's eyes twinkled with a warmth that made Sage smile in response. The ragpicker said, "I am still trying to fit the three of you into my theory. At this point, if I might say, it is just possible that the three of you are a chorus heralding the possibility that 'joy cometh in the morning.' Am I right, Sage?"

Sage just stared as Eich continued, "Something like this," and recited:

> Healing is here! Oh Brother sing it!
> Laugh, oh heart that has grieved so long.
> Love will gather your woe and fling it,
> Over the world in waves of song.

Poem finished, the ragpicker leaned back against his pillows exhausted, the fevered brightness of his eyes now half-shuttered by drooping eyelids. Sage spoke into the silence, "I don't know, Mr. Eich. These days I think I'm more in the bellowing, roaring camp than in the singing one."

"If that is true, John Sagacity Adair, your decisions, your actions, are going to move you away from that which you seek," Eich replied.

"And, just what is it you think I seek?"

"Justice. The bright light of justice in the midst of a confused and confusing world," Herman Eich whispered and closed his eyes.

Later in the day, misgivings about the strike's outcome harried Sage's footsteps as he trudged toward the Mackey lumber mill. Maybe it was time to accept failure and move on. Maybe it was just stubborn bullheadedness and not common sense that kept him going. He wanted to give up, to slough off the uncertainty and likely failure. He also wanted to take some dramatic action, to push the whole mess to a final climax. Stuck, unable to decide what to do, he let the worry go. The only answer right now was to keep setting one foot in front of the other until time and events made the correct decision clear.

When he reached the top of the road leading down to the strike line, he saw invigorated strikers clustered together at the far end. Their inarticulate shouts vibrated in the cold, crystalline air as they responded to the man standing atop Leo's soapbox. Sage stepped up his pace. Once he strode closer, he realized the man on the soapbox wasn't a striker. Instead, that stranger, O'Reilly, was booming out his words and repeatedly punching the air with his fist. Snatches of his words drifted to Sage, ". . . how long is Mackey going to kick us in our rear slats before we take him on? Are we men . . . complacent sheep . . . the slaughter?"

Irritation flashed. Ever since he showed up, this O'Reilly character had worked continuously to snatch the leadership away from the genuine strikers. Sage searched the group, seeking Henry, the union's vice president, who was supposed to be in charge during Leo's absence. Henry looked glum, as did the handful of men who stood beside him.

Sage stepped to the vice president's side and asked softly, "What nonsense is that O'Reilly spouting now?"

"Same thing as always—action, action, action," Henry replied.

"What kind of action?"

"Well, he's a little vague on that point. He's got them agreeing to meet tomorrow night at the saloon down the road where he promises he'll be specific. I don't like it."

"Why? What's got you worried?"

"He keeps talking about the Frenchies and throwing wooden shoes into machinery. Leo's in jail for murder and this flimflammer is talking violence. Things are souring real quick."

Sage didn't like the picture either. Henry was right. This strike was lost if the men pursued violence, because that's where the newspaper reporters would focus their reporting instead of on the strikers' demand for an eight-hour day. Even *The Journal* couldn't avoid reporting strike violence. As a consequence, the strike would collapse, its demise goaded along by police clubs and the selective arrests of the strike s natural leaders—like Henry. Worse, violence would inflame opinions against Leo, leading the public to demand a death sentence.

Henry interrupted Sage's thoughts. "I'm standing here try-ing to think how to stop these men from doing something stupid and I can't think of anything. I've already spoke my piece. It was just like talking to that stump over yonder. They'd rather listen to that O'Reilly there." He spat a stream of tobacco juice into the mud. "Leo's going to be upset about this."

One of the men in Henry's group cleared his throat to say, "Those hotheads decide on taking some foolish action and I'm walking away from this strike. I won't go to jail for no job. Besides, we'll never win this strike by force. Mackey's got enough money to hire all the experienced hoodlums he needs and he already has the police force on his side.

Murmurs of agreement rose from the small group even as O'Reilly continued his oratory, eventually bringing the other men to cheers with his exhortations.

Sage momentarily envisioned the disappointment on St. Alban's craggy, careworn face. His boss and labor leader took ev-ery failure personally and credited every success to others. Sage spoke firmly to the small group of men, "I agree. We need to nip what this O'Reilly fellow is pushing in the bud, men, or this strike is lost. Promise me you'll attend O'Reilly's little meeting tomorrow night." The men all nodded without even showing a glimmer of enthusiasm.

"But talking ain't going to help. We've already talked until we're blue in the face," one of them grumbled.

"We'll see. In the meantime, don't lose hope just yet," Sage said. He patted Henry's shoulder before turning to walk back up the road. As he picked his way around the deepest potholes he muttered to himself, "I wonder how Herman would interpret Mister O'Reilly's sound in the world?"

TWENTY

BITTLER'S ITALIANATE MANSION WAS DARK except for a faint glimmer behind an upstairs window curtain. Bittler was hiding out in that room, Mae reported, because it was the only room that provided no sight line for any sharpshooter who might be stationed outside the house. As his mother promised, the unlocked front door swung open on well-oiled hinges so that Sage was able to make a silent entry into the house. He snapped the lock shut behind him and mounted the carpeted stairs.

When he pushed open the bedroom door, Sage saw the single bed that his mother said was the younger daughter's, a dresser and two chairs: a ladder back and a rocking chair. Bittler occupied the rocking chair, his teeth so busily worrying a fingernail that he was oblivious to Sage's entrance. A nickel-plated revolver lying on the table at Bittler's elbow glinted dully in the candlelight. It was the same gun that Sage had seen tucked into Bittler's waistband when the engineer hailed the cab. Sage snatched the gun and stepped away before Bittler's sleep-deprived brain fully grasped that his sanctuary was breached.

Bittler started to jump up only to collapse into the chair at the sight of the stranger blocking the door and holding Bittler's own gun. Gasping like a beached fish, Bittler's toes pressed him back into the chair so fast that Sage thought it might tip over backward. At the same time, Bittler's heavy brows flew upwards as his small eyes widened within black circles of fatigue and his mouth struggled to form words. "Whaa, whaaa, what do you want?" he finally sputtered, his voice a whimpering quaver that, for a brief instant, tugged at Sage's humane inclinations. That empathy vanished in an instant. How many lives was this man's greed jeopardizing? Besides, for Sage's plan to work, he needed Bittler to fully anticipate these terrible seconds before his death. Sage said nothing, merely watched as the man paled, the muscles in his neck swelling as they readied to cry out his fear.

Now was not the time for Bittler to rouse the household. "I am not here to hurt you," Sage said in a calm, low voice. "I don't work for Mackey."

These two sentences worked. Bittler shut his mouth, his Adam's apple jumping like a frog in a gunny sack, his rigid body relaxing slightly, though he still remained wary. "You! You're that union man who accosted me in the Trade Exchange Saloon," he said after licking his lips with a darting tongue.

"Yes, name's Sam Graham."

"You better scram out of here, Graham. Mackey's men find you here and you'll be sorry," he quavered before resuming his frantic gnawing.

Sage smiled widely, grabbed the other chair in the room, slung it around and straddled it, facing Bittler over its back. He carefully laid the gun down on the bed close to his hand and far from the cringing man's. Bittler eyed the gun, said nothing and made no move.

Sage kept his voice low and calming, "I know that Mackey's men watched me enter your front door. They're out there. My men saw them."

Bittler glanced toward the window and back at Sage. "Oh God," he breathed, "they'll think I invited you here. Oh God, oh God." His chair rocked frantically.

"Probably," Sage said. "But I don't think that makes much difference. That bullet hole in your downstairs window tells me Mackey has already decided how he intends to deal with you and the information you have against him."

"Information?" Bittler's eyes cut to one side.

"Don't play ignorant, Bittler. That dog won't hunt. Not when you've been hiding up here in your daughter's bedroom for—how many days has it been?"

Bittler shifted in the rocker, again gnawing on his cuticle, his fingernails already bitten to the quick.

"Look, Bittler, we know all about the bribes for the shoddy bridge inspections. That's why Mackey has to eliminate you. If you're dead," Sage paused and the intensity of Bittler's gnawing increased. "If you're dead," Sage repeated, "Mackey will tell the world that the workers are the ones to blame for the dry rot. That they conspired to steal the new timbers and let the rotted ones remain in place, all of it with your help."

Bittler started shaking his head from side to side. "He'd never kill me. I've been to dinner at his house . . . "

"Shh . . . ," Sage interrupted, hearing the sound of a hard object striking the window. In the ensuing silence, a faint noise came from the porch below the window. Sage snatched up the gun, stepped softly to the door and opened it halfway. The faint rattle of a distant door came up the stairwell.

A backward glance at Bittler showed that the man was again a cringing knot in his chair. He'd heard the noise too.

The sound of glass breaking and falling onto a wood floor below galvanized Sage into action. He leaned toward Bittler. "Crawl under the bed and stay there," he whispered. Bittler complied with an alacrity that set the empty chair rocking.

Sage stepped carefully down the stairs, his ears straining to identify the sounds he was hearing. Glass being ground underfoot, the rustle of moving fabric. Wheezy breathing, bumping noises and the shuffle of boots issued from the darkness. The sounds came from a room that opened off the left side of the downstairs hallway. As did the pungent smell of kerosene. Its stink hitting Sage's nostrils as he stepped to one side of the archway and peered around the casing.

The French doors to the outside stood open, the faint evening light outlining two dark shapes moving stealthily in the gloom. The same light caught on the side of a metal canister as one of the dark figures sloshed its liquid contents around the room.

"Hurry up," the second figure hissed.

Sage needed to act and quickly, before a match was struck. Not that he really cared whether Bittler lost his house. But the man's wife and daughters were huddled somewhere upstairs with someone Sage cared about—his own mother. As one man flung the kerosene around the other began fumbling in his clothes—likely looking for his match safe. Sage extended Bittler's revolver into the room and with deliberate care thumbed back the hammer so that it made an unmistakable metallic clicking sound.

Both intruders froze, seeming to hold their breath.

"Don't move, or I'll shoot you dead," Sage growled into the silence.

As expected, each man ignored the warning and, as one man, they bolted for the open door. Sage aimed carefully and deliberately shot out one of the door's glass panes. As much as Sage wanted retribution for his cooperage ordeal, he wasn't going to shoot a fleeing man in the back. Besides, shooting them would require too many explanations.

Faint cries sounded above. He ran to the French doors, slammed them shut, pulled the heavy drapes closed and pushed a heavy table against the door to prevent further entry. He raced back up the stairs to find his mother standing in the upstairs hallway, fully clothed, a raised fireplace poker in one hand. Wordlessly he raised a thumb to signal all was well and pointed toward the closed door from behind which fearful cries issued. She headed in that direction.

Charging into the daughter's bedroom, he reached beneath the bed, grabbed Bittler's arm and hauled the yipping man out.

"Hush up. It's me. They're gone." He gave Bittler's arm a shake. "You take ahold of yourself and go calm your family. Then you and I are going to reach an agreement or else I'll toss you off your front porch right into the arms of Mackey's men."

Sage tugged the man down the hallway to the other room. Inside, lamplight fell on a woman's terrified face. Her arms clutched two little girls to her side. He shoved the protesting man across the threshold. When she saw Bittler, his wife slowly straightened, relief replacing the terror in her face. To his credit, Bittler managed to start talking soothingly to his family. Mae Clemens slipped out and closed the door.

"What happened?" she whispered.

"Mackey's men broke in and started throwing kerosene around the parlor downstairs. I stopped them and fired a warning shot as they escaped."

"You sure they're gone?"

"Yup, they didn't expect discovery. Gave them a good scare. I'm hoping it gave Bittler a good scare too. How about keeping his wife and daughters upstairs while I talk to him?"

"Yes, I will, the poor dears will be shaking like aspen in a windstorm. You want me to send Bittler back out to you?

"That I surely do."

As soon as Bittler stepped out of the room, Sage clamped onto his arm and pulled him along the hallway and down the stairs with the man offering foot-dragging resistence the entire way. When they reached the parlor, Sage let go of Bittler's arm and twisted the electricity knob to light the room. Bittler gasped.

"They broke inside," he said. The dazed man shuffled over to where a large can lay on its side in the middle of his expensive Aubusson rug and picked it up. Cautiously, as if afraid the can might nip off the end of his nose, Bittler sniffed its opening. "Kerosene," he croaked.

Not likely to be anything else. The whole room reeks of it. Sage thought, though he kept that sharp retort to himself. No sense in distracting Bittler before the man fully comprehended what had almost happened. Sure enough, the city engineer stood rooted in the middle of the room, first as realization, then horror, raced across his face.

Bittler's stunned expression was Sage's cue. "Snap out of it, Bittler," he barked. "Mackey's men intended to set fire to your house and kill everyone in it, including your children. It's time you face the situation and realize that I am the only one who can save your miserable hide from this fix you've got yourself in."

TWENTY ONE

"How? How can you save me?" Anxiety contorted Bittler's face.

Sage's lips twisted. "Me?" Trust Bittler to care about no one's safety except his own. Again, Sage held his scornful words in check. He needed this man's cooperation.

"Bittler, this is what you are going to do," Sage said as he strode over to a lady's desk against the wall, fished paper and quill pen from its pigeonholes and slapped them down on its writing surface.

He slung a chair before the desk and pointed at it. "You sit here and write down every single bribe you took from Mackey and you list every single bridge that might contain dry rot as a result. Your fancy eastern engineering school taught you how to write, didn't it?"

Bittler began blustering, "I won't write that down! It . . . it will ruin me! I'll go to jail if I write that down!" he protested even as he promptly sat in the chair as directed.

"You'll write it down or else I am going to personally deliver you to Mackey's thugs tonight. On the other hand, if you cooperate, I will send you and your family to a place where Mackey can't find you. You'll be kept safe until Mackey is in jail or until it won't make any difference to him whether you're alive or dead.

Furthermore, I'm not promising, but there is the possibility that I might even be able to keep you out of jail."

For the first time that night, hope glimmered in the other man's eyes.

"Won't they follow us? Won't they figure out where we've gone?" The anxiety in Bittler's voice was sharp. He'd been having some bad days and nights waiting for the axe to fall.

"Nope. I've a plan about that. You best get busy writing. I'm not doing anything at all until you write down everything like I told you to."

Bittler's dark eyes stopped twitching. "Just who the hell are you anyway?" he asked with narrowed eyes. When Sage didn't answer, Bittler faced the desk and bent to writing, defeat evident in the limp curve of his backbone. Sage watched him a few minutes before silently leaving the room to ease open the front door. Stepping to one side of the porch, he gave a low whistle. Within seconds, Fong stood below him. Sage gave his friend whispered instructions. As Fong started to move away, Sage called out, "And thanks for that warning pebble against the window. If you hadn't thrown it, the situation might have turned downright scary."

When Sage returned to the parlor, Bittler's pen was still scratching across the paper. The city's chief engineer continued writing until dawn sent light squeezing around the edges of the closed drapes. He lay down the pen, pushed the papers to the corner of the writing table and rested his forehead on his folded arms. At that moment, Mae Clemens entered the room, carrying a sterling silver coffee pot and china cups on a tray. Sage looked at the four cups on the tray and raised an inquiring eyebrow.

"I received a message at the kitchen door that Police Sergeant Hanke and a Mr. Philander Gray are arriving shortly," she said.

Even as she spoke, a knock sounded on the front door. She deposited the tray on the table that now stood in its new location against the French doors. Returning to the hallway, the sound of her murmured greetings drifted back into the room. Seconds later, two men stood in the doorway, both tall, one hefty, one thin. Bittler raised his head to gaze blurrily in their direction.

"Come in, gentlemen," Sage said, although not offering them a seat on the kerosene-soaked furniture. He gestured at the mess. "As you see, Mr. Bittler experienced a bit of an upset in the middle of the night. Two intruders tried to burn down his house."

The two men wordlessly accepted the coffee Sage offered as Hanke surveyed the scene, his forehead puckering. "Why didn't he call the police right away? Given the chance, we might have caught them," he said.

"I am afraid, Sergeant, that the situation is much more complicated than simple arson. I promised Bittler safety and right now, that means keeping this quiet. I am confident, though, with your help, we are going to catch those two would-be fire-bugs in the near future. In the meantime," he said, gesturing to the city engineer, who shrank back in his chair, his eyes averted, "Mr. Bittler here is asking the two of you to sign as witnesses to an affidavit he has drafted. I believe, Mr. Gray, that you are a notary, are you not?"

Bittler jerked the papers back toward him on the desk and covered them with his arm. "I thought you said the police wouldn't be . . . ," he began.

Sage interrupted. "Sergeant Hanke is here merely to sign as a witness, without reading your affidavit, and to observe that a break-in has occurred. That's in case the validity of the affidavit ever becomes an issue. Mr. Gray is going to notarize the document without reading it, although he will take the affidavit away with him in a sealed envelope."

Bittler dithered a moment before reluctantly uncovering the papers and pushing them forward. Sage took them, read them quickly and handed them back to Bittler. Bittler signed each page before watching with dull eyes as the other two affixed their signatures. Sage folded the pages and sealed them in an envelope. He gestured for Bittler to sign across the sealed flap. That done, Gray accepted the envelope, stowing it in the inside breast pocket of his suit coat. The two men departed without another word.

Hanke and Gray sat at Mozart's kitchen table, shoveling in a hearty breakfast. They both looked up as Sage and Fong entered and demanded an immediate explanation for their crack-of-dawn summons to the Bittler house. They also wanted to know just what actually transpired that morning in Bittler's parlor. Sage told them.

The Bittler family, meanwhile, was gone. By now they were traveling down country roads, jouncing around inside an enclosed produce wagon. He doubted that the driver, one of Fong's tong members, was making much of an effort to avoid the potholes since Bittler regained his arrogance just in time to object to being driven to safety by a "Chink." Sage was certain the city engineer also wouldn't be pleased with his destination—a Mennonite farm south of the city.

To ensure the family's safety, Sage and Fong trailed the wagon through a fine mist until it rolled across the Willamette River and onto the Milwaukie farm road. Once there, the driver clicked up the horse's pace. It appeared the family's departure from their fancy mansion had been unobserved and nobody seemed to be trailing the fleeing family. Most likely, the kerosene-toting intruders had abandoned surveillance outside the house just in case Bittler called in the police.

So, for now, the Bittler's lives were safe. Sage knew from past experience that the Mennonite, Brother Jonas, would open his home to the refugees. Sage would settle up with him later. Mae's description of Mrs. Bittler as a "good woman trying, without success, to act above herself," made him think that rustic farm life might be the calm she needed after the stress of the past weeks. The unpretentious Mennonite farm house, with its scrubbed white oak floors, hand-turned chairs and domestic routine, should give her peace and something useful to do.

Bittler, now, he was another kettle of fish entirely. Sage wished he had a front row seat when it came to watching Mister City Engineer heft a pitchfork of cow manure. And heft he would. Brother Jonas believed every decent man had a duty to work hard every single day except Sunday. The Mennonite was fiercely unforgiving of sloth, even in privileged folk like the Bittlers.

Ida quickly slid heaping plates in front of Sage and Fong. The cook cheerfully filled a plate for Mae Clemens when she arrived minutes later. Mae thanked Ida and said, "I rolled up the rug, put it outside, closed up the house and headed back as soon as Mr. Fong's cousin arrived to watch over things. He'll go for help if anything untoward happens," she told them as she discarded her dripping cloak, hat and gloves. Evidently, the mist had turned into rain. She snugged a wool shawl around her shoulders before sitting down to eat.

Once everyone finished eating, Hanke cleared his throat to say, "One of you better give me a good explanation as to why I violated my duty to report crime in this city."

"Maybe we best continue our talk in the dining room," Mae Clemens said, standing abruptly. "Ida needs this table to roll out her dinner rolls. You know, the ones you like so much, Mr. Gray. Anyways, we've delayed her work long enough." She headed through the dining room doors without a backward glance.

Once settled in the privacy of the empty dining room, Sage related the entire story.

Hanke rolled his eyes heavenward before giving vent, "So, not only am I staying silent about the attempted arson but I also witnessed an affidavit that details a long-running bribery scheme. Are you sure you don't want me to ignore a murder or two while I'm at it? You need to tell me everything. Just so I have a complete list of reasons of why I am going to get fired or maybe jailed my own self."

"Sergeant Hanke, answer me this. If they convict Leo Lockwood of killing old man Mackey, what chance is there that they won't hang him by the neck in the courthouse yard until he's dead?" Gray asked, his question demonstrating that he, at least, grasped the situation.

"Well, I guess they will probably hang him if he's convicted," Hanke conceded.

Gray nodded at Sage, who took up the explanation, lowering his voice as he leaned closer. "I'm thinking that those two men who tried to set fire to Bittler's parlor know who killed old man Mackey." He held up his right hand, four fingers splayed, his thumb tucked against his palm. "Four things make me think this. First, after they trussed me up in the cooperage like a Christmas goose, I heard those two talking. They made it clear that old man Mackey and his son didn't see eye-to-eye on some important things—like the strike." Sage curled a finger. "Second, Bittler's affidavit establishes that son Mackey paid the bribes, not the old man—so the father and son maybe also fought over how to raise their profits." Another finger curled. "Third, those two are working for Mackey and they don't hesitate to kill—they seem to enjoy it. Fourth, they slung kerosene around Bittler's parlor just like it was slung around the Mackey construction office." His hand was now a fist.

"Oh, and," here Sage waggled his thumb, "fifth, someone is going to a lot of trouble to frame Leo Lockwood for old man Mackey's murder. If the frame works, it will kill the strike right along with Leo. Only son Mackey has the wherewithal, motive and vindictiveness to pull that little scheme together." Sage sat back in his chair.

Hanke shook his head, "All you did, Mr. Adair, was give me five good reasons why we ought to arrest those two ruffians and not leave them free to endanger other people, yourself included."

"But think, Sergeant Hanke. I didn't see them good enough to identify either one of them as being at either the cooperage or Bittler's house. Even if Eich can identify them as both my kidnappers, and his attackers, no one's going to believe a ragpicker. You know that, don't you?"

Mae Clemens jumped in. "You slap them in jail now, and I guarantee they'll both be free on bail before the sun sets. After that, faster than rats out a burning barn, those two will either high-tail it down the railroad tracks or someone will send them from this world of woe to make sure they can't spill the beans. Isn't that right, Philander?" she asked.

Gray nodded and she continued, "Mr. Adair, you took the right actions. We need a chance to question those two thugs before anyone else does."

"Problem is," Fong said, "we searched all over town and we never find them. We not know where they pillow their heads so we must wait until they appear again."

For a moment silence reigned. Fong and Sage exchanged calm, clear-eyed looks.

Mae Clemens caught the exchange. "Oh, no you don't. Mr. Adair has been varmint bait too often already. His luck won't last forever. We nearly lost him in the underground."

Silence ensued. Their shared recollection of Sage as a captive in Portland's underground, surrounded by shanghaiing killers, felt like a tangible something in the air. That had been a near disaster.

"It's the only way to draw them out, Mrs. Clemens," Sage said softly. "We know they want me and Chester dead. And, we know that if they want to get paid, they have to kill the two of us. Chester's hidden away. That leaves me to draw them out. We can't let Leo die for something he didn't do. You know we can't."

He looked at Fong, Hanke and finally Philander. "If Leo's going to make it through this, we need to find those two and squeeze the truth out of them."

Before anyone responded, a crash sounded from the kitchen. The swinging doors flew open and two men burst into the room, Ida huffing close behind, flour smeared across one of her rosy cheeks. When she saw all of them gathered there, she merely shook her head and returned to her baking.

Sage leaped to his feet. "Stuart! What's happened to you? Where's Chester?"

Stuart stood a moment, fist resting on the back of a chair, chest heaving, his face dirty and bruised, one coat sleeve hanging in its armhole by a few threads. "Jesus, Mr. Adair, I am so sorry," he said.

"What, Stuart? What's happened to Chester?"

"They burst in right after we walked through the door. First thing I know, these two men are shoving Chester around. One of them hit me. It happened so fast that the boy, there," Stuart gestured toward the young Chinese man standing a few steps behind him, "There wasn't enough time for him to dash up the stairs and tackle them. He sure the hell tried, I'll give him that."

Sage saw that the young man wasn't looking at Stuart, Sage or any of the other Occidentals in the room. Instead, he gazed only at Fong from beneath the eyebrows of his lowered face.

Fong spoke softly, his rapid Chinese words having the effect of relaxing the young man's stance. The young man answered in the same tongue, speaking for a time. When he finished, Fong smiled and said something that made the young man dip his head modestly.

Fong looked at the rest of them, explaining, "My young cousin thinks men hid on second floor until Mr. Stuart and Mr. Chester come back from surveying bridges. At the sound of cries, he run up stairs. He arrive too late. Mr. Chester was gone, taken by two men down back stairs.

"He," Fong nodded at the young man and smiled again, "trailed after them very quiet. They reached cellar and from there, hauled Mr. Chester into underground. He followed, until he has no more match sticks. He thinks, I send men right away, they see tracks in dust. It looks like Mr. Chester deliberately drag one foot. His dust marks helpful only if we hurry. This is busy part of underground. Other feet brush away marks if we don't hurry."

"Clever thinking," Sage said to the young man who smiled shyly. "It makes sense to follow those tracks. I'll happily pay every man who looks for them," Sage offered quickly.

After Fong said a few words to him, the young man nodded and disappeared back through the kitchen's swinging doors.

"He go to round up Chinese posse," Fong said. "I lead them." He clapped his damp hat back onto his head and exited through the kitchen.

Later that night, Sage made sure his boots thudded hollowly on the wooden sidewalks as he moved south along the dark street. From out of the small houses came the sounds of ordinary life—voices, laughter, the clatter of cookstove lids being settled back onto replenished fireboxes. Sage's human shadow moved along the opposite side of the street, with cat-like stealth. One of Fong's "cousins" was keeping watch.

He was on his way to attend O'Reilly's saloon meeting. Part of him hoped that he never made the meeting. He wanted those two thugs to grab him again giving Fong's men an opportunity to follow. Surely they'd take him to the same place they had Chester. He tried to think of where to find Chester, yet came up with nothing. The city was too big with so many empty buildings, as well as shady operations, in which to imprison a man with no one the wiser. Their greatest likelihood of success lay with Sage serving as bait. Meanwhile, the underground was Fong and his band's search area and above ground was where Hanke and his men were looking. It was a grim task. Both groups of searchers knew they might find a dead body rather than a live man. And Philander, well, Philander was thinking—always a good thing.

Sage's thoughts drifted to the meeting ahead. If he made the meeting without being kidnapped, the next best thing would be somehow diverting a disaster on the strike line. Tonight, what little flame remained of the strikers' spirits needed a good fanning. At the same time, O'Reilly's rabble-rousing needed kiboshing before that flame flared into an uncontrollable conflagration.

A broken board caught his boot and nearly sent him onto his face. Damn. As his mother would say, he was "dithery as a yellow jacket buzzing fried chicken." Where was Chester? Was he still alive? Had they trussed him up and left him lying somewhere that was exposed to the elements, just like they'd done with Herman? What if Mackey's thugs didn't try to snatch the "Sage" bait? He felt sick at the thought. Sage slowed his steps, turning his back on the street to stare into darkened shop windows—doing everything he could to make it easier for them.

TWENTY TWO

Entering the saloon, Sage waded into thick tobacco smoke, the pungent smell of workingmen's woolens and men's voices thundering bravado. Henry's little group of supporters stood glumly bunched in one corner while the Irishman O'Reilly, and the men he was goading into action, filled the room's center.

Sage and Henry exchanged looks as Sage took up a solitary position against the plank wall. A few of the men around O'Reilly cast curious looks or nodded toward Sage before their attention returned to the boisterous Irishman.

As if Sage's arrival was the signal, O'Reilly climbed atop a chair and spread his arms wide, patting the air with his palms to quiet the room. After a few fits and starts, the voices at last stilled and O'Reilly began speaking.

His voice was rich with the Emerald Isle's musical lilt. That alone drew you to him, Sage thought. There was, however, more to the package, like the mischievous dancing of his light blue eyes. Certain men possessed that characteristic others called a "magnetic personality." O'Reilly had it. Sage had seen that personality before and didn't trust it. It appeared to be a gift outside its possessor's control. Those who possessed it, when you came to know them, seemed to be uneasy in their skins. Maybe too many unearned successes left a fellow anxious waiting for that inevitable evening-up-the-score failure. Regardless, Sage's experience told him that these so-called "magnetic" people rarely measured up to the promise of their personality.

O'Reilly's voice had softened into a tone of cajoling sympathy, "Well, boyos, 'tis up against the wall we are. Your stomach's mighty tired of making acquaintance with your backbone, doncha' know? For sure now, we're nearly done in. What say we take a little bit of Mister Boss Man Mackey for ourselves before we go? Give him a wee lesson that he'll think on in the dark hours of his night."

The men cheered while Sage wondered exactly what "bit" of Earl Mackey's anatomy the cheering men thought appropriate to claim.

O'Reilly supplied the answer. "Your labor made the Mackeys rich even before you pulled your guts together and struck the bastards," he said. "Each one of you knows at least one comrade who came to harm because he fell from a bridge or maybe he just fell from a life too hard to endure." There was vigorous nodding all around. O'Reilly raised a fist to punch through the smoke that swirled above his head and thundered, "That yon lumber mill is yours by right. Its walls are soaked with your sweat, tears and yes, even your blood. That mill is not Mackey's birthright, it is his reward for squeezing the life out of men like you! It exists by the sweat of your body and your brow! It is yours by all that is right!" Hoarse cheers rang out and the men began murmuring excitedly to each other. Not all of them, though. Frowns creased the faces of Henry and his stalwarts.

The words are right enough, Sage mused, but the direction he's aiming the men is all wrong. Was O'Reilly hoping they'd storm the mill and take it over? Or, burn it down? Did St. Alban or some other labor leader send O'Reilly to the strike line? Nah, no way. St. Alban, and the other leaders he knew, would see right through to the danger posed by a man like O'Reilly—personal magnetism or no.

If the Irishman was not a labor movement man, it raised the question, "Just who the hell was he?" One of those fair-weather labor agitators who reveled in excitement only to vanish whenever things became tough or boring? Folks like that were just another form of dry rot. Fair weather supporters and glory hounds were no different from the rotted bridge timbers he and Chester discovered. Lean against them in a time of need and you'll find yourself falling. They would always save their own cowardly butts first.

Sage studied the man, his eyes squinting at a sudden thought. Of course, O'Reilly might be playing another, more dastardly, role. Figuring that out, however, would require more time and investigation. Sage stepped away from the wall and headed toward the center of the room. The men moved aside to let him pass.

O'Reilly, his eyes softening with sympathetic warmth, called, "Hey now, here comes a man who carries a heavy, heavy burden. It being his uncle, a fine man, indeed, who might swing from the courthouse gallows. One more victim of the Mackeys and their greed. Let Leo Lockwood be the last! Let us act for the future!" With that, O'Reilly stepped down off the chair and gestured for Sage to mount it.

The men clapped and cheered at O'Reilly's sentiment only to begin muttering once they saw Sage's grim expression.

Sage climbed onto the chair and took the time to briefly lock eyes with every man in turn. The room fell absolutely silent.

He began speaking in a low voice, one devoid of O'Reilly's oratory flourishes, "Men, you know me as Leo's nephew. I don't know most of you all that well. Like O'Reilly here, I've never had the pleasure of working beside you in the driving rain or blistering sun so I can't pretend to know your exact hardships. That said, for weeks now, I have stood beside you in this damnable wet muck. I've listened to you talk of your families and their hard times. Mostly, I have come to know each of you through my uncle's eyes and through the words that came from his heart. I know he's thinking of you now as he sits in that dark cell. I sent him word of this meeting."

Sage paused, letting silence underscore the importance of what was coming. "And I know, sure as I know that rain will fall tomorrow," Sage's next words rolled out slowly and distinctly, "that he does not want you acting like O'Reilly here is trying to convince you to act."

The men shifted uneasily on their feet while Sage let those words hang in the air for a beat. When he spoke again, his voice was even softer, "A humble man, a fine human being I've just met, told me something that I believe speaks to this situation tonight. That humble man told me that your yearning for justice is like a song in the world. You are good men. The song that you sing is not the roar of anger or the scream of hate. Your song soars, lifted up by what you know to be right, good and just."

As he continued, Sage felt the words flow upward from somewhere in his solar plexus, seemingly bypassing his brain so that his ears heard them as if they were being spoken by someone other than himself.

"Each of you began this strike with that song in your soul. You've lost that song. This man," Sage jabbed a thumb toward O'Reilly, "just who is he? We barely know him. What song is he singing? I know the answer to that. You know it too, if you stop to think about the feelings his words are stirring up in your heart. It's the screech of hate, anger and bloodlust. That's the song O'Reilly's singing tonight."

Sage glanced down at the Irishman. O'Reilly's face blazed red and his blue eyes glared up at Sage, chilly as a snowy arctic sky. Sage looked beyond him into the strikers' faces. "The last thing Uncle Leo wants to see through those iron bars is the sorry sight of you men being herded into the cells next to him. The last thing Leo wants is to know that your families are alone and fearing the future like his own wife and children are tonight. If that happens, he will believe that he failed, that his sacrifice and Rufus's sacrifice, yielded only failure, destitution, and despair."

Sage paused before adding one more thing, a fillip of an argument calculated to dissuade any of those still inclined to raise a ruckus, "And, don't kid yourselves. If you men turn violent like O'Reilly here wants, you might as well throw the noose around my uncle's neck yourselves. You take to violence and the public will buy the lie that the rich folk sell—that union men are ignorant, brutal and uncivilized. And they will conclude, therefore, that my uncle is an ignorant brutal, and uncivilized man. Is his death something you want to carry on your conscience for the rest of your life?"

He paused again to look into each man's eyes, gratified to see realization dawning and the fevered hatred dying down. He finally looked directly at O'Reilly. Without looking away from that man's glowering hostility, Sage said to the others with quiet firmness, "Go home, men. Go home to your families now."

He stepped off the chair but his eyes remained locked on O'Reilly's even as the men shuffled out, subdued as mourners leaving a funeral. Within minutes, only he and O'Reilly remained, their eyes still locked, the only sound a distant clink as the bartender quietly stacked glasses behind his counter.

O'Reilly's mouth compressed into a narrow, thin-lipped, gash. "You son-of-a-bitch," he spat out. Despite the venom in the other man's words, Sage also detected a hint of admiration in the curse. O'Reilly paused, as if speechless in his anger, before he slapped on his hat, jerked his coat off a chair back and strode from the saloon, letting the door slam shut behind him.

When Sage departed seconds later, a sharp, short whistle sounded from the darkness alongside the building. He moved tentatively in that direction. His Chinese protector stepped into sight and immediately back into the shadows. Sage moved to the building's corner and listened.

"Man staying at Mr. Fong's provision shop is asking for you," informed the soft, accented voice issuing from the darkness. "He say he remember something that might help."

Herman Eich lay propped up on large pillows atop his cot. Spots of red stained his cheekbones, beneath eyes aglitter with fever.

"You are not looking so good, Mr. Eich," Sage observed.

"It is comforting to know that what I feel happening internally is congruent with what is happening externally," Eich responded, his voice bemused and slightly dreamy. "But before the charming Mrs. Fong's medicine drops me back into that black nothingness, I need to tell you something."

Sage leaned forward, fearful that unconsciousness might claim Eich before he'd passed on his information.

"I remember," Eich said and closed his eyes.

"Remember?" Sage nudged when the silence continued.

Eich stirred, and his eyes opened. "Yes, I remember where I saw that other man, the leader at the cooperage. I first saw him the day after old man Mackey died. He looked like a man of means, not like a workingman. That is what fooled me—he was dressed different and in a totally different locale."

"Where? Where was it that you encountered him?"

"Outside Mackey's mansion. He stormed out the rear gate of Abner Mackey's mansion. Almost knocked me over."

"You're talking about that third man, the third one involved in kidnapping me?" Sage pushed.

Eich's eyes closed and he nodded tiredly. "Daniel, we need to . . . ," he started to say, only to have oblivion slacken his mouth before he finished speaking his thought.

Sage touched the rough hand of the sleeping man, "Don't worry, Herman, we'll look after Daniel," he murmured.

There was a rustle of silk and a whiff of jasmine at his side. "Please, Mr. Adair, Mr. Herman needs sleep now. He terrible sick. No getting better."

For the first time since arriving, Sage really looked at Fong's wife. Deep shadows lay beneath her eyes and her ivory skin was too pale.

"You are tired, Kum Ho. You need to rest."

She smiled, an ironic twist to her lips.

He interpreted the look. "My mother will come here to lend a hand as soon as possible," he said, patting the tiny woman's forearm.

TWENTY THREE

EICH'S INCOHERENT WORRY ABOUT Daniel still lingered in Sage's mind when he stepped into Mozart's foyer shortly after the restaurant's closure and just ahead of a heavy rainstorm. Overhead, a fresh coat of pale green paint gleamed atop the foyer's embossed tin ceiling.

"Wonder what he'll be painting next?" Sage muttered to himself.

He heard voices in the kitchen and moved toward them, hoping Fong was there with a rescued Chester in tow. No such luck.

Fong was there, noisily slurping up a bowl of soup. Mae Clemens sat across the table from him, her work-reddened hands cupping a mug of tea, her face weary.

"Didn't find Chester, I take it," Sage said as he took a chair at the table.

"My men followed dust trail through underground until the boots go above ground, close to Mackey lumber mill."

"You think they're holding him in the cooperage?"

"No, we broke cooperage window, crawled in and looked. He not there. We think maybe they are holding him somewhere in lumber mill. My men now watch from river. Cousins tie small boats to pilings under lumber mill dock. Hard to stay in one place because water travel high and fast. One cousin is good swimmer. They throw Chester in water, cousins will fish him out."

Sage pictured the poor "cousins" hunkered down in their small wooden row boats, bailing with numb fingers as rain streamed down between the wharf planks. Not the safest place from which to launch a rescue. "Those are good men you have helping us out, Mr. Fong," he said. "Please let them know of my gratitude." Fong uncharacteristically dipped his head and pride gleamed in his dark eyes.

Sage raked his fingers through his hair, "We better find Chester quick before those two kill him. How the heck are we going to search for him inside the lumber mill? It's been guarded 24 hours a day since the fire."

"How about we make distraction for guards? Give us time to sneak inside, look around?" Fong asked.

Before Sage could respond, the back door into the kitchen rattled beneath the pounding of a fist. Sage jumped up, pulled the door curtain aside and opened the door. "What's the matter?" he asked Leo's son who stood there, hatless and dripping wet, his dark hair plastered against his scalp.

Sage pulled the boy inside the kitchen, where his clothes dripped water onto the linoleum. Mae silently handed the boy a clean dish towel. He took it yet failed to use it. Instead, he held it in his chilled white hand, looking at it as if he had no idea how it got there. Mae took the towel back and gently dried the boy's face.

Sage cleared his throat and the boy's fearful eyes met his, "Has something happened to Leo, to your mother?" Sage asked.

The boy shook his head, his eyes wide and fearful, his chest heaving from exertion or fear. "Ma said to come tell you the police raided our house. They took away something from our back yard."

"What was it they took away? Did you see what it was?" Sage asked, feeling apprehension scrabble up his spine like a startled squirrel up a tree.

"I did. Some kind of can, a big one. Like a man carries kerosene in."

"Was it your family's kerosene can?" Sage asked.

"Nah. Ours is green and we keep it in the shed. This one was silver and I never seen it before."

"Where'd they find it in your backyard?"

"By our back gate. I think somebody dropped it there a few hours ago because it wasn't there when Ma sent me out to feed the chickens tonight."

Sage exchanged looks with Fong and Mae Clemens. Their faces showed that they also understood the implications of a strange kerosene can in Leo Lockwood's backyard.

"Did you hear or see anyone out back of your place tonight?" Sage asked as the shivering boy accepted a cup of hot sugared tea from Mae Clemens.

"No. None of us heard a thing," he said. Voice turning mournful, he asked, "This is bad for Pa, isn't it?"

Sage sighed. "Someone is surely doing their best to make it bad for him, Bobby. Tell you what, I may know the men who are making these bad things happen to your father." The boy's face brightened.

"Tell your mother to talk with all your neighbors first thing tomorrow. See if any of them noticed someone prowling around back of your house. If someone did, ask your mother to send word to me and to your father's lawyer, Mr. Gray. You promise me you'll do exactly that?"

"Maybe tomorrow, I'll stay home from school and help her," the boy said.

Sage shook his head. "No, you keep up with your schooling. That's what your father wants. Your mother is the one who needs to be asking around. She's more likely to get people to cooperate."

Minutes later, the boy headed back out into the weather, a large paper-wrapped ham tucked underneath his arm.

"Looks like Mozart's menu'll be a little short on ham tomorrow," Sage teased his mother.

She shrugged. "Let 'em eat bacon," she said, twisting the knob on the only electric light fixture, plunging the room into darkness and forcing Fong and Sage to vacate the kitchen.

❈ ❈ ❈

Sleep's oblivion spanned only a few hours before Sage was up and dressing hurriedly. The plan was to arrive at the lumber mill just before daybreak. Sage and Fong headed for the stairs intending to slip out the restaurant's front door until Mae stopped them. "No, you can't go out that way. Daniel's already down there painting and he's going to wonder why the two of you are creeping around wearing matching black getups."

"Good god, Mother! Why are you telling him to start work so early?"

"I didn't tell him anything. He just appeared at the kitchen door. Ida was rolling out her pies and let him in."

"Ordinarily, charity is admirable, Mother" Sage said, "but having a stranger hanging about all the time is beginning to irritate. I wish you hadn't given him so many paint jobs just now. It's turning out to be more than a little inconvenient."

"Me?" Her voice rose with incredulity. "I'm not the one giving him the jobs. I thought you were."

"No, I've not spoken to Daniel except in greeting," Sage said and both looked at Fong, who raised his hands and shook his head in the universal gesture of denial.

"Not me tell him," he said.

For a moment, they just stared at each other until Sage shook his head wearily. "There isn't time to discuss it now. It's only a little while before daybreak. Let's be on our way, we'll figure Daniel out later."

He and Fong slipped down the hidden staircase to the cellar and through the tunnel into the alley. Once out and trotting down the street, Sage asked Fong, "Also, whose paying for all that paint?"

"Maybe Mister Herman," Fong responded.

That makes no sense, Sage thought to himself. Anyway, inexplicable as Daniel's presence was, now was not the time to ponder it. He snugged his collar tight against the drizzle and followed Fong's dark, swiftly moving figure. Black clouds roiled overhead in a silvering sky. Rain began to crash down, fat cold drops rebounding upward to soak their trouser legs.

They slipped into the lumber mill yard by climbing up from the gully. The smell of fir pitch was pungent even in the cold, damp air. Bark bits abounded, firming up the mud. Ahead, about twenty feet toward the middle of the yard, debarked logs filled the countless cradles that loomed on either side of the narrow, chip-covered pathways. The rain began to let up, the fat drops falling more and more infrequently.

Sage jumped when Fong called out the soft "shaak, shaak" of the stellar jay. An answering jay call responded from beyond the log cradles. A rhythmic clank of metal on metal sounded at the far north end of the yard. A low guttural oath came from Sage's right and a man stepped out of the shadows between two log cradles. Raising a whistle to his lips, he let loose a shrill blast. Two men hurried out the mill door. The three met, talked and quickly moved together toward the far end of the yard, heading away from the gully edge where Sage and Fong crouched.

As soon as the three guards disappeared into the gloomy canyons between the log cradles, Sage and Fong hastened to the mill door. They slipped into a huge room lit by brightening skylights high above.

The space was large and wide open. High stacks of cut lumber ranged in rows across its expanse. Apart from the splat of indifferent raindrops on the tin roof, the only other sound was a mechanized whine in the distance. It reminded Sage of a mass of buzzing insects. They stepped cautiously in that direction, each pausing only long enough to snatch up a short length of two-by-four. They moved silently across the plank floor toward a large doorway opening and into an adjoining room.

About thirty feet away, half-hidden behind a stack of lumber, a steam-driven band saw thrummed at the far end of a moving metal conveyor belt. No log lay upon the belt as it rattled toward the band saw's teeth. A man's angry voice sounded over the rattle and huff of the machinery. As Sage and Fong edged closer, Sage discerned words and recognized Chester's voice. He was cussing someone out with all the vigor of a teamster driving a balky mule.

"You good for nothing lazy scallywags, you lily-livered spawns of Lucifer . . . ," A flesh-smacking punch cut off Chester's shouting.

Using the stack of lumber as cover, Sage and Fong inched their way forward, one on either side of it. When Sage reached the stacks corner he peered around it, ready to duck out of sight if anyone faced his direction.

Chester sat on a log round that was likely the band saw operator's daytime perch while he waited for the next log to arrive. They'd cinched Chester's arms behind his back and tied his ankles together. Blood trickled from the corner of his tight-lipped mouth.

As Sage watched, one of the two men standing in front of Chester gave him a clout on the ear, shouting, "You shut your damn mouth, or I'll feed you to that saw so slow you'll be able to watch yourself cut in two an inch at a time." Sage recognized the voice. It was Wheezy, from the cooperage.

Chester remained defiant. "Don't matter to me none, I'll be dead sooner or later whether you kill me fast or slow."

At that moment, over the gnashing of machinery, a scream sounded that was neither human nor cat, instead falling somewhere in between. It was wild enough to lift a brave man's hair. Fong, creating a distraction.

Sage didn't hesitate. As the two men whirled toward the sound of the unearthly screech, Sage glided forward, swinging his two-by-four, giving each captor a whack on the back of his head. They fell, unconscious, their only sound soft "umphs." Turning, Sage saw that Chester was wide-eyed, his mouth agape in surprise. Seconds later he grinned and joy lit his eyes. "By golly, my eyes are telling me lies 'cause I can't believe what I'm seeing. Boy, am I glad . . ."

"Shhh, no time. We're breaking you out of here," Sage said, moving toward him. Fong clambered atop the pile of lumber, turning to watch the outside door in the neighboring room. Sage hurriedly cut the ropes binding Chester's feet and hands.

"Oh, oh, my feet are yipping 'pins and needles, pins and needles!'" Chester gasped as he stood upright and tottered.

Sage grabbed the man's arm and steered him around the unconscious men and toward the side door opening onto the wharf. "Believe me, I know exactly what you're feeling. Was there myself, not long ago. There's no time, we're leaving here now. Their reinforcements are on the way!"

"Hurry!" Fong hissed from atop the lumber pile, even as he started slithering down to the floor, "guards coming."

The three of them slipped through the door opening onto the wharf and Fong closed it quietly behind them. Outside, the gray waters of the river swept past in silence. There was not a single lumber pile in sight to provide them cover. Fong gestured for them to move further down the wharf, in the same direction as the river flowed. They'd covered no more than seventy-five feet before the mill door slammed open, banging against the building. A shout sounded. Sage glanced back to see the three guards spilling out the door, their leader fumbling in his heavy coat, probably for a gun.

Fong raced ahead, veering to the right, away from the mill wall and toward the river. He reached the edge of the wharf, grabbed onto two short, upright, posts and swung himself over the edge, dropping out of sight.

Sage tugged harder on Chester's elbow, finding he no longer needed to hurry the man along. Chester was hobbling at a fast rate. Bullets kicked splinters from the planks beneath their feet, giving both men more encouragement than needed to further speed their flight. They reached the posts and Chester slung himself over the side and down the wooden ladder with Sage so close behind him that he stepped on Chester's fingers. The zing of a bullet passing overhead made both men slide the rest of the way to the ladder's bottom rung. There, two small boats jerked against the ropes holding them to the ladder. Fong guided Chester's feet into his boat and cast off before the rescued man got fully seated. Rushing water immediately pushed the boat further under the dock. All three men reached and grabbed, using their fingers to steer the boat away downstream among a forest of the creosoted pilings. Sage dropped into the remaining boat, barely managing to grab a cross brace before the boatman released the rope, and he too started pulling the boat along among the pilings, his eyes snicking upward at the thick planks overhead.

As the two boats bumped their way among the pilings, the thud of running feet sounded overhead like a giant's thundering steps. Looking back toward the ladder, Sage saw two boots descend. The sight of those boots galvanized him into action and he too started grabbing, pushing and pulling, desperate to increase the number of pilings between their boat and the gun-toting man on the ladder.

Seconds later, the swift current shot them out from beneath the wharf's far end to float away fast and free. Sage clutched at the gunwale as the boat began rocking in the roiling water, its thin sides at the mercy of tree limbs and other debris riding the river's mad dash to the sea.

He took a deep breath, trying not to think of the boat capsizing, of his winter clothes and heavy boots pulling him down to the bottom. He raised his eyes from that watery threat. To the east, the clouds lifted and a golden dawn limned black mountain edges. Like a hot air balloon, Sage's spirits lifted at the sight of those distant peaks and of a grinning Chester in the nearby boat. It's a brighter dawn today than yesterday, Sage crowed to himself before immediately sobering. Recovering Chester was just one problem solved. There was still Leo, the strike and all those rotten bridges.

TWENTY FOUR

"I'D SURE THE HECK LIKE TO KNOW why we didn't haul those two scallywags away with us," Chester grumbled. "We shoulda took 'em straight to the police. Once I told them how those two kidnapped me and was going to kill me, and Stuart here backed me up, those two'd be locked up in the hoosegow right next to Leo!"

The three of them sat in Stuart's new hotel room close by the railroad yards. Stuart had insisted on also moving so he could keep his new friend company. Now Sage was on the receiving end of both checker players' scowls.

Sage felt their frustration. He didn't like seeing those two killers get away with their shenanigans either. Still, it was the best move. "Look, fellas, if they're arrested right now it does us no good at all," he told them. "First thing we know, they'd make bail and be out of town so fast all we'd see is their backsides disappearing down the railroad tracks. Besides, they're just taking orders. We need to identify the man giving those orders. Mr. Fong and Mr. Eich both say there's a third man. He's the one we have to find and catch. Otherwise, this isn't going to stop."

"Well, since we up and skedaddled, I'd sure the heck like to know how we're going to find this mystery man of yours."

Chester crossed his arms over his chest, not ready to let go his peevish outrage.

"Ah, that is where our Mr. Fong and his cousins always prove themselves invaluable. It wasn't until this morning that we knew exactly where to find those two. So, while we floated away down river, more of Fong's men stayed in hiding around the lumber mill, waiting for them to come out. Don't worry, we'll soon know everywhere those two go and everyone they speak to."

Fong was waiting when Sage returned. "Time we exercise now. Keep thoughts focused on movement from core of body and thoughts will become still," he said. Sage obediently changed his clothes and climbed the stairs to the attic. Fong worked Sage hard at the snake and crane, repeating the long version of the fighting exercise two times and engaging Sage in the two person drills Fong called "pushing hands," until Sage reached the point of no thought, his body moving between action and reaction, his mind freed of the strike, murder, and all of the missing puzzle pieces.

Nearly two hours later, Sage was wiping the sweat from his brow and slowing his breathing. Fong, however, continued to perform the slow movements, his face as cool and serene as when they had first started. He began speaking, his voice rock steady. "When young boy, I travel with my family to Poyang Lakes, beside palace of Lao Tzu. It was early winter. Great white cranes flew from the north ahead of snows. In early morning, when mist thick on ground," Fong's hands paused to sketch a thigh high wave of fog, "my father and I crept through the grasses toward lake. Because cranes' beaks down among grasses, searching for insects, we able to creep close. Something disturb them, maybe hiss of our breath, maybe snap of grass stalk. Their heads lift up and, from each bird, one black eye stared at us. As one they stretch wings wide, rise into sky, leaving only call floating on wind and bird shadow across the sun. We carried no net. Otherwise, one of them stay behind."

Sage waited for more, but Fong remained silent, moving at the same excruciatingly slow pace through the various positions. Sage cleared his throat. His friend stopped moving and met Sage's gaze.

"I am thinking," Fong said, "that sometimes a man searches so hard for one obvious thing, he fails to notice what is close to hand."

Sage nodded. This was a message he understood. "You are wondering whether we are so busy finding Chester and chasing after these two men that maybe we are missing something?"

Fong nodded. "It is just feeling," he said. "Nothing more."

Fong's description of those great white cranes stepping through the morning mist teased at Sage's thoughts until he entered Mozart's dining room and spotted Philander Gray. The lawyer sat at his favorite table underneath the musician's balcony. Behind Gray, at least one plaster wall above the mahogany wainscoting shone with a fresh coat of cream-colored enamel paint. So, Daniel's paint brush was now laying siege to the dining room proper itself. Sage looked around for the sorrowful painter. Only a faint fresh paint smell remained—Daniel, his ladders, brushes and buckets were nowhere in sight.

One look at the lawyer told Sage that Leo's situation had worsened. For once, Gray was not shoveling in his food. Instead, he was morosely herding a single pea back and forth across his half-full plate.

"Lockwood's wife failed to find any neighbor who'd seen someone nosing around Leo's house while carrying a kerosene can," Gray said as soon as Sage sat down.

"What proof is that empty can, anyway?" Sage asked.

"Pretty damn good proof when the lettering on the bottom identifies it as coming from the Mackey lumber mill."

"That doesn't make sense. Leo's not going to toss evidence like that into his backyard where it's visible to any passerby. Nobody's that stupid."

"The prosecutor says Leo dumped the can there after the fire, planning to hide it somewhere else but got arrested before he could."

"Why take it back to his house at all? That makes no sense."

Gray shook his head. "One thing I've learned, and what every police officer knows, is that most criminals don't exactly plan out the details like you and I might when we imagine doing a particular criminal act. The difficulty is, I'm not finding a scintilla of evidence that's in Leo's favor. Not a whit sufficient to cast reasonable doubt. This case is beginning to concern me and, I tell you, that's a feeling I don't experience often."

An energetic swoosh of the kitchen's swinging doors drew Sage's attention. Mae Clemens was heading toward them at a brisk pace. Her hair straggled loose from its coil and her face was pinched with worry. She gave a perfunctory nod in response to the various patrons' greetings but kept her eyes fixed on Sage.

"Mr. Adair, Mr. Gray," she said when she arrived at the table.

Sage stood up. "What's the matter?" he asked, dread a stone in his chest.

"It's Herman, he's fevered and won't settle down. He says he has to talk to you."

Sage nodded at Gray, who waved him on his way, and immediately headed toward the stairs to talk to Fong who was meditating in the attic. When Sage entered, Fong unfolded his legs and stood with a fluid grace that belied his middle age.

"I must go see Herman, Ma says he's taken a turn for the worse and needs to see me. I planned to take this around to Merrill, at his bicycle shop," Sage said, as he pulled from his pocket, Stuart's list of those trestles Chester found in need of prompt repair. "Will you see that he receives this list of dangerous bridges?"

Fong took the paper. "I take it myself to Mr. Merrill at bicycle shop."

"Thanks," Sage said and turned toward the stairs.

"Take Herman strength!" Fong called after him.

Mae Clemens was waiting impatiently at the kitchen door, already cloaked and hatted. "We need to hurry. Sage, I'm afraid he's not going to make it," she threw back over her shoulder as she hurried down the stairs and rapidly strode down the alley.

Minutes later the provision shop's entry bell tinkled softly, summoning Mrs. Fong from the inner room. Lines of worry creased her forehead. "I ask for needle man to help us, because Mr. Eich is so sick," she told them, in an almost apologetic tone, as she stepped aside to allow their entry.

Once inside, they froze in the sickroom doorway, both taken aback by the sight before them. Eich lay motionless on the cot. Bending over him was an elderly Chinese man. He wore a long black silk robe and a round silk hat. The tightly braided silver queue trailing down his back jumped a little as he rapidly rolled a long, extremely thin needle back and forth between his palms. Even as they watched, he plunged the warmed needle into the unconscious man's head.

Sage started forward, only to have his mother's fingers grip his forearm. Mrs. Fong saw the movement and stepped toward them, her eyes beseeching as she struggled to explain.

"We try many herbs. Nothing break fever. Sometimes in China, needle doctor break fever. Ask cousin go for needle doctor. He fix many people very good," she explained, gesturing at the old man, who was briskly rolling another needle between his palms. This one, he plunged into the back of Eich's hand.

Sage hesitated, transfixed by the sight of the Chinese man efficiently inserting one thin needle after another into the ragpicker's body. Either the needle insertion was painless or Eich was too far gone to feel anything because his body never flinched. Only the sound of his labored breathing, now a gasping wheeze, indicated that he still lived.

Mae spoke softly, "Sage, Herman is so sick I don't think he ll be hurt further by those needles. I'm near to my wit's end. There is nothing more I know to do. I think he has pneumonia from being out in the cold. Unless his fever drops and his lungs open up, we'll lose him." She was whispering, her worried eyes fixed on the sick man.

Sage pulled her close to his side. "What was it that he want to tell me?" he whispered into her ear, trying to distract her from the fear stiffening her body.

"I can't rightly say. He was all agitated, frantic to talk to you." She took a deep shaky breath and continued, "What he said made no sense. He'd say 'rage is a bellow.' Or, he'd clutch at my hand and make me promise I'd 'succor the poor man.' Or, he'd ask for you," her voice wavered. He looked at her face. Her chin trembled in an effort not to cry.

"Oh, Ma," he said, wrapping both arms around her and resting his cheek against her hair. "He'll make it," he said, his assurance coming from hope, not from knowing.

After a few minutes in that sick room, it seemed clear that Eich would remain unconsciousness for some time to come. Seeing no way his presence could help the situation, Sage departed, leaving his mother and Mrs. Fong to watch over the needle doctor's peculiar ministrations. Not that he expected the bizarre treatment to make a difference. Despite his reassurances to his mother, Sage felt a weary resignation over the ragpicker's likely fate settling into his bones. So much so that the thought of returning to play Mozart's convivial host gave him an itch to head in another direction. So, he did. He changed course and headed west. He'd call on Portland's bicycle king to find out whether Merrill had shown Mayor Williams their original list of unsound bridges.

Merrill's exuberant greeting was a disconcerting contrast to the hushed despair Sage had left behind him in the Fong's provision shop. "Mr. Adair," Merrill exclaimed, "You are a soothing sight for sore eyes. I received the second list you sent over with your Chinaman. First thing tomorrow, we'll be taking a look at those bridges too. There's already some good news for you on that front." Merrill paused to peer closely at Sage. "So, is something the matter, son? You look like your best friend died."

"That's awfully close to the truth. He's pretty sick. We're afraid he's not going to make it."

"Sorry to hear that." Merrill's face momentarily sobered before he continued, "Well, let's sit you down." Merrill escorted Sage to a chair next to his desk before bellowing, "Abner, fetch us some hot coffee from next door. And buy yourself some hot chocolate while you're at it." A boy appeared, a thick dab of black grease on his chin. He took the coins proffered by Merrill and hustled out the door. Within minutes, Sage was watching steam rise from two mugs of coffee sitting on the desk.

"I wish there was a way to help your friend," Merrill said, "but sometimes sending up a prayer is all a body can do."

"Thanks, Mr. Merrill." Sage said, touched by the man's genuine sympathy. After a pause he asked, "So, what's this good news?"

Merrill laughed. "Ah, well, like I told you, our new mayor is a little too old to be clambering up and down ravines. Despite that, he's no dummy. He brought along one of his grandsons and the two of us climbed in and out of that gully to poke rods into the bridge timbers. We confirmed what you said. Dry rot riddles the trestles' supports but fresh creosote covers it up so that, from a distance, they look brand new. Once Mayor Williams heard that, he trotted directly back to City Hall and wrote a letter firing Horace Bittler, the city engineer. Funny thing, though, when they tried to deliver it, Bittler was nowhere to be found. One of his neighbors said the whole family decamped at dawn a few days ago, riding in, of all things, the back of a produce van."

And here I thought we'd gotten the Bittlers away with no one the wiser. Wonder what Bittler is doing right now? Sage thought to himself and his mind conjured up a pleasurable picture of Bittler in Brother Jonas's barn, forking hay or shoveling manure. However, all Sage said to Merrill was a disinterested, "Hmm, wonder where Bittler went?"

"Well, Bittler will learn soon enough that he's been fired," Merrill said, eyeing Sage more intently. "Anyway, Williams is in a high dudgeon and swears that, by tomorrow, a new city engineer will be closely inspecting all the rest of the trestle bridges. Your list of the problem bridges is going to give the new engineer a leg up on inventorying the situation. If we're lucky, he'll be competent and not appointed just because he's the mayor s nephew or a political crony's brother-in-law." Merrill leaned back in his chair, his face alight with a satisfied smile.

"What about Earl Mackey?" Sage asked.

The smile dropped off Merrill's face. "Mackey told Williams, that he had only recently discovered that Bittler and the union work crew had been conniving to cheat the repair jobs. He insisted they'd conspired to steal and sell off the new bridge timbers and to creosote over the dry rot. Mackey claims he knew nothing whatsoever about the scheme until yesterday."

"And Williams believed him?"

Merrill gave him a pitying look. "They play golf together and belong to the same so-called 'gentlemen's' club. What do you think?" he asked.

TWENTY FIVE

"I BELIEVE YOU, JOHN, I BELIEVE YOU," Johnston said, his tone making clear his impatience. "It's just that there's not a damn thing to be done about it. There's no way to print a story like that without solid evidence." Regret knitted the newspaperman's eyebrows. "I need more proof that Mackey bribed Bittler. Remember, given Earl Mackey's political clout in this city, his business cohorts will rush to defend him as will *The Gazette.* The mud will fly through the air like muck in a feedlot stampede. I don't mind slinging a little mud myself now and then, you know that. In this case, though, I'll need more mud on my side than just the written say-so of that absent and self-confessed crook, Horace Bittler."

Johnston's regret was genuine, Sage knew that. The newspaperman stood up for the working man at every opportunity—in fact, Johnston's well-advertised commitment to the "little guy" accounted for *The Journal*'s growing circulation numbers. Even so, he couldn't expect Johnston to stick his newspaper's neck out without more evidence to back him up.

"So I guess Earl Mackey is going to breeze through this entire disaster without a single hair on his pomaded head being messed," Sage said, frustration giving his words bite.

"Except for the fact that he's lost his father," Johnston gently reminded him.

"Yah, well I've got to wonder just how much pain that loss caused him. In fact, I'm not too sure his hand wasn't in it."

Johnston held up a hand, "Whoa, Sage. Unless there's solid proof of that particular allegation you need to be careful who might be around when you give tongue to it. If Mackey hears that you're alleging patricide, he'll take you to court. And, he'll win. Mackey has the reputation of being a generous, public-spirited man. He and his wife are regulars on *The Gazette*'s society pages because they fund one charitable cause after another. The jury will remember those good works and they'll tend to believe him, unless you can offer irrefutable proof that he's behind the murder."

Sage rose from his chair to pace the small space in front of Johnston's desk. "People like Mackey always construct an admirable public exterior," he said. "Poke beneath that exterior you'll find moral rot. Take Andrew Carnegie, for instance. People think he's a great public benefactor with all those libraries he funds." Sage kept talking even as the more calm part of his mind knew that he was preaching to the choir. It didn't stop him. Sometimes a man needs to hear the truth spoken out loud, even if he's the one doing the talking.

"What you don't hear about is how Carnegie acquired all that money he parses out. How he speeds up production in his steel mills until his workers collapse from exhaustion. That damnable Taylorism time-management system he uses sucks the last living ounce from a body. 'Scientific management' my backside. There's not a whit of difference between that scheme and an overseer with a damn whip!" Sage hit the top of a bookshelf with his fist. "Carnegie epitomizes evil, that's how I see it. His obscene level of wealth comes from sucking the life out of his workers. He uses just a fraction of his ill-gotten gain to act the beneficent God so people will throw rose petals at his feet. Carnegie, Mackey and the other robber barons are all cut from the same bolt of cloth! They turn my stomach."

Johnston, his elbows planted on his desk, calmly eyed Sage across a bridge of folded hands. Once Sage resumed his seat, his outburst over, Johnston said mildly, "I sympathize with your views, Adair. I hold the same ones. You know I do." Johnston leaned forward over his desk, his eyes regretful. "I am also a businessman responsible for keeping this 'voice of the people' we've created going. I can't risk the future of this newspaper on a shaky story. If I did, and lost the paper, the city's only daily would be *The Gazette.*" The newspaperman straightened and said with finality. "Bottom line, John, there's no way I will print your story until it's well supported— however much I might want to expose Mackey's rotten activities."

❀ ❀ ❀

Sage walked into a near empty Mozart's just after the dinner hour. He paused at the threshold, noticing that new cream-colored paint now coated all the walls above the dark mahogany wainscoting. When he looked for an indication of where Daniel's handiwork might next appear, he saw nothing. Maybe the sad, peculiar man was done with painting.

"How in the world did Daniel manage to finish painting that entire room in such a short time?" Sage asked his mother when he entered the kitchen and found her stirring the contents of a steaming pot. He sniffed and stepped closer to peer over her shoulder. Creamy chocolate pudding, one of his favorites.

"He arrived here again at the crack of dawn and worked without stopping. He finished an hour before dinner started." Mae lifted the pudding from the heat and began spooning it into small dishes. "Say, you've been taking care of his pay, haven't you?" she asked, looking at him.

"You mean we haven't paid him?"

She bristled, "What is this 'we?' You carrying a mouse in your pocket? I know I haven't paid him. I thought you took care of that."

"No, not me. And who's been buying the paint?"

She shrugged her shoulders.

"Fine job were doing watching out for him. Maybe that was the point Herman kept trying make—that we needed to pay the man." Sage looked around. "Where is our industrious but forelorn painter, anyway?"

"Last I saw Daniel, he was carrying the ladder down into the cellar. Dinner was hectic and I never saw him again. Maybe he's still down there puttering around."

Sage headed toward the cellar door. "I'll see if he is and I'll make sure we settle with him before he leaves tonight."

The cellar yielded no evidence of the painter, only the musty smell of its dirt floor. Surplus canned foodstuffs for the restaurant were stacked neatly on the wall shelves that hid both the second stairwell from the third floor and the tunnel leading to the alley.

Lighting a gas jet, Sage looked for Daniel's painting equipment. Only the ladder leaned against one wall and, come to think of it, that was Mozart's ladder. A few near empty cans of the paint sat on a shelf. Otherwise, Daniel's buckets, drop cloths and paint brushes had vanished, leaving nothing to show that Daniel's painting project was still underway. Back upstairs he searched the small storage closet near the restaurant toilets and found nothing there. Next, he looked in other logical places where Daniel might store paint buckets and the like, even climbing into the musician's balcony. There he got a surprise. Colorful flower garlands filigreed freshly painted walls. Sage stepped closer, amazed at the artistry in the painted flowers. "Beautiful," he muttered to himself. "I wonder if he'd paint a few of these decorations on the dining room walls?

Returning to the kitchen, he told his mother, "His painting gear isn't in the cellar. Does he usually take it home at day's end?"

She was at the stove, stirring a different pot. He looked over her shoulder. Beef barley soup. His stomach growled. She laid down the spoon and said, "No. Daniel always neatly stacks his painting gear in the cellar. He washes his brushes in the kitchen sink, dries them carefully and takes them down into the cellar." Concern wrinkled her brow as she tossed him a roll, picked up the spoon and began stirring again.

"Well, he's left nothing behind this time. Not a single brush." Sage stood silent for a moment, chewing the roll as he pondered over the painter's strange behavior before saying, "Have you seen

expensive broadcloth suit. Sage, however, remembered him clearly—remembered the man's exhaustion and his sorrowful, pinched face. Tonight, the man was easy and joking with his friend. Probably a colleague. Yet, the price the doctor paid for his compassion was there, in the lines around his eyes, in the pensive way his mouth drooped during the conversational lulls.

Compassion was at that doctor's core, Sage decided. Wonder what sound compassion makes? Maybe a soothing croon, he surmised. The memory of Eich's fevered face slid into his thoughts.

Near the center of the room a young couple dined in what seemed a celebration since, given their simple clothes, Mozart's appeared above their financial means. Excitement enlivened the young woman's face as she eagerly looked about. Her partner's gawking was more restrained but his sparkling eyes and uneasy fingering of his shirt collar gave him away. Sage asked a passing waiter to present a glass of champagne to each of them. His reward was their surprised pleasure at the gift.

Sage's interlude of quiet contemplation ended with Philander Gray's entry into the restaurant. The lawyer's face was grave and he waved away Sage's offer to show him to a table.

"Don't feel like eating right now, Adair. Been to see Lockwood."

"What's wrong? Is Leo sick or something?"

Gray shook his head dolefully, pursing his lips before saying, "Well, if you said he's sick with worry, you would be on the mark."

"Poor Leo. Damn, I wish there was something more for me to do. I'm hoping Fong shows up soon with some good news," Sage said. "His men are trailing those two thugs wherever they go. I expect him to report in sometime soon."

"We better come up with something awful darned fast," Gray said. "The prosecutor has informed the judge that he's ready to begin the trial the day after tomorrow."

"That's too soon," Sage said. Panic hit hard as a log flying out the end of a chute. "We need more time to find those two and their boss, tie them to Earl Mackey, and make them confess to killing the old man. It isn't possible to accomplish all that in one day."

"Whether we accomplish it or not, Leo's trial starts the day after tomorrow, sure as rain will fall in November," Gray responded.

TWENTY SIX

THE DARK FORM GLIDED INTO Sage's room just before day lightened the sky. Sage was awake. With Leo's trial just 24 hours away, Sage had stared into the dark all through the night.

"Not to worry. It is only me," Fong's said, somehow knowing that his friend lay awake.

Sage lit the oil lamp, its flaring yellow light catching in the dark hollows beneath his friend's eyes. Fong had been ceaselessly trying to track Mackey's three thugs. That effort, coupled with the strain of housing the desperately ill Eich, left the man looking exhausted. Sage didn't know Fong's age. He'd always thought it improper to ask. He guessed the other man to be somewhere in his mid-fifties. Most days, his impassive countenance and quiet strength made him seem younger than Sage felt. Not today.

"Sit, Mr. Fong. You look like you've been to hell and back," Sage said. Throwing back the covers, Sage pulled pants on over his long johns.

Fong slowly eased himself into the wooden rocking chair as if his bones were aching or about to snap. "And, you look like Chinese ghost scared by demons," he replied tiredly, with just a hint of his usual twinkle.

"Have you news?" Sage asked. "Don't tell me we lost those two galoots."

Fong shook his head. "We followed them to Covington Hotel." Sage knew the Covington. Older and lacking the Portland Hotel's prestige, the Covington was still considered a respectable, middle-class hotel. It catered to businessmen and financially comfortable traveling families. Not the type of place he'd expect to find the two men he'd come to think of as "Wheezy" and "Whiny."

"Strange to think that the two of them are staying there."

"Oh no, they are not staying there. Covington is where third man staying."

"Great! What's his name?"

"It took some time to find out. The only Chinese man who works in hotel is down in laundry and he belongs to different tong than mine. First, I obtain approval from tong leader for him to help me. He try to discover the man's name." Fong smiled briefly. Sage recognized the problem. It was hard for the hotel's only Chinese employee to ask questions about a guest without attracting the wrong kind of notice. Fong cleared his throat and spoke, "Laundry man pretty certain third man is staying in room 309. He says number 309 is only single man staying there who is younger than forty years."

"What's his name?"

"Charles O'Connell is name hotel staff call him by."

"Did you stay and watch for him to come out?"

"I stayed for many hours. Many ways to exit that hotel. I am not sure he still there. My cousins follow other two bad men when they leave hotel so I stay to watch by myself. I pace back and forth between two sides of hotel like rooster locked out of hen house until cousin come to assist. I tell man to stand watch. Describe to him this O'Connell . . . told him to look for single man, of younger age and follow."

Sage grinned. "Good work! Unless this O'Connell fellow realizes we're watching him, he won't feel the need to change hotels. He's not going to suspect that a Chinese man would be keeping an eye on him. That's the last thing he'd think of." Sage reached for his boots. "If he's not there now, he'll turn up there sooner or later. What happened to the other two, the ones we clouted at the lumber mill? Any luck in finding out where they are holed up?"

Fong gave a tired smile. "Oh yes, we know the boarding house where they are staying. It's up in Northwest Portland. They are not there now."

"Oh, they managed to give your cousins the slip?"

Fong smiled again. "You maybe like this, Mr. Sage. Remember prison cell in underground where those shanghai men kept Matthew prisoner?"

Now there was a memory. Of course Sage remembered that cell. A few months prior it was a holding pen for all those poor souls the crimp Mordaunt had drugged, mugged and otherwise kidnapped from Portland's streets. Before Sage, Fong and Sargeant Hanke came to his rescue, Matthew had spent a few days on the dirt floor of that cell, nearly insensibile from opium, along with other shanghai victims.

"They're down there? How did they fetch up there?"

Despite weariness, Fong's eyes managed a twinkle. "Yes, they are down there," he said. "You said you wanted to question them. We not own a cooperage or a lumber mill like the Mackeys. So, when they came out of saloon staggering first one way and then other, two cousins tap them on side of heads. When they fell down, cousins helped them into underground. Cell still there." His face sobered. "I think maybe shanghai men are using it again. I am sorry. We stopped watching it last few days."

Sage didn't doubt that the cell was in use once again. They'd done no more than slow the shanghai trade when they broke up Mordaunt's crimping operation. That was the discouraging fact about humans. Whenever there is money to be made, there will always be an unscrupulous somebody eager to step into the breach—no matter how disgusting the endeavor.

"Have they regained consciousness yet?"

"Just before I came here, they start to make groaning sound so they are awake by now. I think listening to underground rat noise going to make them 'spill beans.'" He smiled his toothy, wicked smile from which Sage gathered that some of that "rat noise" would be Fong's cousins helping the prisoners' fear grow.

"What if the shanghai men turn up expecting to find an empty cell?"

Fong laughed. "If shanghai men come, we make them fall over each other's feet to run away. In underground, we Chinese are masters. Not to worry. We know how to frighten people away when we need to."

❀ ❀ ❀

Sage moved out through Mozart's cellar tunnel shortly after first light while Fong exited out the kitchen door, heading home to rest. They'd decided the two thugs might benefit from a longer stay in the underground cell. The Stygian blackness, the scuttling of rats and the fear of being shipped to the Orient might inspire them to be truthful when questioned.

Climbing up into a misty morning and turning to lower the trap door, Sage froze. Johnston's words from the day before hit his tired brain like a lighthouse beam. He dropped the trap door and stood in air so damp that it left droplets on his mustache, as he pondered the publisher's words in connection with the strike, testing the logic of his sudden insight. "Mackey's public persona . . . was that the key? Was a criminal conviction all that important?" he asked himself. Hope surged. If what Sage suspicioned about the elder Mackey's death was true, maybe it was possible to save the strike and Leo at the same time.

Unexpectedly resolute about his next course of action, Sage stepped up his pace. His heart lightened as his spirits rose for the first time since they'd rescued Chester. He stopped in at the bricklayers' union hall. There he obtained the permission necessary to accomplish the first part of his plan. Going on to the cul de sac, he found only Henry and a few steadfast strikers still manning the strike line.

"Few" was the correct description. No more than seven men slowly circled in the picket line, defeat bowing their shoulders. Even a weak sun break failed to enliven their steps.

"Howdy, Sam, any news about Leo?" Henry asked, as soon as Sage reached the group.

"His lawyer says the trial starts tomorrow," Sage said and the other man's face paled.

"Dear Lord, is there no way to save him?" Henry asked. The men crowded around, each face weary and careworn beyond its years.

"Believe me, I'm working on that. Right now, that's not anything you men are in a position to help me with. Besides, you're doing enough by coming down here and keeping the pressure on Mackey. I'm here because I have a plan that should win this strike tomorrow," Sage said, sweeping his hand in an arc that encompassed the end of the cul de sac. "To make it work I need each of you to undertake one more task. Go out and find all the guys. Ask them to gather together one more time at the bricklayers' hall, Second and Yamhill, at three o'clock this afternoon. Tell them we intend to expose us a little dry rot and win the strike tomorrow. Don't invite or tell that O'Reilly fellow if you come across him. It's vital he not know what we're up to. Be sure everyone knows that."

Maybe if Sam weren't Leo's nephew and maybe if they weren't at the end of their collective rope, they'd have told him to go to hell. But he was, they were and, so, they didn't. Instead, they meekly dispersed, heading out to find the strikers who'd either stayed home or were out drowning their sorrows in a mug of five-cent beer.

The sight of them trudging away up the road stabbed into Sage's heart. It was going to be long, hard work to restore the pride and optimism the Mackeys had stolen from them.

A scuffling sound caught his ear. Turning around, he saw Earl Mackey and a few of his bodyguards standing on the porch of the partially burned construction shack a hundred feet away. He thought Mackey exposed his teeth in a grin. Sage didn't stick around to make sure. Instead, he pulled his hat brim down, buried his chin in his collar and headed up the road. He didn't want Mackey looking too closely at his face, since they'd be meeting soon.

❀ ❀ ❀

A few hours later, Sage exited Mozart's during the dinnertime rush. This time he wore businessman's attire so that his passage through the Covington Hotel's lobby wouldn't draw attention. And it didn't. Sage confidently strode through the hotel doors, across the lobby and up the wide stairway, his peripheral vision on the desk clerk, who glanced up briefly before returning his attention to the newspaper draped across his counter.

The third floor was quiet as Sage stepped softly down the carpeted hallway to the door numbered 309. He knocked softly, figuring the O'Connell fellow was likely gone. If the man answered, Sage planned to say he'd knocked on the wrong door. That way, he'd see the man's face.

The door remained closed. He strained to hear sounds inside the room. There was nothing. He took a pliable sliver of whale bone from an inside pocket. After making sure the hallway was empty, Sage slipped the flexible piece of bone between frame and door until there was a metallic snick. He twisted the door's ornamental brass knob and pushed the door open. After one final glance down the hallway, he stepped into the room, quietly closing the door behind him.

Inside, an ornate iron bed stood against the long wall, a table beside it. Gas wall jets jutted out here and there while a hardwood dresser created a narrow pathway at the bed's foot. A tall oak wardrobe filled one corner of the outside wall, a sink hung in the other corner. Obviously, the hotel maid had come and gone since the bed's coverlet was professionally taut. Sage dropped onto his knees to look under the bed. Nothing, not even dust fluffs. Mae Clemens would approve. He crossed to the dresser and pulled open its three drawers. Each drawer held neatly stacked garments. The abundance of clothes meant that this O'Connell fellow was not a passing-through traveler. Still, nothing indicated who he was or why he was in Portland.

Sage sighed. Only the wardrobe remained to be searched. He crossed the room and tugged its door open. Inside, a metal rail sagged under the combined weight of tightly packed suits, shirts, pants and a heavy, long black coat. He quickly slid the hangers along the rail, his fingers searching the pockets of every garment. As he riffled through the coat's pockets, he noticed a crumple of brown fabric on the floor of the wardrobe. Shoving the black coat aside, Sage reached down to pull out a working man's jacket, shaking it out to study it closer. He'd definitely seen it before.

"Who the hell are you, mister?" the voice snarled into his right ear as an icy gun barrel jabbed into his neck.

TWENTY SEVEN

THE INSTANT COLD STEEL TOUCHED his skin, Sage reacted. Hours of training with Fong took over. His weight shifted to center on his back leg, making the gun barrel slip off of his neck into the space in front. Sage twisted, his left arm slicing sideways in "warding off" and sending the gun flying through the air. The sight of the man's face caused no hesitation because Sage already knew who he fought.

The other man, his face straining with intent, lunged forward even as Fong's voice rolled through Sage's mind like a calm wave: "Best time to attack your enemy is when he is on the attack, because his Yi is on attack and not on defense. Sage's right hand scooped down, swooped up—first repelling the punch, then grabbing his attacker's right wrist. Sage twisted to the right, moved his left leg behind the man's right leg, pressed his upper arm against the other's ribs and shifted his weight forward. The man fell backward onto the bed and stayed there.

"What the hell kinda move is that?" O'Reilly asked from his supine position.

"I believe it's called 'part the wild horse's mane,'" Sage answered, his voice calm, his breathing even. He bent down, snatched up the gun and held it loosely in his hand. The thought of Fong's approval of this outcome made him smile slightly. This self-congratulatory moment was brief. O'Reilly had been able to sneak up behind him. That meant Sage was not going to avoid more of the forehead-thumping alertness-training Fong insisted Sage still needed. Fong was right, once again. In his mind, he heard Fong's patient voice murmur, "Like crane, Mister Sage, you too intent on searching for insects," or some such bird-based lesson.

O'Reilly struggled to sit upright on the mattress. "Just what might you be doing in my room?" he asked, his brogue thick.

"When I entered, I didn't know this was your room. After all, how could any of us know that an itinerant 'working man,' such as yourself, lived in such luxurious surroundings? Let alone possess a wardrobe stuffed with the very finest of worsted suits?"

O'Reilly said nothing, merely sending Sage a narrowed look from his ice-blue eyes.

Sage continued on. "I guess this means you're working for Mackey. What are you? Dickinson?" The detective agency was the arch-enemy of every man who united with his co-workers to get better hours, wages and working conditions.

The cold, watching eyes narrowed further.

Sage wagged an admonishing finger in the man's face. "Don't trouble to deny it. Back East, agent provocateurs like you crawl out from under the rocks every time there's a labor dispute. Funny how all of you agent provocateurs use the same tactics. Sow discontent among the strikers, spur them into acting rashly."

A smirk lifted one side of O'Reilly's face. "It's not my fault if those losers don't learn any better. They always start fighting amongst themselves and acting stupid sooner or later. I just help things move along faster, according to the boss's schedule. What's that saying, 'The sooner begun, the sooner done?'"

Sage noticed the Irish brogue no longer softened the man's speech. "Your name's not O'Reilly or O'Connell is it?"

"It's O'Reilly, same as your name's Sam Graham. I'm betting that we're both mercenaries in this war—just on different sides."

"Except, unlike you I don't try to murder people and I'm motivated by something other than greed," Sage said, not bothering to suppress the contempt he felt.

"I never tried to murder anybody!" Indignation sharpened O'Reilly's voice. He started to rise up off the bed.

A vision of a wet Herman Eich tied up in the ravine hut flashed through Sage's mind. He raised the gun so it pointed at O'Reilly's midsection. "Nuh, uh. You stay right where you are." O'Reilly ceased moving. Sage decided to say nothing about Eich's near fatal encounter with O'Reilly's thugs. It was better for O'Reilly to continue thinking that the ragpicker was nothing more than a nosy bystander.

"Cut the lies, Mister O'Reilly." Sage said instead, sarcasm thickening his words. "I'm the guy your two flunkies planned to stuff in a barrel and dump in the river. And, of course, there's that big, sharp bandsaw blade those two planned to use on Chester."

O'Reilly's laugh barked and he shook his head. "A one-way train ride out of town was the worst we planned for you and that Chester fellow. I specifically instructed my men to just scare the bejesus out of the two of you. That's all. Glad to see they loosed your innards some. Reason enough for me to make use of them again."

The urge to pummel the smirk off O'Reilly's face balled Sage's fists. But, he made himself breathe deeply and relax. Now was not the time to go for personal satisfaction. "I'm supposed to believe that crap coming from someone who's proven he's crooked as a rattler in a rock pile?"

O"Reilly shrugged. "You may hate my side of this war, but I don't hold still for murder and neither does the company I work for." O'Reilly talked past Sage's snort of disbelief. "'Course I also don't hesitate to defend myself," he added. "Anyway, you're a fine one to throw accusations around. You best look in that mirror over there," O'Reilly gestured toward the mirror atop the dresser. "Seems to me that your suit is a mite too fine for Leo Lockwood's unemployed, so-called, 'nephew.' I'd say there are at least two liars in this room."

O'Reilly nailed him on that point. Sage folded his arms across his chest and changed the subject to the one that mattered most. "Why'd your boys kill old man Mackey? He raise some objections to taking you on board?"

O'Reilly shook his head. "You're chasing the wrong squirrel up the tree on that one, Graham. He didn't know his son hired me on board. Besides, Lockwood killed Mackey. We only steered the police in Lockwood's direction. We all know Lockwood went to the construction shack, found the old man there and killed him.

"I suppose you'll also claim your two men didn't try to burn down Horace Bittler's house the other night."

O'Reilly's lips twisted. "Damn fools. I told them to scare the man into leaving town, not try to burn up his damn house. You ever noticed that no matter however clear your orders, men still must somehow put their own peculiar stamp on them? Just like a dog having to hit every bush. I already told them no pay for that job since they were stupid and damn near got caught."

O'Reilly shot Sage an inquiring look. "Why, I bet you're the fella who shot at them. Sure enough Bittler wouldn't have the gumption to face them down. You scared them pretty good too," he said. "They're out looking for you right now—not to kill you, of course. Just give you a little thank-you present. Since you are here with me now, I suspect they never found you.

O'Reilly's eyes turned chilly as he said, "By-the-bye, I didn't appreciate your fine performance the other night. It ruined me with the strikers."

The man's shoulders lifted and dropped dismissively. "Doesn't matter all that much, don't you know? You only had a few men picketing this morning. That strike of yours is deader than a doornail," he added with a smug smile.

Sage didn't respond, distracted as he was by the thought that O'Reilly might be telling the truth about not killing Abner Mackey. And, he realized, O'Reilly also didn't know his two men had fallen into "enemy" hands. Good. Maybe he'll stew a bit when they don't show up.

Sage asked a question of his own. "So what's the next step you plan on taking in this 'war' of ours?"

O'Reilly spread his arms wide and grinned. "Oh, my work is done here. We figure we've won this war, hands down. Those strikers are all out of fight. Their president is going to be kicking the air in a few days. Their leaders won't find another job anywhere in the city and the rest of them will crawl back to Mackey with their tails between their legs. Even better, Bittler has bolted to parts unknown and I hear tell that he's out of a job now too, so he won't be coming back. All in all, the agency's client and I are quite happy with the outcome." O'Reilly's grin widened. "Yup, it looks to me that our little war is over and I won. Fact is, just before I came back to find you riffling through my belongings, I stopped and bought a ticket on the morning train to San Francisco."

He pulled the train ticket from his pocket and waved it in the air. "Job well done is what I'd say." He smiled wide. "Completed it in record time with a minimum of fuss. Agency will give me a bonus, I expect."

Sage's blood surged to an instant boil but he forced himself to move casually toward the door, pausing only after he'd opened it. He turned to lock eyes with O'Reilly. "No man was ever so much deceived as by himself," he said, paraphrasing Grenville, and had the satisfaction of watching confusion replace the smirk on O'Reilly's face.

Ben Johnston was at *The Journal's* offices, hard at work. With events unfolding at such a rapid clip, timing was now crucial. It took only a short explanation before Johnston agreed to print the list of bridges needing repair and the fact of Bittler's firing in the next day's newspaper. "So long as one of my reporters confirms dry rot in a few of them," Johnston cautioned, always the ever-vigilant guardian of *The Journal's* reputation. Sage didn't mind. Since there was already one toadying newspaper in town, it was important that *The Journal* retain its reputation for carefully verifying its facts.

Sage arrived at the bricklayers' hall just before three o'clock that afternoon. All was in readiness for the Mackey strikers. In short order, over thirty men gathered. Their facial expressions ranged from weary despair to mulish obstinance. Still, they listened as Sage talked and within a few minutes, smiles had transformed their faces.

"Don't you think the police will come drive us off?" asked one doubter.

"By the time Mackey thinks to send for them, it will be too late. He'll have recognized that he's boxed in and if he raises a ruckus, he'll lose control over who finds out."

"Well, I, for one, don't see how doing this can hurt us any. Leastways, we'll be doing something different for a change. We won't be down at that darned mill wading through the mud," said another man, reaching for one of the stakes. "Let's start to work, men," he urged.

With murmurs of assent and shuffling of feet, the men moved forward, their rough hands picking up the tools of their trade and setting to work. Henry took charge with renewed vigor, vowing all would be ready by six o'clock the following morning.

Back out on the street, Sage's worry now centered on the next task before him. Failure of that task meant he would be no closer to finding Mackey's murderer and Leo would be much closer to hanging. He was still mulling over the various approaches to take when he reached Fong's provision shop.

Mrs. Fong stood behind the counter, waiting on two black clad men. All three looked toward the door, and in the dim light Sage saw the men's eyes narrow and their stances stiffen. Mrs. Fong spoke rapidly in Chinese—the tone of her voice permitting no opposition. The two men nodded and headed out the door, giving Sage a wide berth where he stood idly fingering a stack of linen handkerchiefs.

Once the street door snapped shut, Mrs. Fong came from behind the corner, her face weary. She led him to the living quarter's door, gestured him through it, and shut it behind him.

His mother was dozing in a hard-backed chair beside Herman Eich, her head hanging forward. The silence was no longer laden with the ill man's labored breathing. Sage squinted, his heart lurching when he failed to detect a rising of Eich's chest. He stepped carefully toward the cot, trying not to wake his mother. If Eich was dead, she'd know soon enough. Sage laid the back of his hand against Eich's cheek and felt warmth. Eich twitched under the touch and relief whooshed out of Sage, so loud that his mother stirred.

"Oh, it's you. Herman's doing much better. I think we're through the worst," she said.

"That's great news," he said, squeezing her shoulders. "Has he said anything more?"

"Not since you came last time. I expect he'll be awake come morning. You come back tomorrow."

In whispers, Sage told Mae about his confrontation with O'Reilly and about the strikers' activity at the bricklayers' hall.

"You've done good, Sage. The trick will be forcing Earl Mackey to act before he has time to scheme a way out."

"I plan on hitting his front porch right after the paper comes out. Fact is, I figure on being his very own personal paperboy."

❀ ❀ ❀

Leaving the shop minutes later, Sage took up a post on a nearby street corner. He jumped when Fong's voice sounded next to his ear, "Right on time, Mr. Sage. Good trait, timeliness. But, there remains problem—still not much good at being alert."

Sage whirled around to see Fong's black clad figure already striding toward an alley where there'd be a stairway down into the underground. As he followed the black-clad figure, Sage knew for certain that he was in for more hours of Fong's "alertness" training. He felt his forehead contract in anticipation of Fong's deadly accurate punches.

The cellar stairs ended in an opium den. A few dim candles revealed the dark forms of men lying atop ranks of short wooden bunks stacked three-high against the cellar walls. According to Fong, the shortened bunks forced the smokers to lie on their sides so they wouldn't choke on their own vomit. Apparently opium rendered people unconscious and sick at the same time. Thankfully, only dreamy murmurs sounded in the cloying smoke, along with the burble of water pipes and the scrape of Sage's boots.

As he dogged Fong's silent heels the length of the room, Sage sensed heavy-lidded eyes following their passage. His skin crawled at the mental image of a sharp knife hurtling through the air toward his back. Once they'd passed through another door and into the underground proper, Sage released the breath he'd been holding.

Fong paused and whispered, "Sorry, Mr. Sage. This is quickest way to holding cell."

"That's all right," Sage whispered back. Traversing the opium den's gauntlet took the edge off whatever anxiety he felt upon entering the underground's musty darkness. Still, for a moment, the familiar fear jittered through him. Not because of the shanghaiing experience. No, his fear originated years ago, when he was nine years old and a coal mine explosion buried him deep inside a mountain's dark heart.

Fong waited quietly as Sage quickly took himself through the mental paces he'd recently developed to counteract this old fear. He listened to the scuffling sounds of life overhead. Next, he breathed slowly through his nose and relaxed until the thudding race of his heart subsided. When Fong struck a match to a kerosene lantern, Sage felt no overwhelming rush of relief. Instead, he found himself more than ready to move deeper into the underground. He found himself eager to confront the two men who'd attacked him and Chester. They held secrets he wanted to learn. Tonight was the best and, maybe, last opportunity to prove Leo innocent of the old man's death.

TWENTY EIGHT

SAGE STEPPED CAREFULLY, TRYING NOT to stir the decades-old dust beneath his feet. He kept his breath shallow and breathed through his nose because he didn't know what was in that dust. Once, Fong told him that many of Portland's Chinese willingly entered this underground to die if they became seriously ill. They hid here to avoid discovery, tended to by other Chinese who rightfully feared Chinese illness being used to justify wholesale deportations. He worried whether deadly disease vapors, like consumption, still lingered in the dust. Not knowing the answer, Sage kept his mouth clamped shut.

Ahead, Fong moved confidently forward, his hand satiny gold in the light of the lantern he held aloft. Minutes later they passed, without stopping, the vague forms of the cousins guarding the two captives. By now, Sage knew that the two men in the holding cell probably sensed a lightening of the darkness—although not quite enough to trust their eyes. Next, they'd start to believe that someone approached, their stomachs beginning to knot as their staring eyes confirmed that the light was real and growing stronger. A single question would torture them a thousand times a second: Did salvation or danger approach?

Sage tapped Fong's shoulder to make him stop and turn. "I need your advice. How is the best way to play this?" Sage asked, his voice low.

"Ship name of *Reefer* is in harbor. Men call it a 'demon ship,'" Fong answered in a whisper.

"Why a 'demon ship?'"

"There was bad storm at sea. Ship lost rigging and drifted many days. All provisions gone very soon. Many died," Fong answered.

"That happens to a lot of ships in the Pacific."

"Ah yes, that is true. One difference, about this ship. When *Reefer* reach port, survivors not look hungry." He paused to let the import of his statement reach fruition before continuing, "The same men still on board. No other captain want to hire them. *Reefer* ship is short many sailors. Much talk in North End about what happen to missing men. Two in cell probably hear talk about it."

Fong bared his teeth in a humorless smile before starting forward once again.

They neared their destination. The lantern light shone on a pair of white-knuckled hands wrapped around the cell bars and on a brand-new nickle-plated padlock. The most disturbing thing about this cell was that it had been deliberately constructed as part of the building's original brick foundation. A few months ago, Sage wanted to demolish it. He'd thought its destruction might ease Matthew's nightmares. Once Matthew regained his equilibrium, however, Sage reluctantly abandoned that idea at Fong's urging, "Mister Sage, we may need cell sometime. Cousins and I keep watch and free every man kept here. Pretty soon shanghai men not use it."

A few feet from the cell, Sage took Fong's lantern and stepped forward. He stood in front of the bars and raised the lantern to illuminate his face clearly.

A wheezing voice growled from just inside the bars. "God damn it! Didn't I tell you we got kidnapped because of the Mackey job? That son-of-a-bitch ain't no shanghaier. I told you it weren't no damn shanghaiing!"

"Don't be so quick to celebrate, my man," Sage said. "As a matter of fact, the strikers ain't been paid for weeks and it just so happens that a friend of mine is trying to crew a ship. He's paying top dollar, especially for men of your ample stature. Maybe you two have heard of her—the *Reefer*?"

From deeper inside the cell, beyond the light's edge, the second man, more than likely "Whiny," whimpered.

An hour later, Sage and Fong made their way aboveground. The *Reefer* threat did the trick. Claiming they'd signed on only to cause a little fright, they started talking without further encouragement. Their protestations corroborated O'Reilly's claim that he'd given them instructions not to kill anyone. Wheezy, a Californian named James Parks, spoke most convincingly on that point.

"Hell, I knew how much chloroform I gave you. We even punched out a knothole to make sure you'd hear us jawing. With that Chester guy, we was only going to chloroform him and dump him in a boxcar heading east." Parks' offended churlishness gave his words a ring of truth. He claimed their plan at Bittler's house was to stand at the bottom of the stairs hollering "fire" until the Bittlers stirred. Once they knew the family was awake they planned to toss their match and leap out the front door. Of course, they didn't seem to think their treatment of Herman Eich was anything worth mentioning. Sage said nothing to them about that near-fatal attack. The ragpicker was safer if they believed him dead, or at least unconnected to the strike.

They'd also confirmed that Sage was correct about O'Reilly and about their own involvement in the strike. They identified O'Reilly as the one who'd sent the message luring Lockwood out of his house. The purpose of that tactic was to give them an opportunity to jump him when the streets were empty. They'd admitted to dropping the kerosene can over the fence into Lockwood's backyard. And, it was Parks who'd told the police he'd seen Leo with the kerosene can near the fire.

The two speculated that they'd missed ambushing Lockwood either because he arrived early and killed Mackey or else because he'd gotten there late, seen the fire and snuck away. Either way, he'd sidestepped walking into their trap. As far as they were concerned, the Mackey fire was unexpected and unwelcome. On this point, they were convincing. Their jaws dropped and their faces flushed with anger when Sage accused them of Abner Mackey's murder. Their indignation seemed genuine.

Sage reached the street, checked his pocket watch and saw that it was nearly midnight. Despite the late hour, he needed Philander Gray to help him decide what to do with the two miscreants. So, Fong headed east across the river with a message for Philander while Sage strode westward, once again looking for Sergeant Hanke. The plan was for everyone to meet up at the hotel where Chester and Stuart had holed up. Fong's cousins would escort James Parks and his partner through the underground to the same hotel.

By one-thirty in the morning, Philander held two confessions, each bearing an illiterate man's mark in lieu of a signature. Sergeant Hanke was escorting Parks and his partner to yet another cell, this one in the city's jail. Sage felt no hatred toward James Parks and his sidekick. Given land and seed money, both men might have been contented farmers. Truth was, poverty tended to push moral choices further from a poor man's reach. Still, the little discomfort he felt about the fate of Parks and his friend dissipated when he remembered Herman Eich's flushed face and Chester's unstinting bravery even as he faced down that whirring bandsaw blade. Herman and Chester, after all, knew poverty too, yet they'd both chosen to lead honorable lives, making the moral choice time and again.

Sage and Philander stood in the lobby of the shabby hotel, conversing softly. The night clerk slept, his cheek resting on his crossed forearms, a newspaper draped over his head to block the light.

"This new information means we'll be able to delay Leo's trial for a few days," Philander said. "But, we won't be able to win his freedom or stop the trial. Passion is still running too high over Abner Mackey's murder. To appease the public's anger and thirst for revenge, the police need some poor guy in jail and going to trial. In the social circles that count politically, people considered Abner Mackey a likable old gentleman. I plan to ask for a bail hearing in light of those two men's confessions. I predict, however, that the judge isn't going to release Leo because he admits he was at the scene of the fire. So, Leo's not in the clear, yet. You still need to find the real murderer."

Sage sighed, weariness had settled in, making his bones ache. "I was afraid you'd say that." He slapped his workingman's cap onto his head. "Well, right now I've an early morning visitation to orchestrate. Once that's over, I'm going after Mackey's killer." He paused to ask a final question, "How many days' delay in the trial hearing is the judge likely to give you?"

"Three if we're lucky, more likely two. That prosecutor is eager to strut his stuff," Gray replied.

The press room still radiated heat from the night's print run. Unexpectedly, Johnston stood just inside the door, ready to hand Sage a freshly printed and rolled newspaper. He further surprised Sage by following him out of the building.

"What a minute," Sage protested, raising a hand to stop Johnston from proceeding. "No need for you to go. You know, if things go our way, you can never report this story."

Johnston's lips spread in a wolfish smile. "I remember that little fact. But I recall you saying that, at one point, Mackey is likely to look out the window and see the picketers. I suspect he'll pucker up even more if he sees me out there reading the placards and interviewing the men."

Sage saw the potential impact of Johnston's idea immediately. He chuckled and cuffed the newspaper publisher's arm, saying, "All right, then! We'll take you up on your offer and many thanks to you!"

The morning air was dry, still and tingling cold. The sky overhead was an unblemished vault of icy blue. A good omen, Sage told himself as the cable car clanked jerkily upward, hauling the strikers and their hand-printed picket signs into the hilltop neighborhood with its ostentatious mansions. The strikers' party spirit coaxed smiles from the sleepy domestics riding the cable car on their way to work in those mansions.

Earl Mackey's huge house loomed a few blocks east of the cable car stop. Its squat Corinthian pillars supported the broad, east-facing porch anchoring the top of a brick-paved circle drive. On either side of the porch, small-paned windows flamed orange with the rising sun. As Sage studied it, he thought it was big enough to make a decent orphanage.

While the workers stayed gathered a few houses down, just out of sight, Sage headed up the drive accompanied by Chester. They mounted the front steps. Sage slapped an open palm against the mahogany door. A few minutes of that noise and Mackey himself opened the door wearing his bathrobe and a snarl.

"Just what in God's name are you doing, pounding on my front door this early in the morning?" he demanded, his jowls quivering.

"Just delivering your paper, Mr. Mackey," Sage said, doffing his workman's cap.

Mackey reached out stubby fingers to snatch the proffered paper even as his face registered recognition, "Say, I know you bums! You better get the hell off my property or I will see you thrown in jail! You're those damn strikers!" He started to shut the door only to have Sage's quickly inserted boot prevent its closure.

"Funny you mentioning jail," Sage said. "You ought to glance at that newspaper headline, Mackey, before you brush us off."

Mackey glanced down and his mouth dropped open. Two-inch headlines blared, "*Scores of Roadway Bridges Near Collapse.*" When his hand released the door to hold the paper level, Sage pushed it open wider. At the movement, Mackey looked up from reading, "What exactly is it that you want?" he asked, his tone mulish.

"We're here to talk a deal."

Mackey hesitated before stepping back into the hallway and motioning them toward an inner door that opened into a drawing room. Inside, satin chairs and brocade settees cluttered the room. Cloths draped every table, their swirling colors fighting for attention among the ornate mirrors, marble floor statuettes and knickknacks covering every flat surface. A bank of floor-to-ceiling, small-paned windows faced the street, heavy velvet drapes pulled partly shut. The pastel washes of a sylvan mural covered the other two walls.

Only one short wall was bare of riotous color and competing patterns. On it hung rows of photographs. Stepping closer, Sage saw that each picture showed Mackey and his wife smiling proudly and standing beside various noteworthy politicians and socialites.

Sage stopped his perusal of the wall when he heard Mackey toss the paper to the floor. "Phish, that article doesn't mean anything. My name's not even in it," Mackey blustered, "You're wasting your time and mine." He stepped forward as if to herd them toward the door.

Raising a hand, Sage stood his ground. "Before you dismiss my offer, please know that I've obtained an affidavit from Bittler, stating you bribed him to approve the bridge construction work your company performed. In that affidavit, he swears that you paid him to keep his mouth shut about how your 'special finishing crew' painted the rotten timbers with creosote. Then, he wrote that you turned around and sold the city's new bridge lumber a second time to someone else."

Mackey flushed, his eyes shifting around the room as if seeking for a way out. His face hardened. "Bittler's just lying. He's pushing the blame off himself," he said, even as he halted in his movement toward the door.

Sage smiled. "One thing's for sure. Those bridges are rotten through. And I wonder what a skilled accountant might find if he compared the volume of lumber you sold compared to the amount of raw logs you actually purchased? I bet your financial records would make some mighty interesting reading for a sharp-eyed accountant." Sage stepped to the window and yanked its velvet drapes further apart. "Anyway, once people read those signs out there, who will they blame next time a bridge collapses or when their neighborhood bridge is so unsound they have to get out of their carriages and walk across it? How are you going to explain away so many unsound bridges that your company supposedly repaired just months ago? Some of those inconvenienced will resent having to walk in the rain. Not to mention there's the fact of the two dead innocents and the city's destroyed fire wagon. All because of a bridge repair you supposedly oversaw."

Mackey's face flushed, his lips clamped and his eyes flicked sideways. When he stepped to look out the window that flush drained away. Outside, the strikers were milling about on the sidewalk. Each striker held a sign reading either "Earl Mackey's Bridges Falling Down" or "How Many More Deaths on Earl Mackey's Head?" Even worse was the sight of the town's new muckraking newspaperman, Ben Johnston, moving among the strikers, his long neck craned forward, his hand scribbling down whatever they said. Mackey gasped and his hand clutched the curtain.

Sage stepped closer to Mackey, speaking directly into the man's ear. "Do you imagine that once those bridges start collapsing, those folks on that wall of yours," here Sage gestured toward the photographs, "will want to associate with you? Especially when everywhere they turn, they'll see those same messages, outside their clubs or those fancy shindigs you all like to attend?"

"Wait, you better not be spreading that lie around town like that. I'll sue you!"

"Ha! A win in court it yields you nothing. These strikers are penniless, thanks to you. Besides, our lawyer tells us that truth is a defense to any claim of slander. And Mackey, once a jury looks at all the facts, they'll find our signs more truthful than any excuse you might concoct. Besides, even if you won in court, there is still the court of public opinion. Can you really believe that battle is winnable in that particular court?"

Mackey backed away from the window and carefully lowered himself down onto a brocade settee. "What's the deal you are offering me?" he asked, his tone subdued, all resistence drained out of him.

Sage gestured to Chester who stepped forward to hand Sage a piece of paper. "All we want is for you to sign this paper."

"What is it? What does it say?"

"It states that you agree to a labor contract with the union that includes an eight-hour, six-day workweek at the same rate of daily pay they received before the strike, plus an extra sixteen cents per day. Same thing the men asked for when they laid down their tools."

"If I sign it, what's my gain?"

"We burn those signs out there before anyone else sees them and Mr. Johnston loses his notes. You'd better hurry. Your neighbors will be stirring shortly—their servants are already hard at work cooking them breakfast."

Mackey's jowls bunched as he snatched the pen and paper from Sage's hand, slapped the paper down on a side table, scanned the words and scrawled his signature across the bottom of the sheet.

He flung the pen down and tossed the paper toward Sage. "Now get out of my house," he hissed through clenched teeth. He turned his back to them, facing the wall of photographs.

Sage nodded at Chester, who snatched the signed contract and sped from the room. The sound of the front door opening and closing marked his exit. Seconds later, a faint cheer sounded from outside. Chester probably waved the signed contract in the air to signal victory.

"You too! You get the hell out of here right now!" Mackey snapped over his shoulder at Sage.

"I'm leaving but first, there's a question I want to ask: What kind of a man orders his own father killed?"

Mackey's eyes blazed. He whirled and lumbered forward, his fists balled so tightly that his knuckles blanched white. For the first time that morning, Sage tensed in anticipation of a physical attack.

"I asked O'Connell to teach Lockwood and the strikers a lesson, that's all!" Mackey said, spittle accompanying his words, his face fire wagon red. "You take that allegation back or

I swear I'll ram your teeth down your throat and I don't care what happens."

Sage stepped back. "You're not what anyone would call an honest man. Why in the hell should I believe you?" he asked.

Mackey's face lost expression. He stumbled backwards until he again sat down on the settee. His chin crumpled and his eyes filled. From out of his pocket his fumbling fingers pulled a gold pocket watch. He stared at the watch face as he rubbed it with his thumb. "My poor papa," he whispered, burying his face in his hands, the watch's chain trailing from between two of his fingers like a golden string.

When he raised his chin to look at Sage, his pebble brown eyes glittered with tears and his tone was unequivocal, "I loved that old man. I disagreed with him sometimes but I loved him. He was a better man than me." Mackey stared at a point somewhere just past Sage and kept talking, his voice thick with emotion. "I wish I'd died in his place. It's all my fault. He wanted to end the strike—to reach agreement with the strikers. He said that it was tearing his heart out, especially after than man died. That's why he was there at the mill that night. We argued for hours. Finally he told me he was still the boss and he was going to work out the numbers on a new offer to strikers. Me, I kept fighting with him to the last. I was determined to win that damn strike at any cost. I stormed out of his house. I told him . . . I told him to go to hell."

Mackey covered his face and sobbed, his body shaking, his voice muffled as he said, "If I'd done like Papa wanted, he'd be alive today. I would have been down at the shack, working up the offer with him. And, Lockwood couldn't have killed him."

The man's disintegration was complete. Much as he didn't want to, Sage finally accepted the fact that Mackey did not order his own father murdered. Fong had been right, once again.

TWENTY NINE

LAUGHTER AND HEARTY BACKSLAPS greeted Sage when he rejoined the men outside. Some grinned their relief while others stood off by themselves, tears falling from eyes looking into the distance. Sage and Johnston gleefully shook hands before Johnston resumed collecting the men's reaction to their win.

The jubilation stilled as one by one, they noticed the man who stood on the mansion's front porch. Despite the indignity of addressing them while in his bathrobe, Mackey's bulk and his scowling face remained commanding. He raised a finger, pointed it at the men and shouted, "Don't think you're the bosses now! You men report for work at 7:00 a.m. sharp on Monday or you'll be out of a job!" He reentered the house, slamming the door to the sound of cheers.

As the cable car followed its lifeline down into the flatlands, its operator, a union man himself, added his baritone to the strikers' singing. Sage glanced over the edge, about midpoint in the thousand-foot-long trestle, and stopped singing. It was a long way down. Uneasily, he wondered whether punk riddled the timbers beneath the cable car. Nah. No way would Mackey daily jeopardize his own family's safety. "Not bloody likely," as his Brit friend, Laidlaw, would say. That's one thing you could always count on when it came to the rich folks. They'll always take care of each other and their own family's interests.

Once off the cable car, the group strode through the bright early morning toward their favorite saloon. Their joyful racket in the crisp morning air stirred loose a few angry shouts from second story windows. Closer to the saloon, where the upscale homes gave way to simple working-class clapboards, their procession brought other working men and women onto their porch stoops to join in the cheering.

Late morning found a somewhat inebriated Sage yearning for sleep. His ears still rang from the shouts and songs of the victorious men. His throat ached from his own participation in the revelry. He made his way to the alley, down into the tunnel and up the secret stairway to Mozart's third floor. Once there, he fell onto his bed and flipped the coverlet over his body without bothering to remove clothes nor boots.

Then, his mother was shaking him. "What happened?" she demanded.

"Mackey gave in. The strike is over. The men return to work on Monday," he mumbled as he struggled to sit up. On the small table, tucked into the bay window area, stood a silver coffee pot and plate of toast, a clear message that she believed it was time he left his bed. As he spread preserves on the toast, he told her about his confrontations with O'Reilly, O'Reilly's men and finally, with Mackey himself.

"I like imagining Mackey's face when he looked out that window and saw Johnston amongst the picketers," she said, chuckling. "I'm holding good news too. Herman's definitely on the mend. Last I saw him, he was sitting up, sipping Mrs. Fong's beef tea."

"I'd better go see him," Sage said, tossing down his napkin, shoving his chair back.

"Hold on a minute," Mae Clemens said, laying a restraining hand on his forearm. "Take a look out that window there. You've slept through till near eight o'clock at night. It's too late to go wake the Fongs now. She's exhausted and so is Herman for that matter. There'll be time enough in the morning." Her finger tips flew to her mouth. "My word, I forgot. I came to tell you that Philander is waiting for you downstairs."

Sage jumped up, stripped off his workingman's outfit and started throwing on clothes suitable for his role as Mozart's proprietor. "No need to hurry," she assured him, "He's ordered his supper and you know what that means. He'll be here at least an hour. That man surely loves to eat. Don't know where he stows it, he's thin as a rail. Good thing he's a lawyer and can afford all the provisions he tucks away."

Philander was, indeed, still forking in his food when Sage took the seat across from him. He listened to Sage recount recent events, pausing in his methodical chewing only to take a sip of wine.

"How about we go see Leo tonight? Give him some good news, at least," he suggested. "Something to take the sting out of the bad news that the judge only granted a two-day trial set-over."

The faint street lamp light filtering through filthy casement windows only enhanced the depressing impact of the jail's dank stone walls, iron gratings and trickles of water pooling in the corners. Unexpectedly, a dense pack of humanity covered the corridor and open cell floors. An overwhelming stench of wet woolens and unwashed bodies forced Sage to breathe through his mouth. Men lay sprawled upon newspaper mats, heads on their boots, bodies curled beneath wet overcoats. Some tossed fitfully midst others who were awake and muttering to each other or to themselves. Sage and Philander picked their way toward Leo's cell past the dull-eyed gazes of the sleepless, whose fingers scrabbled beneath layers of filthy clothing on the hunt for biting vermin.

Once they reached the clear space in front of Leo's cell, Philander offered an explanation. "Winter nights, the city warehouses the homeless here, rather than leaving them on the street. Otherwise, every morning, we'd be stepping over dead bodies. Such an unwelcome sight for our good citizens on their way to church, is it not?" he asked, his cynicism unmistakable.

Not for the first time, Sage wondered at the reason for the lawyer's abiding dedication to the downtrodden. As good a lawyer as he was, Gray could choose to use his legal education in much more lucrative ways. Yet, he didn't.

Sage looked back up the corridor with its carpet of bodies and shook his head. He'd known of the practice since many cities were using it. It did save some from the perils, both physical and mental, of sleeping on the streets during wintertime. Still, Philander was right. Warehousing the homeless on the jail's floor was also a way to hide the community's moral shortcomings.

There was a rustle from inside the cell as Leo struggled up from his bunk at the sound of Gray's voice. He approached them with the timidity of a dog that hoped for a handout, while fearing a kick. Sage reached through the bars and Leo responded by clasping Sage's hand in both of his. For a moment, the two men stood there, Sage's eyes smarting. He fought for control. Pity, without more, would only add to Leo's burden. Besides, what was it his mother always quoted? Right. "Friends help; others pity."

"Is there news?" Leo's quavering voice held none of the confidence he'd projected all those weeks during the strike when he'd stood on his soapbox successfully exhorting his men to remain steadfast.

Philander's confident voice cut in before Sage thought of a reply, "Yes, there is some good news. We obtained confessions from the two men who dropped the kerosene can over the fence and into your yard. They also said, their boss, that man O'Reilly. . ."

Sage interrupted, "You remember him, Leo? That Irish fellow always trying to rile the men up? Said he'd traveled down from the Idaho mining fields?"

"O'Reilly," Leo parroted absentmindedly.

Momentary panic surged through Sage. Was Leo's mind deranged?

Leo's flaccid demeanor didn't give Philander pause because the lawyer quickly seized the thread of conversation. "Yes, as I started telling you, it turns out that this O'Reilly was the one who wrote the message asking you to come to the Mackey construction shack. He was a Dickensen agent provocateur trying to goad the men into violence so the police could beat the dickens out of them and end the strike."

A spark of hope lit Leo's brown eyes. Sage fought the urge to reach through the bars and grasp the man, to shelter him from the disappointment heading his way.

"Problem is, Leo, you've already admitted that you were there, near the head of the cul de sac, around the time the fire broke out. So, the judge won't drop the charges against you or stop the trial." Philander's voice was gentle as he continued, "But, given that so much of the evidence against you has collapsed, I will try again tomorrow to obtain your bail. If nothing else, the bail hearing will give you a few hours away from this dungeon." He gestured at their surroundings. "Even wet streets and rainy skies are better than this."

Leo's face fell. Seconds later he roused himself, his spine straightening and his head coming up as if he'd tapped into a source of renewed strength. When he spoke his voice was stronger, "I know you'll help me out of this, Mr. Gray. I'm sure you'll eventually find a way to return me home."

Philander leaned closer to the bars. "Truth be told, Leo, John here is the one who found out about O'Reilly and those two men. He delivered the whole kit-and-caboodle to me, all tied up like a Christmas parcel."

Gratitude glowed in Leo's eyes. "Thank you, Mr. Adair. And thank you for seeing after my family. My wife's told me all that you've done. The money and food you send her keeps her spirits up and my family afloat." He looked at Philander. "What about the real murderer? Was it Earl Mackey or that O'Reilly and his men?"

Philander shook his head slowly. "I'm afraid not, Leo. But, keep your hopes up. John here is still looking. He has a real knack for solving problems like yours."

That bit of news hit Leo hard. His body sagged for a second before he gulped a deep breath and lifted his chin. "I trust you fellows," he said. "The two of you will spring me out of here. I'm certain of that."

Sage jumped in, telling Leo about Mackey signing the contract. That news snapped the familiar Leo further back to life. "Hip! Hooray!" he exclaimed, and danced a little circle in his cell. "By golly, that's the best darn news I've heard since I've been in here. Lordy! Imagine that? We won the strike!" Tears pooled in the union leader's eyes and trickled down his pale cheeks, reminding Sage of the men who'd stood that morning on the hill above the city, tears of relief in their eyes. Sage's heart ached even as his determination hardened.

Unstoppable mental images whirling through Sage's mind kept sleep at bay. Leo's haggard face. Mackey's sobbing grief. Joy lighting the strikers' careworn faces. The sneer twisting O'Reilly's lips. And, it seemed like Sage's every shift in position aggravated one small pain or another. Finally, he threw off his tangled bed clothes, struck a match to the lamp wick, and started pacing the room.

Idly, he stared at his face in the bureau mirror, fingering the shock of white at his temple. It was a permanent reminder of that careening sled ride down the backside of Chilkoot Pass. He'd lain nearly unconscious in the snow, blood dripping from his head, his leg broken in two places. Crippled and alone in the empty expanse of the Yukon winter, death loomed inevitable. Determination alone kept him going. Inch by painful inch, he'd crawled through the snow until he reached help. He needed some of that fortitude now.

Lifting the lamp higher and leaning forward, Sage saw that fatigue sagged his features as much as it did Leo's and Fong's. "No," he vowed firmly to his reflection. "I won't give in. We are going to free Leo, period," he declared in a voice that boomed unexpectedly loud in the quiet night.

Downstairs, a search of the pantry yielded Sage a piece of pie and a cool glass of milk. Leaving his dishes in the sink, along with a mental apology to Ida, Sage carried his lamp through the swinging doors into Mozart's darkened dining room. Sitting down at the small table beneath the musicians' balcony, Sage cradled his head on his folded arms. Soon the soft flutter of the lamplight nudged his eyelids closed. In that flickering golden haze his mind drifted into a morning of sunlight and spreading mist. In the distance, the glistening stalks of tall grasses nearly concealed the dense white of a crane's sinewy neck as her beak foraged for seeds and bugs.

What was Fong's point about that memory? Sage's tired mind turned that question over gently, like a half-forgotten pebble in his palm. "So busy looking, the cranes didn't notice the danger around them" or something like that. More words tumbled through his head, not a one of them the answer.

Sage sighed, opened his eyes and straightened up. "Might as well head upstairs," he said aloud, taking up the lamp and starting to rise. With the movement, the flame flared, its light catching the gleam of the newly-painted wall above the wainscoting—Daniel's gift. In that instant, another light flared even brighter in his head and he knew. Shock dropped him back into his seat where he sat silently as each piece slipped snugly, irrevocably into place. He knew who killed old Abner Mackey and why.

THIRTY

HERMAN EICH LAY ON THE COT, the pillows at his back angling him nearly upright. When he saw Sage, he smiled wearily. Once Eich expressed his gratitude for rescue and care, he lapsed into silence. Neither man spoke until Sage asked, "So, at what point did you realize it was Daniel?"

Eich didn't hesitate, "I think the night you rescued me from that hut. When I lay on my cot and I was barely conscious, going in and out. Daniel was above me, tending to me. He leaned close and I looked into his eyes. In them I saw despair, hopelessness, and shame, too. I knew then what had happened. And, he knew that I knew."

Eich's long boney fingers stroked the embroidered silk coverlet. "Mrs. Fong tells me that Daniel came to sit with me many times while I remained unconscious. Once she told him I was improving, that I would remain among the living, he never came again."

"Mother said that in the midst of your fever , you kept saying 'rage is a bellow.' Were you talking about Daniel?"

"Hmm, I don't remember saying that. It does sound like what I was thinking. Daniel's suffering seemed so restrained. I kept thinking that if he'd just let out his grief, he might live again. Instead, he bottled it up, he withdrew further. I knew part of it was guilt over his family's death, yet I sensed there was also a burning anger that seemed unquenchable—something he refused to talk about. I kept thinking that if he screamed his throat raw, he'd feel better. Just from letting it out. Instead of improving in spirits over time, though, he seemed to withdraw more, becoming even more agitated in his behavior."

Sage was pulling it together even as he formed the words, "Last night I realized that I saw Daniel for the first time when Chester and I inspected for dry rot down in the Marquam Ravine. We stood there talking about the dry rot, about how the Mackeys creosoted over the rotten timbers and made money selling the lumber a second time to someone else. A man popped out of that abandoned hut and raced away up the hill. I thought he was one of those madmen who live like hermits. I barely saw his face and it was dirty and unshaven. Still, I nearly recognized him when you brought him, all scrubbed clean, into Mozart's kitchen that first time. I wonder why I didn't realize it sooner. Of course, he was the man I'd seen in the gully. He'd been camping out in that hut, staying close to where his wife and baby died. That's why he immediately thought of looking there for you." Sage sighed heavily. "Anyway, I think he overheard what we said when we stood underneath the bridge. And, if he did, I'm sure he believes that if the fire wagon hadn't fallen through the bridge, his wife and child would still be alive. Knowledge like that would make any man vengeful. Chester and I gave him a target for reveng—Mackey. The wrong Mackey, as it turns out."

Eich rubbed a hand across his face. "I thought if I found something for him to do, took his mind off what happened, he would eventually move beyond the grief. Instead, he seemed to go deeper into it," he said.

"If he killed old man Mackey, that explains why he didn't come out of it. We've been talking every day at Mozart's about the murder, about the dry rot and the bridges. Who knows what he overheard? Now that I think of it, I bet he hung around painting just to eavesdrop on what we said."

"And so, because of my grand idea, he learned that he'd killed an innocent old man," Eich said, sadness heavy in his face.

"I'm sure he did. And he also learned another innocent man is likely going to die because of his actions. But you had no way of knowing that would happen."

"Where is Daniel now?"

Sage shook his head. "I don't know. I looked for him at your shed when we realized we'd been so busy that we'd forgotten to pay him for his work and for the paint he used. He wasn't there. He's fixed the place up for you—new blankets, pillows, caulk in the cracks and whitewash. It'll be a lot warmer. Daniel's not there, though, and all his belongings are gone."

Eich sat straight up in bed, urgency strengthening his voice. "Sage, you need to find him soon. He lacks sufficient funds to turn his back on a week's worth of wages and still buy me new blankets."

As Eich spoke, a thought raced through Sage's brain. "You think he intends to kill himself?" he asked.

"I'm certain of it. He's a young decent man with guilt lying far too heavy on his soul."

In less than an hour, Sage located Sergeant Hanke. Shortly after that, the two men slid down the ravine bank toward the abandoned hut. Hanke moved no quieter than he'd moved in the past. Even a near-deaf person could hear their approach. Certainly their noise alerted Daniel because, when they got within twenty feet of the hut, he burst out its open doorway and disappeared around the far side. They quickly reversed direction. Still, he made it onto the broken bridge at least sixty feet ahead of them. When he reached the middle of the span, Daniel faced them, his eyes staring pinpoints of brown.

"You come any closer and I'll throw myself off this bridge and you'll never get the proof you need to free Mr. Lockwood."

Sage and Hanke slowed as they be stepping across the bridge, stopping only when Daniel slung one leg over the rickety railing, his face a mask of determination. Sage glanced toward the ravine bottom, littered with trash and bone-breaking rocks. He raised both hands, palms out to calm the man.

"It's okay. It will be all right. The whole city will soon know about Mackey's phoney bridge repair scheme. People will understand why you did what you did. If a man has a good reason, he's not hung."

Daniel's laugh was harsh, defiant. "Ha! How will they understand when I don't even understand why I killed that poor old man in such a horrible way? He told me he'd done nothing wrong. He begged me. Clarisa . . . Clarisa, she'd be so ashamed of me." Daniel yanked his leg off the railing, shouting, "You just leave me be!" as he whirled and trotted away across the bridge, heedless of the loose boards and man-sized holes.

Sage and Hanke thudded after him, never quite catching up. Hanke shrilled his police whistle but no reinforcements appeared. He dropped further behind. Cold air seared Sage's lungs as he gasped for breath and strained to keep up. Daniel raced on with Sage close behind. As they pounded down block after block, the heavens opened and sheets of rain slammed down. Sage tucked his chin into his collar to avoid breathing in water.

A block from the river, Daniel paused at a construction site. He glanced behind, located his pursuers, then stooped to shove bricks into his overcoat pockets. Standing erect, he staggered forward wobbling under the extra weight he'd taken on. He thudded up the ramp onto the Morrison Bridge, his feet drumming on the wood decking. When he reached midspan he halted and turned to face Sage, who also halted with one hand on the bridge rail to steady himself as he tried to catch his wind.

Daniel's harsh voice carried to Sage across the twenty-five feet that separated them. "I was selfish, thinking only of myself. If I'd been upstairs to help with the baby . . . Clarisa, she was so tired . . . I knew it. . . The candle . . . She'd asked me to buy an oil lamp but no, I was too busy and didn't have time. Ha! Oh no, not me, the good husband and father. No, not me helping her out with the baby. I told her I needed my sleep for work the next day. Didn't want anything to interfere with my great plans. I had just got a new job painting the inside of one of those hilltop mansions. I was thinking that I was finally on my way to being a painter for the rich nobs in this town. I planned to outdo myself on the job, win more referrals so that soon, I'd be able to buy a house for me, Clarisa and Daniel. Maybe even hire a woman to help Clarisa out." Self-loathing gave his words a bitter bite as tears ran down a face twisting with pain.

Sage caught his breath and eased erect, searching for words capable of forestalling the event he feared was about happen. "You still have gifts to offer the world, Daniel. Those flowers you painted on the balcony—that's something good you can give people. Something beautiful."

Daniel's face twisted. "You like those flowers? That was the pattern I planned to paint on Daniel's nursery walls in our new house. Instead, I painted them on Mozart's balcony to be with the music. Two beautiful things side by side. Like Clarisa and baby Daniel in their grave." His voice broke. Sage stepped toward him, hand outstretched in supplication.

Daniel moved quickly, slinging a leg over the top of the railing. "Don't come any closer, Mr. Adair. You do, and I'll jump and you won't be able to save Leo Lockwood."

"What about Leo?" Sage asked, even though he knew the answer. He needed to keep Daniel talking—he needed to slow down the man's frenetic momentum.

"He didn't kill Mr. Mackey, I did. I guess you figured that out, otherwise you wouldn't be here with that policeman."

"I didn't know until this afternoon."

"Mr. Eich knows too. I saw it in his eyes." Daniel's voice became pensive. "He has warm eyes Mr. Eich does, but his eyes are so full of sorrow. Guess he's seen too many fools in his days."

"We figured out why you killed Mr. Mackey. You overheard us talking about the dry rot the day we inspected underneath the Marquam Ravine trestle."

"It was a mistake tying up that old man and setting the fire. A dumb stupid mistake. Just like the mistake I made leaving Clarisa all alone upstairs to care for Daniel when she was so tired. Just like the mistake I made running outside to yell for my neighbors to fetch the fire wagon. It was wrong to run outside like that. I should have gone upstairs the minute I woke up and smelled smoke. I should have died with them."

Daniel stared upriver, his lips pressed into a grim line of self-disgust. His chest heaved with a deep sigh and he looked at Sage. "Once I started painting at the restaurant, I overheard that you went down to the Mackey strike so I stayed around, eavesdropping every chance I got," he said. "That's how I found out that I'd made a mistake. That old man didn't know anything about the rotting bridges. He tried to tell me that. I called that poor old man a liar. He told the truth didn't he?"

Should he lie? Given the intensity of his despair, would Daniel spot a lie? Sage took a deep breath and held it before sighing it out. "Yes. Only Earl Mackey, the son and not the father, hid the bridge rot. But Daniel, there was no way for you to know that. It took us a long time to discover that," Sage said, his voice gentle as he sought to give the agitated man comfort.

A half sob escaped from Daniel. He twisted to stare down into the sullen gray water below.

Sage inched forward slowly, hoping to grab the man around his waist while he was distracted by the water flowing below. Daniel raised his head, a knowing look in his eye. Sage halted.

Daniel spoke directly to Hanke, who now stood quietly just behind Sage. "It's all buried beneath the dirt floor of that hut in the ravine—Mr. Mackey's watch, a length of the rope I used to tie him with, and my written confession. Look for a tin box with the top waxed shut to keep out the damp. Dig on the uphill side, in the far corner. I was planning to send a note to the police telling them where to find it."

He looked back to Sage. "Thank Mr. Eich and Mrs. Clemens and Miz Ida for their kindness to me. You too. I wish I deserved it. You are good people. Real good people." In the next instant, quick and silent as silk sliding from a chair, he disappeared over the bridge railing.

Sage and Hanke froze, rain pelting their faces, before jumping to the railing and searching the rushing water below. Nothing floated below except bits of bark torn loose from log rafts. No arms flailed in the air grabbing for life. Racing across the bridge, dodging a carriage and van, they peered downstream. Nothing there either, except for the disappearing pockmarks of relentless rain upon the water's surface.

THIRTY ONE

One week later

ONCE AGAIN THE STEADY PELT OF RAIN dinged the tin above their heads, filling the shed with its noise. "Another gray winter afternoon at the bottom of the heavenly downspout," Sage grumbled in his mind as he hunched over his cup of tea. He hated the thought of Eich enduring months of this noisy, penetrating damp. Even Daniel's skillful efforts failed to completely eliminate its pernicious presence. The endless damp would bring death to healthier men than the ragpicker this winter.

He looked at Eich, who rested quietly on his cot. The man's watching brown eyes glowed with an inner warmth. Sage cleared his throat. "I'll be glad when this damnable winter is over. Seems like more rain than usual," he said.

Eich raised himself off the cot to take up a piece of wood, open the door to the potbellied stove, and poke at the dying embers. "I don't know but that I like the winter best. That's when nature reveals her elemental structures. The shape of her bones. The powerful havoc of her skies. The promise of renewal in every raindrop." He laid a log upon the flames and returned to the cot.

Sage shifted on the tall stool. "Ah, I bet you'll be glad when it stops raining. It has to be hard pushing that cart through the mud and all."

Eich lifted his hands, palms up. "There is some discomfort, I admit. Still, I don't mind it. I think of rain as a life-giving force. Maybe that comes from my youthful trudge across the Southwest desert. Nearly died of thirst. Nothing out in that country except stone, gravel, stone and more stone. You ever think about how many different kinds of raindrops fall to the earth here in the Pacific Northwest? A man needs so many different words to describe them."

Sage shook his head. "When I worked in the woods, I thought on it a bit. It wasn't something that gave me any pleasure. These days, I just try to stay out of the wet." He shifted position again. "Even so, I bet the men are glad to be out working in it today. Mackey's rushing to repair the bridges all around town before any more of them collapse. He's got crews working seven days a week, ten hours every day. For the first time though, they're receiving pay at time and one-half for those two extra hours and for that extra day thanks to the labor contract Mackey signed."

"I expect that after that strike, they are glad to be making the extra money, no matter what the weather or the hours. Probably ran up a passel of debt. Delayed buying their kids winter coats and boots," Eich said. "I expect their families are knowing joy and contentment for the first time in months. And just in time for the holidays."

"Leo hardly has time to see his wife and kids, he's so busy. You are right, though. There's laughter again in their homes, I'm sure." Sage swallowed more tea, finding it cool.

"So, the city's contracted Mackey to repair the bridges he supposedly already repaired?" Eich asked.

"Yes, another one of those hush-hush agreements. He's footing the cost of the lumber and almost all of the labor. The city isn't going to lose any money on the deal. Just because Mackey might be guilty doesn't mean he's stupid. His lawyer served him well. He's also buying the city a brand new fire wagon. That purchase will, in all likelihood, cause *The Gazette* to heap fulsome praise on his head for his charitable beneficence. He'll come out of this smelling like one of the city's proverbial roses. What a surprise."

"His own greedy actions cost him his beloved father, that may be punishment enough," Eich mused. "And, redoing all the bridges will lighten his pockets considerably. So, what about the crooked city engineer? Any word on him?"

"Bittler? His house is up for sale. He departed Brother Jonas's farm as soon as the furor died down. He and his family caught the train in Salem, heading south. Never even came back to Portland. Mackey probably found Bittler a job down there in California just to insure Bittler stays away permanently." Sage sighed. "Feels like a lot of injustice remains securely in place."

"Well, winning the strike is economic justice, not just for the strikers but for every other man who works construction in this city. Besides, another thing you've accomplished is to find yourself a metaphor for your ongoing battle." Eich observed.

"A metaphor?" Sage asked.

"Dry rot," Eich said, gesturing toward the window. "We humans look around and we think what we see is exactly as we see it. That it is, as it is. We think we see life's essential characteristics, no real secrets are hidden from us. Given the ugliness of what you fight, where you travel, you know different, don't you? You, Sage. You and your mother and Mr. Fong. The three of you dig beneath the surface. You confront the ugliness that taints the lives of both the bad and the good. You expose corruption, injustice, greed to the light and air, so society has the opportunity to cut it out. And, that is exactly what needs be done to stop dry rot, isn't it, in both wood and in society?"

"What about the hatred, the need for revenge that I feel sometimes? Aren't those feelings part of that ugliness, part of the rot?" Sage asked, "Seems like they tend to undercut whatever noble inclinations underlie my goal." He looked into his cup and realized how afraid he was of hearing the answer and yet, of how much he needed to hear it.

"Revenge, hatred, jealously, anger, hmm." Eich swallowed some tea, before saying, "I'd say that no man's motivation can be pure all the time. We are, after all, only imperfect human beings striving for perfection. Not a single one of us ever achieves it. That's our lot on this earth. So, yes, those emotions will always be there. Sometimes, they work to good effect. They keep our heads above the water long enough for our feet to find the bottom."

The ragpicker's brown eyes seemed penetrating as they searched Sage's face and he said, "Our feet, though, must find that bottom. To continue striving for justice and humanity over the long term, our feet must rest on beliefs that are more solid, more life-affirming than either hate or revenge." A wide smile eased Eich's craggy face and loosened the tension. "It's like finding a thing of beauty inside a dustbin. The discovery makes digging through the muck worthwhile."

Sage stood, setting his mug down on the workbench, allowing his fingers to trail across a porcelain plate, the nick in its edge already filled, smoothed and ready for paint.

"I feel bad about Daniel," he said, giving voice to painful thoughts that had been nagging at him. "I should have realized sooner what that poor man was going through."

"That sorrow is mine also, " Eich said, leaving the words hanging in the air for a beat before continuing, "We'll never know if we didn't missed saying a word or performing a deed sufficient to pull him back from the edge of that precipice. That unanswered question is a pebble we will carry in our shoe until the day we are through. At times, each of us who knew him will likely take that pebble out to sorrow over."

Sage sighed. Maybe, if he'd lied about Abner Mackey's innocence in the bridge rot scheme, Daniel wouldn't have jumped. Sage sighed again. That unanswered question was more like one damn sharp rock that he'd be carrying in his shoe.

He looked at the older man and felt his guilt give way to gratitude. Eich's acknowledgment of their shared burden somehow comforted Sage. He felt his heart edge toward making peace with the loss of that talented, devastated, young man.

Sage slapped his hat on his head. "I guess I best be going. Mother won't be too happy if I, yet again, abandon her to handle the dinner crowd by herself." Sage moved toward the door and Eich rose from the cot to show him out. When Sage pulled the door open, a sun break momentarily dazzled both men. The bright light magnified myriads of water droplets clinging to every blade of grass, every fir needle, every exposed limb. Sage paused, transfixed by the unexpected beauty.

Eich reached out to touch Sage's arm, saying, "And so, we shall both continue to toil, my boy. You exposing the dry rot. Me converting bits of refuse into small pleasures for those whose lives need them most."

Sage clasped the older man around the shoulders and squeezed before he realized he'd formed the intention. He released Eich saying, "All of which means never-ending work for both of us. Fine, impossible tasks we've chosen for ourselves. How long before we are both able to take a rest from confronting the infernal ugliness in human beings?" he asked, not expecting an answer.

Eich gazed out into the sparkling day and quietly recited, "Deep in the caves of the heart, far down, running underneath the outward shows of people, dwells the organic growth of God, Himself, in time."

Sage said nothing, though his immediate rueful reaction to that optimistic view of human evolution was one of grudging acceptance. It was going to take a very long time, then. He gazed at the slanting sunbeams coaxing twists of silver mist skyward. "The organic growth of God," he muttered. He wasn't sure if he really understood that idea or even accepted it. Still, the words felt gentle, promising—almost a blessing. His spirits rising like the mist, Sage stepped across the threshold and into sunlight.

THE END

Historical Notes

1. In October 1902, a number of bridges across Portland's ravines and swamp land began collapsing, one of them taking a fire wood wagon down with it. The city engineer, who had been also implicated in a sewer pipe fraud, was thereafter fired by the new "clean sweep" mayor. The replacement city engineer's inspection revealed that many of the city's bridges were unsound. The list of bridge flaws in this story is an amalgamation of that city engineer's actual findings.

2. Like so many public services needing continued support, the monied interests lobbied against the taxes needed to keep them sound. In Portland, public taxes built many trestles over swamps and ravines to aid Portland's developers as they busily extended the city's borders by selling land and houses on the outskirts of the settlement. These bridges ended up in a deplorable state. This was because, once they'd sold all their property, those same developers successfully fought to repeal the taxes needed to maintain

the bridges. Lastly, the scam of covering over rotted bridge timbers existed but it was not necessarily the practice responsible for Portland's October 1902 bridge collapses.

3.   Fred T. Merrill is loosely based on the real Fred T. Merrill who made his fortune selling bicycles. He served as a city commissioner from 1900 to 1905 and was known for representing the interests of common people and for taking stands against corruption and big money interests. He did, indeed, put the "kibosh" on Standard Oil's plans to site oil tanks on the east-side river bank across from the city's downtown. In 1898, Merrill challenged sixteen horses to race against his bicycle, a contest that he subsequently was considered to have won. All other facts and personally traits attributed to Fred T. Merrill are fictitious.

4.   The scene of horse riders bursting from a building and riding down strikers was taken from a real incident that took place on a date later than in this story. In July 1913, six policemen on horses rode down on women cannery workers who were striking for $1.00 per day wages. At least two of the women were sent to the hospital.

5.   The character of Herman Eich is based on a real Herman Eich who was lovingly called the "Ragpicker Poet of Portland." The real Herman Eich was an an-archist, ragpicker and poet who died in 1896, at a young age, while riding the rails in Idaho as a hobo.

6.   New Odessa did exist as an utopian community in Southern Oregon, although there is no evidence ty-ing the real Herman Eich to that early experiment in communal living. A group of Jewish idealists, originating in Odessa, Russia, traveled on foot across Panama, up the coast by steamer and then down the Willamette Valley by train. They built New Odessa

between Roseburg and Grants Pass, near Glendale, Oregon. The real New Odessa lasted from 1882 to 1887 before disbanding.

7. After *Dry Rot* was written it was discovered that, in December 1902, the Portland Carpenters Union won a strike that had an eight-hour workday as one of its demands.

8. The struggle for the eight hour workday lasted decades. It was first achieved in 1836 by striking carpenters in Boston. Before the federal law was passed in 1938, countless workers lost their lives at rallies, strike lines and through ambush, because they were demanding an eight-hour day, forty-hour workweek. Since the early 1980s, there has been a concerted effort made by large corporations to eliminate both the eight-hour day and overtime, since they would rather work people longer than hire additional workers.

9. Fire and the threat it posed played an important role in Pacific Northwest history. It is rare to find an early settlement that did not experience a serious conflagration. For example, Lakeview, Oregon, lost 75% of its structures to fire in 1900.

10. As the labor movement grew in strength it became common for the owners to engage the services of management spies and provocateurs whenever there was a labor dispute. The Pinkerton detective agency had its beginnings in 1850. As late as 1969, Pinkerton was planting agents into Portland strike lines. For example, during a roofing company strike, one of the agency's agents was responsible for the arrest of some strike sympathizers who were caught with Molotov cocktails in their vehicle. The Pinkerton agent walked free, even though some of the accused alleged that he'd been the one most actively promoting violence.

About the Author

S. L. Stoner is a native of the Pacific Northwest who has worked as a citizen change agent and as a labor union and civil rights attorney for many years.

Acknowledgments

I want to start by thanking the readers of this series. Their enthusiasm and support has encouraged Sage to keep adventuring and fighting the good fight.

To the extent this series accurately reflects history, that is due to those who have done their best to preserve the past. In particular, I want to thank the staff of the Oregon Historical Society and the Portland City Archives. These organizations deserve our gratitude and our support.

This book in the series received special assistance from Joel Rosenblit, Sally Frese, Helen Nickum and Denise Collins. Many heartfelt thanks to each of them, particularly Helen and Denise who read every single word with such great care and red pens in their hands. Any remaining errors are solely my own.

Family members, friends and my colleagues in the labor movement, both old and new, remain the loving foundation of this series. Fortunately, they number too many to name here without forgetting someone. It is their beauty, intelligence and humanity that lights these pages.

I visualize Herman Eich as a born teacher. I tried to convey him as possessing that mastery, passion, kindness and humility that enables him to send his teachings straight to the heart. While working on this book, I thought about the born teachers I have been privileged to know. Fortunately for me, there were many but three in particular are in my life right now and I want to acknowledge their gift to myself and to the world: Caroline Miller, Jill Khovy and Jeff Patterson.

Last and most important, the greatest credit continues to go to George Slanina, whose unwavering support, kindness, and pithy observations make this series possible.

Other Mystery Novels in the Sage Adair Historical Mystery Series
by S. L. Stoner

Timber Beasts

A secret operative in America's 1902 labor movement, leading a double life that balances precariously on the knife-edge of discovery, finds his mission entangled with the fate of a young man accused of murder.

Land Sharks

Two men have disappeared, sending Sage Adair on a desperate search that leads him into the Stygian blackness of Portland's underground to confront murderous shanghaiers, a lost friendship and his own dark fears.

Sage Adair Mysteries coming soon . . .

Black Drop

Crisis always arrives in twos. Assassins plan to kill President Theodore Roosevelt and blame the labor movement. Young boys are slated for an appalling fate. If Sage Adair missteps, people will die. Panic becomes the most dangerous enemy of all in this adventure.

Request for Pre-Publication Notice

If you would like to receive notice of the publication dates of the fourth Sage Adair historical mystery novel, *Black Drop*, please complete and return the form below or contact Yamhill Press at www.yamhillpress.net.

Your Name: _____

Street Address:_____

City: _____ State: _____ Zip: _____

E-mail Address: _____

Yamhill Press, P.O. Box 42348, Portland, OR 97242
www.yamhillpress.net

Author Contact: slstoner@yamhillpress.net